A River Of Resentment

Kristen King

Silvester & Eve Publishing

CONTENTS

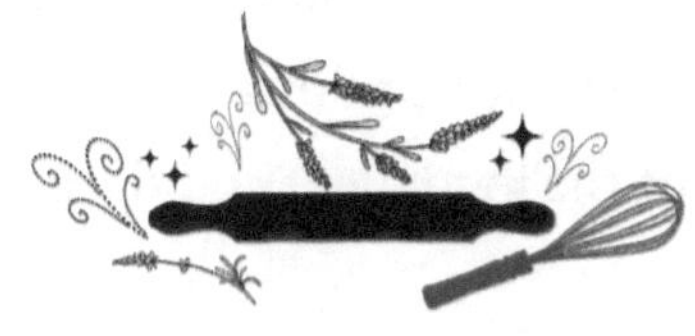

Penny's Soothing Rye Bread

1 Tbsp active dry yeast

1 cup warm water

3 Tbsp molasses

2 tsp caraway seeds

2 tsp salt

2 Tbsp applesauce

2 Tbsp cocoa powder

1 cup rye flour

2 1/2 cups bread flour

olive oil spray

cornmeal for sprinkling

Pour the yeast into the warm water while chanting,

Bubble with purpose, bubble with care.

As bubbles form on the surface, the yeast will dissolve. Add the molasses to the mixture. One at a time, combine the other ingredients into the mixture with a wooden spoon, each time saying the name of the ingredient and the chant,

For good measure, comfort, and warmth.

Once the dough is well combined, flour a kneading surface and drop the dough onto it. Knead the dough with the heel of your hand, stretching it away from you and then pulling it back over the top of the dough ball. Continue this process for about five minutes until the dough is smooth.

Lightly spray the inside of a large mixing bowl with olive oil spray and place the dough ball into the bowl to rise. Cover the bowl loosely with a damp towel. Place your hands on the sides of the bowl and whisper to the dough,

Rise like a mother bear. To nurture, protect, and love.

Allow the dough to rise at room temperature or slightly warmer for about an hour. After the dough has risen, punch the center of the dough down to release some air. Drop the dough onto a floured surface and gently knead a few more times until shaped.

Place the dough into an oil-sprayed loaf pan and let rise a second time for about half an hour. This time, leave uncovered and whisper to the dough,

Once more for good measure and for our comfort to grow.

After the second rise, place the dough on a flat baking sheet lined with parchment paper and sprinkled with cornmeal. Cut a couple diagonal slits across the top of the dough about a half inch deep.

Pour a cup of water into a separate shallow baking sheet and place in the oven on the lower rack. Add the flat sheet with the bread dough into the oven on the upper rack.

Bake the loaf on 400 degrees Fahrenheit for about 40 minutes or until the loaf sounds hollow when tapped with a knife. Let cool for at least 15 minutes and enjoy.

CHAPTER 1

Sulfur loomed in the air of the hearth room as Autumn leaned in closer to Mrs. Allan. The woman trembled as she played with the strap on her purse. Her body appeared tense even though her son, James, stood over her.

Autumn placed her hand on Sorcha Allan's and gave her a gentle smile to encourage the story. While Autumn sensed the bad omen coming, her tabby cat familiar, Tavish, licked his paws at her feet, happy to have his witch beside him.

"It's all right, Mrs. Allan. Anything from your dream that you can remember will be helpful." Autumn sat back a bit to give her some space.

"Oh dear, after all these years of having premonitions in my dreams, I never got used to it. These horrible ones, especially."

Autumn's cousin and shop co-owner, Simone, pulled the curtains back to the hearth room of their shop, Parchment and Pine, and walked in with a tray full of teacups and a pot of water. She poured and handed a cup to Mrs. Allan, then stood beside her cousin.

"Anyway, I've learned it's best to deal with them as soon as possible. No sense in keeping them to myself since the dreams always manifest. That's why I sent James over to you with the last one he had."

"We understand, Mrs. Allan. This is a hard thing to deal with, but Autumn is a great listener. She'll help you make sense of it, and then we'll all do what we can to make things right." Simone eyed her, waiting for the details to pour out.

"Well, I felt like a voyeur in my dream, as I usually do. It was almost as if I hovered in front of the scene as it appeared to me. I've had the dream twice now, which tells me it's getting closer to coming to fruition. The more often I have the dream, the sooner the events transpire." Sorcha took a sip of her tea as her hands shook.

James pulled a small ottoman over to his mother's chair and put his hand on her forearm.

"Just walk through each piece of the dream step by step." James helped place the teacup back on the table as his mother still struggled to settle her nerves.

"I moved up the river in my dream, almost like I dropped in directly beside it. Very little light remained, but I could tell that the rapids were stronger than their usual calm. The closer I got to the water, the more I could make out a figure floating on the top of it." She shook her head and covered her mouth with her hand.

James looked at Autumn with concerned eyes. "My mom feels these dreams deeply. She takes on emotions connected to the events in the dream, like they really happened to her. I guess it's part of the gift. It's not just seeing but emphatically feeling what happens through the dream."

Autumn narrowed her eyes curiously at James's explanation. She was understanding more not only about his mother's gifts but about James's inherited abilities as well. The two of them had grown close over the last few months, but she still wanted to know more about him.

Sorcha continued. "As I got closer to the figure in the water, I noticed it was a man sprawled out, face down, floating on the ripples. He didn't move, just lay lifeless there, caught on some kind of boulder in the river."

Sorcha unzipped her purse and dug around for a tissue to blot her nose. "It was getting dark in the dream, and I couldn't make out much. Yet, I felt fear, and I tried to look around to see if anyone else was there. All I could see were trees lining the river trail and the dark shadows they made."

She took another sip of her tea and then raised her index finger in the air. "Oh, but when I turned back to the water, I noticed something there."

Autumn nodded at Mrs. Allan to proceed. "Okay, what was it you saw?"

"Black, opal-like shimmers in the water. They shined like dark specks of glitter just under the surface, and the specks trailed under the man's body and down the river."

"Black specks of glitter? Like magic sparks in the water?" Simone came around to the other side of Autumn's chair and stoked the fire to keep it going.

"I can't be sure of anything. It just looked murky but with dark shimmers that weren't right for the river." Sorcha sighed and patted James's hand before looking at Autumn and Simone. "Oh, girls, I'm so concerned that someone is going to get hurt, but I don't know who. What can we do?"

"It's okay, Mrs. Allan. We've got a few things that stood out from your dream, so that'll give us a bit to go on. Simone and I will walk through the details and talk with our mothers for any more insights. I don't want you to worry, all right? Just go home with James and take care of yourself. You can let us know if you have the dream again and if anything new arises. For now, let us try to piece things together."

Autumn got up and went over to help Mrs. Allan out of her chair.

"Thanks, Autumn. I'm gonna take my mother home and get her settled in for the evening. She needs to rest and shake off some of this fear she's still feeling from the dream." James opened up the curtains and led his mother to the front of the shop to retrieve their things.

"Yeah, of course. I'm glad you both came by and shared with us, but just take care of your mom, okay?" Autumn grabbed James's arm and moved in front of him. "And thanks for trusting me again with these dreams."

She looked at him with her bright green eyes that sparkled in the evening light, and he had to stop himself from leaning closer.

"Autumn, I trust you implicitly. You never have to worry about that." He shuffled the shop door open and escorted his mother out. "I'll stop by again when I get a break from the restoration, okay?" He waved at her and walked away.

Autumn smiled, thinking she might conjure up the break he needed from working on the downtown restoration if it meant seeing him sooner rather than later.

Simone made her way to the front of the shop and peeked out the front window. "Well, aren't we becoming quite the place for advice on magical matters?"

"Yeah, apparently once the four energies activate in your bloodline, you end up being a beacon for anything out of balance. I mean, it is a good thing they came to us, but I have no idea how we're going to help right now. All I can focus on is the sulfur smell taking over the shop with foreboding energy. It's awful! Can you smell it? I didn't want to say anything while they were here." Autumn held the front door open to bring in some fresh air.

"I don't smell anything, but give me a minute and maybe I can help with that." Simone shimmied around Autumn and out the front door. She lifted her hands up at her sides and whispered something under her breath as she fluttered her fingers down gently.

Tiny raindrops fell on the pavement in front of the shop, slowly getting stronger. The rain brought with it a hint of freshness in the air, and Simone smiled at her cousin.

"There. Now, you can send some of that crisp rain smell wafting through the shop if you'd like."

Autumn laughed. "Good call on the rain. The best way to wash away any negativity." She swept the air into the shop with one hand while propping the door open with the other. "Wind and rain work swiftly hand in hand. Purify this space with a gentle blowing band."

A breeze pushed through the shop door and brought with it the scent of falling rain. The sulfur slowly dissipated in the air, and all that remained was the freshness of a light rainfall.

"Ah, much better! Thanks for that." Autumn closed the front door and made her way to the back counter of the shop. "Now, about this dream, where do we start?"

"I don't know about you, but aside from the likelihood of a dead body, those black shimmers in the water definitely stood out to me." Simone cleaned up the tea set from the hearth room and joined Autumn back at the counter.

"I agree. There's definitely something to those shimmers, but I think we better start with the basics. We know a man's involved at the river and that it was dark. Let's lean into that for now and maybe keep an eye out for anything strange around the water."

"Sounds good. Don't forget, Eve is coming by my mom's house tonight for a little magic practice, and I was hoping to get some help packing my things to move into Gran's house, too."

"Of course. We can all help and talk about this dream while we're there. This may be the perfect way to bring Eve into our new coven and see how all our gifts come together." Autumn opened up a new window on the shop computer and typed into the search "Hollow's Glenn river walk."

After all that had come to pass last time with James's dreams, she didn't want to take any chances leaving this one to sit for long.

CHAPTER 2

The doorbell rang at Aunt Jo's house, and Autumn galloped down the stairs to open the door. Eve, their newfound coven member and earth witch, stood waiting on the other side with large reusable grocery bags slung over both shoulders and filled to the brims.

"Glad you made it! Come on in. It's pretty chilly out there." Autumn pushed the door open wide and waved Eve inside. "What's all this you brought?" She helped Eve pull the bags off her shoulders and peeked inside.

"Oh well, when you invited me, you said we might dabble tonight, and for me, that means herbs and spices and wonderful smells and textures. So I brought some materials." Eve gave Autumn a big, excited grin that showed off her dimpled cheeks. She squeezed her hands together at her chest, waiting for a similar reply.

Autumn laughed and nodded. "Right, that makes sense. Okay, well, let's put these things in the kitchen for now. Simone's upstairs and needs a bit more help packing first. So if you wouldn't mind throwing a few things into some boxes, then we can get to the fun stuff."

Eve agreed and picked up the bags with Autumn to take into the kitchen. Aunt Jo stood with Autumn's mother, Penny, at the kitchen island, chopping vegetables for a hearty lentil soup. The two women were glad to finally be back in each other's company after several years apart.

"Oh, Eve! How are you, dear?" Jo came around the island to wrap Eve in a warm hug. "It's so lovely to have you this evening. The girls mentioned you'd be coming by tonight, and Penny and I are just so excited that you'll be joining the girls in, uh . . . well, whatever you'd like to practice." Jo threw her hands up in the air and turned back to the island. "Now, we'll be having a nice warm soup and some homemade rye bread this evening if you'd like to stay for dinner."

"Thank you, Ms. MacKinnon, but I can really only stay for a little while. I need to get back and help my mother prep some dough for the morning orders at the Forest Brew. We've had a few large delivery requests come in now that the holiday season is underway."

"Oh, I know. Parchment and Pine has had several invitation and holiday party orders this week. It's about to get really busy, but that's a good thing." Autumn opened the bags Eve brought and laid out some jars of vanilla beans, coconut sugar, cinnamon sticks, and whole nutmeg.

"This is the heavy one. I figured you probably already had a mortar and pestle, but this is the one I use for dabbling with my own spells. So I brought it since I'm used to this one." Eve pulled the heavy black stone tools from another bag and placed them on the island. "Oh, and these dried apples and honeycomb pieces should be just the thing for a sweetening spell I've been meaning to try." Eve looked at the three of them sheepishly and shrugged her shoulders. "There are a few customers in particular that I'd like to be sweeter during the lunch rush, so I thought I might try my hand at setting out a few spell jars on the tables and the counter. Who knows? Maybe they'll end up being sweeter than usual, and it'll help my mom get through the day easier."

Penny came over and rubbed Eve's shoulder. "You have a kind heart, Eve, and I can see that you genuinely want to care for people. I like that. Why don't you girls go help Simone while we get dinner on the stove, and then you can have the kitchen island for your workings, all right?"

Autumn nodded and led Eve through the house and up the stairs. Tavish greeted them at the top of the staircase with a meow.

"Hey there, Tav. I told you I'd be back." Autumn scooped up the cat and brought him along into Simone's room.

"There you are! Hey, Eve." Simone waved to her from the bedroom floor as she wrestled with closing a box. Always the scrappy one, she brushed her black bob out of her face and acted like she'd conquered a beast. "I've shoved as much as I could into these boxes, and now I just need to wrap up my painting supplies in paper so the jars don't break." Simone pointed to her flat worktable underneath the window.

"Okay, Eve and I can get started on that while you tape up the boxes." Autumn walked over and gently placed Tavish down on the windowsill beside the table. "There you go, cutie. You can be our little helper, okay?"

Eve walked over to the table beside Autumn and started looking through the labels on the paint jars. "Wow, I didn't know you painted. These colors are gorgeous."

"Oh yeah, I do a little of everything, but abstract painting and photography are my favorite. I got my undergrad degree in graphic design, though, and now I'm almost done with my masters. There's just something about creating something out of nothing and being able to express anything at all. It's freeing and empowering, you know?" Simone taped the last box up and sat on top of it with a sigh.

Eve turned a mason jar of ruby-red paint in her hand and thought about Simone's words. "I guess I feel that way about my baking. I get to create whatever makes me happy and choose how all the ingredients come together. It's kind of like your canvas with the paints you choose."

"Exactly. Those recipes are just pouring out of you because you have a gift that wants to be let loose. And that's why we're here tonight, right? To practice letting our gifts loose?"

Simone jumped up and rubbed her palms together in anticipation.

"Yes, Simone. That's why we're here." Autumn rolled her eyes at her cousin and put a few jars rolled in paper into an empty box.

"All right, then, let's get the last of these paints wrapped up and get to it." Simone raised her dark eyebrows and looked at them. "And don't forget, Autumn, we need to talk about everything that happened today. Eve should be part of the conversation, along with our moms. If you're interested?" Simone looked up from wrapping a jar to see Eve's expression.

"Are you kidding? Of course I want to be part of it. Although, I don't know what help I'll be, but I'll definitely try." Eve did her best to keep her excitement in check, but the girls sensed her childlike heart was exactly what their coven needed.

"Well, that's settled, then." Autumn pushed the box toward the middle of the table for the girls to fill with the wrapped jars. She crumpled some newspaper and pressed it into the edges and folded the top flaps together to close it. "That should work. We can grab these boxes later and bring them back to Gran's house. I mean . . . our house." Autumn grabbed her cousin's arm and squeezed it tight.

"I can't believe we're finally moving in together after all these years. It really is the start of a new era." Simone put her hands on her hips. "And Eve, you're part of that, too. We're gonna do some amazing things together. I can feel it."

Autumn nodded and picked up Tavish. "Come on, you two. We've got a lot to talk about and some magic to practice." She snuggled the cat into her chest and made her way downstairs to the kitchen with Eve and Simone behind her.

"Oh, something smells amazing in here." Eve looked over at the simmering pot on the kitchen stove.

"You know you're welcome to stay if you'd like." Jo turned from the stove to face the girls.

"The bread is still baking in the oven, but I'm headed into the garden for a moment. I need to whisper a few things to the trees before the frost comes. I don't want them to be stressed as winter begins." Penny gave Autumn a wink and threw on a maroon chunky knit cardigan before heading out the back door.

"Right, why don't we prep the ingredients for Eve's spell before Mom gets back in?" Autumn started pulling some of the spice jars closer to them on the counter.

Eve tipped her head toward Simone. "I mentioned to Autumn and your moms that I'd like to test a sweetening spell. Basically, the ingredients go into the spell jar one by one. You say a little something to set your intention, and then tie the jar up with some twine to let it all steep together like tea. It never gets opened again, though, until the spell has finished. Then, you can dispose of the materials by sending them back to the earth. Make sense?"

"Yeah, I like it. Can we make these spell jars for any intention?" Simone bent down to look at the jars at eye level.

"Sure, I guess. These are some of my favorite spells because they're simple yet powerful. You just need to know the right ingredients and have the feeling behind the words to make it all come together." Eve opened the jar of cinnamon sticks, closed her eyes for a moment, and breathed in deeply. She then grabbed the mortar and a metal grater and began shaving an entire piece of nutmeg.

"Tell us how we can help." Autumn leaned over the mortar as Eve grated the spices.

"Autumn, you can measure out some honeycomb pieces and dried apples. Simone, you can prepare the jars by cutting the twine. I also have a coffee bean in a jar somewhere. You can use it to inscribe the outside of the jars with a symbol to represent the Forest Brew customers. The intention will be to make them sweeter when they come in."

"And I'll pick the music," Jo said with a smile. She walked over to a touchscreen sitting on a bookstand on the counter and sorted through a music playlist. "Oh, I have just the thing for us." With the touch of her finger, some Celtic fiddle music played in the background, and Jo clapped her hands along with the rhythm.

"Oh, there's no stopping her now. She's found her rhythm." Simone smiled and shook her head with the music as she marked the jars with a symbol that looked like a coffee-mug-shaped Celtic knot.

Jo shook her head at her daughter, lifted the hem of her skirt, and kicked her feet around in combination with the music.

All three girls stopped to clap along as Jo danced around the kitchen, legs going as quick as they could carry her.

With red cheeks, Penny pushed through the back door. "My goodness, what am I missing here?" She shrugged her cardigan off and onto a wall hook as her sister came around to greet her with open arms. They latched hands and did a sidestep around the kitchen island together before coming back to the stove to stir the simmering soup.

"Well, that was my exercise for the evening! I just couldn't resist the sound of that fiddle, though." Jo lifted a wooden spoon from the pot and leaned over to sample the soup. "Mmm, just right."

"The scene is just perfect in here, you know? Glorious scents from a big pot cooking away on the stove, music of our ancestors filling the air, and the workings of magic strewn out everywhere in between. This house grounds me in so many ways." Penny came over to Autumn and hugged her daughter tight.

Immediately, the stress seeped through Autumn's body and into her mother. "Oh dear, perhaps I spoke too soon. You're so tense. What is it?"

Autumn swallowed hard and looked around the room before landing on her aunt, Jo. "We had a visitor at the shop today."

"Who was the visitor?" Jo grabbed a large glass pitcher of peppermint iced tea before eyeing Autumn curiously. She gasped deeply when the vision hit her. "Sorcha."

CHAPTER 3

Autumn leaned over to take a glass of peppermint tea from her aunt. She gave her a grateful nod before looking at Simone to continue the story.

"Sorcha's all right, Mom." Simone moved around the island to help her mother pour the tea into more glasses. "She and James came in after she had a bad dream and wanted us to help her make sense of it."

Autumn placed a cinnamon stick into six mason jars as she listened to Simone recount the story. Penny turned the music down and continued filling spell jars alongside Eve at the kitchen island.

"As soon as I looked into Autumn's eyes, I saw Sorcha with a worried expression in my mind. Why didn't you mention something sooner? You let me go on dancing through the kitchen and didn't mention a word. Last time James came to us with a dream, everything changed." Jo sat down on a kitchen stool and took a sip of iced tea to calm her nerves.

"I know, Aunt Jo. It worried me, too, but I didn't want to ruin the evening if we could salvage some part of it. Simone and I planned to bring it up tonight, but you were so happy about the family dinner that I wanted to give it a while. Plus, I'm not sure what to make of it yet." Autumn pulled the mortar and pestle toward her, threw some cardamom pods in from the provisions Eve brought, and started grinding them furiously.

"Well, we can all see that something's going on, so just let it out." Penny pulled her bread out of the oven and set it on a cooling rack so she could focus on Autumn.

"Mrs. Allan told us about a dream she's had twice now. She saw a man floating in the river, and he appeared to be dead."

"Dead? As in not alive?" Eve stopped pouring teaspoons of coconut sugar into the mason jars and stared at Autumn with a fearful look.

"Yes, Eve. Dead, as in not alive." Autumn gave her a sympathetic look and brought her attention back to Aunt Jo. Eve shuddered and went back to her measuring.

"She described feeling fear in her dream like she was actually there. Mrs. Allan mentioned the details of the dark trees around the river trail and the rapids carrying the body over the top of the water. She even tried to look around for anyone else in the dream, but there was no one else except . . ." Autumn tried making sense of it all as she was saying it out loud, but beyond the dead man, this was the part that concerned her most of all.

"Go ahead. We need to know everything." Penny braced herself to listen.

"There were shimmers in the water."

"You mean, magic shimmers? Sparks?" Eve perked up in recognition from her own magic.

"Maybe, but Mrs. Allan described these as black, opal-like shimmers," Simone interjected with intensity in her voice. "It didn't sound like any magic we would be doing. Possibly something a lot more sinister, at least that's how it felt when she described it."

"Yeah, Simone's right. I could smell sulfur in the air the whole time James and his mother were in the shop. It was so overpowering that Simone had to make it rain just to get the smell to go away."

"Wow, you made it rain? That's . . ." Eve searched for the words in disbelief as they all stared back at her. "Sorry, of course you made it rain. Good strategy. Don't mind me, just keep going."

"Anyway, we don't have much to go on, but obviously Mrs. Allan seemed pretty scared that this would all come to pass. Simone and I were thinking of looking around the river for anything strange, but other than that, we don't know where to start." Autumn handed the ground cardamom over to Eve to suggest it was ready for the jars, and Eve took it appreciatively.

Simone came around the island to help Eve lay out the rest of the ingredients.

"If she's had the dream a couple times now, that means it's nearing closer. I'll go check on her tomorrow and get a feel for the state she's in. I know Sorcha usually takes on a great deal of emotion from her dreams, and this one most likely has a deep hold on her. Let's sleep on this tonight, and then perhaps Simone and I can connect with the water and see what we can find out. Penny, what do you think?" Jo smoothed out the apron lying over her lap and glanced up at her sister.

"I think you're right. Sleeping on it will be the best course of action for now. We can receive more insight with a clear and open mind in the morning. So let's finish up these spell jars, have a bowl of soup, and plan for an early night. There's no sense in worrying tonight."

As they all nodded, the doorbell rang. Jo perked up right away.

"Oh, I completely forgot. I also invited Lainy over to have dinner with us tonight. We need to get to know her better now. She's family, after all."

Jo took off her apron, smoothed back the side twists in her graying brown hair, and went to the front door to greet their guest. The others all looked at each other as they fiddled with the spell jar materials.

"Well, the timing may be awkward, but it's good that she's here." Autumn shrugged and placed a pinch of nutmeg into a few jars. "She needs to feel more like part of the family after being lost for so long. Besides, I wanna know more about her."

Jo came back into the kitchen with Lainy right behind her. The girl stood with her dark-brown locks curled and hanging over her shoulders. She wore a burgundy-colored fitted crew neck that gave her a tidy, structured appearance. Yet, when they all looked at her, each one of them could see the warmth radiating from her.

"Everyone, Lainy's here to join us this evening." Jo smiled and waved her into the kitchen toward one of the island stools.

"Thank you, Jo. Hello again, everyone." Lainy nodded and waved her hand as she looked around the room before stopping on Eve. "Oh, I'm sorry. I don't think we've met."

"Right, I'm Eve. I run the Forest Brew coffee shop and bakery with my family. I'm just here, uh . . ." She stopped and glanced over at Autumn, unsure of what to say.

Autumn moved closer to Eve and grabbed her shoulders. "She's practicing magic with us tonight. We thought we'd try our hands at a sweetening spell. Have you ever done one?" Everyone paused what they were doing to eye Lainy.

Taken aback by the stares, she stuttered as she spoke. "Uh, no, actually. Although, maybe I should have attempted it on my sister a time or two." Lainy froze and locked eyes with Autumn. "Sorry, I shouldn't have brought her up. I just meant that it's not really the magic I grew up doing, so I'm not familiar with that." She slid onto the stool and crossed her arms over her chest.

Autumn put her hand on Lainy's forearm. "It's okay. Why don't you tell us a bit about the magic you are familiar with. How about that?"

Lainy's face softened with Autumn's tone. "All right, well, I think you all know I'm a fire witch. When I was little, I found fire to be so mesmerizing. I would light candles every night at the dinner table. Whenever we'd have a fire in the fireplace, I stared at the flames for as long as I could stay awake. They just felt so connected to me."

"Wow, I've never known a fire witch before, and I never realized you had fire gifts in your family." Eve cracked a few bits of the honeycomb into the jars while listening.

"We actually just recently found out ourselves," Penny intervened to keep the conversation light. "It turns out Lainy is a long-lost relative with the gift, so we're doing our best to welcome her into the family and learn as much as we can. Plus, now we know Autumn has all four of the points: earth, air, fire, and water. We just haven't seen the water come out yet, but it'll happen."

Penny sliced the rye bread and placed the pieces carefully on a wooden cutting board in the center of the island. Jo pulled several ceramic bowls from the cabinet and placed them beside the cutting board, along with some spoons.

"We can talk and finish this spell while we eat." Jo waved them all over toward the bowls. "Grab some soup from the stove while it's hot, and Penny has rye bread here for you. Once we all have a bowl, Eve can direct us on how to proceed with the spell, all right?"

Eve gave Jo a big smile. This would be the first time she cast a spell with anyone besides her mother. The butterflies swirled in her stomach, but she felt like she was exactly where she needed to be.

They all gathered around the island with their soup and stood quietly for a moment, lapping up the hearty warmth.

"Oh, Mom, this soup is exactly what I've been craving, and the bread is amazing, Penny. Thanks for this." Simone closed her eyes and savored the bite she took.

"I felt you might need a good lentil soup to start the winter season. I know my girl." Jo squeezed Simone tight and then went over to sit on a stool beside Penny. "Now, Eve, tell us how this spell goes."

"Okay, we have all the glass jars prepared, and our intention is to make the lunch rush customers at the Forest Brew a little nicer when they come in." Eve glanced at Lainy, trying to catch her up. "Each of the jars now contains cinnamon sticks, ground nutmeg, coconut sugar, and cardamom. I'll say the words as I drop the honeycomb pieces into each jar. Simone, if you could rub a drop of almond oil over the symbols you inscribed on each jar, then that will seal the intended recipients of the spell. Then, all we'll need to do is tighten the lids and seal them off with this twine. Autumn, you can do that if you'd like."

Eve pointed to each of the materials as she spoke, and they all nodded their heads in agreement. "Oh, and Lainy, I've never done this before, but since you're a fire witch, you could seal the jars off for us with some melted candle wax. Would you like to do that?"

Lainy straightened her back and rose off her stool. "I'd love to, yes."

Jo walked across the kitchen to a small glass-doored cabinet that sat waist-high under a hanging wall clock. She pulled out a pink chime candle and a green one.

"Which color works best for this kind of spell?"

Eve leaned over to check the candles and raised her brows, surprised at Jo's intuitive choices. "They'll both work brilliantly, so we can try them both. Let's see which one works better for us."

Jo placed the candles in front of Lainy and gave her some long matchsticks to light them.

"I think we're all set. I like to start by closing my eyes and grounding my energy if you want to do that with me." Eve closed her eyes, and one by one, they followed her.

"Spirit of the earth, connect us to your energy. Ground us in our magical workings so that we may be strong and protected in our intentions." She opened her eyes and took a deep breath. "Just imagine your feet growing roots into the earth below you. It'll help stabilize you as you do the spell." Eve gazed at the women around her, eyes closed and concentrating on the spell. A sense of happiness swept over her, and she couldn't help but smile at the thought that this was now her coven.

"You can open your eyes now." Eve grabbed a few pieces of honeycomb and began sprinkling them into the jars. "With each piece, may the Forest Brew be sweetened. With kindness, let the people's appreciation be deepened." After each jar had its ingredients, Eve picked them up to eye level and swirled the ingredients together. "Simone, it's your turn for the oil."

Simone grabbed the almond oil and dabbed some on her fingers. She rubbed the symbol on each jar as Eve continued saying the spell two more times.

"Now, Autumn, seal the jars with the twine." Eve took a spoonful of her soup and watched Autumn carefully wrap the twine from the bottoms of the jars to the tops with a bow. "Nice, and now Lainy can melt the wax over the top of each bow."

Lainy dipped her rye bread into her soup and took another big bite before hopping off her stool. She lit a matchstick and went for the pink candle first. The wax from the candle dripped over the top of the twine and sealed over the lid of each jar.

"Now, don't those look lovely?" Penny studied each of the jars on the island and then lifted her head to Eve. "I'm impressed."

Eve sheepishly grinned and then refocused her attention. "Okay, let's finish the spell." She cleared her throat and grabbed Autumn's hand beside her. They each locked hands and waited for Eve to proceed.

"Energy of the earth, thank you for hearing our intentions and providing your support. As we place these jars, may the spell activate and the intentions be met. So shall it be." She dropped her hands, and the others followed.

"Wonderful! Now, we can help you pack these up to take to the coffee shop tomorrow. Oh, and Simone, are you still planning to take your things to Gran's house tonight? It'll be so dark when you get there." Jo gave Simone a worried look.

"Actually, I think I'll just go for a run tonight to help me sleep, and I'll probably just stay here one more night, if that's okay."

"Of course, dear. You know you can stay as long as you'd like. Autumn, stay tonight as well since you're already here. None of you need to rush off, but I do want to get my crystals under the moonlight before it gets too much later. You'll all have to excuse me. Just leave the dishes in the sink, and I'll get to them." Jo kissed Simone on the cheek and waved her hand at them as she left to collect her crystals.

"You know, now that I think about it, this gives me the perfect opportunity to go speak to the river. Maybe I can have a little chat with it on my run and get some insights." Simone put her bowl in the sink and started heading out of the kitchen.

"Tonight? Are you sure?" Autumn called to Simone with nervousness in her voice.

"Exactly. The moon will be out, just like Mom said, and that'll make my intuition clearer. I'll be back in no time." Simone's voice trailed off as she jogged up the stairs.

"I don't get it. Why is this the perfect opportunity to talk to the water?" Lainy narrowed her eyes at Autumn.

"Because it's about to carry the secrets of another death." Autumn scooped up Tavish off the floor and walked to the back garden door with him. She peered out the window and saw an orange full moon rising over the tree line. Tavish brushed his wet nose on her cheek, and she looked at him, knowing there was more to come out of this still-developing night.

CHAPTER 4

Simone laced up her barefoot running shoes, put her phone in the side pocket of her leggings, and headed out onto the river trail behind Jo's house. She usually came out to get some exercise when she couldn't sleep, and Hollow's Glenn provided the safest and most serene place to get in some late-night jogs. There was something about nature surrounding her on all sides that made her feel more at ease. Plus, just like her mother, Simone recharged her energy with the light of the moon.

Even though she wanted to do some investigating around the river tonight, she also needed the water to calm her thoughts and remind her to flow with life. After all, she was finally about to move out of her mother's house, graduate from her master's program, and start up a coven with Autumn and Eve. Simone could see big things on the horizon, but she didn't want to get ahead of herself. She enjoyed staying in the moment and letting the tides take her wherever she was meant to go.

As she picked up her pace down the river trail, the tall lantern lights lining the path flickered above her. They illuminated long swaths of the path and a small portion of the edges, but the trees beyond that and the river beside her were mostly dark. Her breaths quickened the harder she ran, and she mimicked the pace of the water beside her, only going in the opposite direction.

Simone knew the path well and recognized that she was on the straight half-mile stretch before it curved into the trees ahead. After that, the path would make its way underneath a downtown bridge and up the hill toward the old lumber mill.

She sprinted through the rest of the straight trail and then slowed to a walk when she got to the trees. Simone put her hands on her hips and controlled her breath. The light was fainter at the curved part of the trail, but the moonlight made its way through some trees.

She walked over to the river and watched as the rapids flowed downstream at a steady pace. The water had just barely iced over at the edge, but it still worked its way through steadily. She crouched down and dipped her hand into it. Simone could barely tolerate the temperature, and she felt sure no one could sustain it for over ten minutes, even this early in the season.

The moon sat higher in the sky than before she left the house, so she continued up the river, looking for anything strange about the water. Nothing seemed out of place, so Simone went back to the path and continued jogging through town. She had to get more energy out, otherwise there was no way she could sleep that night.

She pulled out her phone and set the stopwatch as she jogged in place. Then, she took off, gaining speed with each pound of her feet on the trail. The downtown bridge passed over her, and the shadow loomed above for a few seconds before she came out on the far side. Simone looked over to the town water fountain and flower beds as she passed them by. Her gran's bench sat between the river trail and the fountain.

"Hey, Gran," she whispered under her breath. "It's a beautiful night to be surrounded by the trees, don't you think?"

Simone kept a steady pace, making her way up a slight hill along the path. The wind picked up, and the evergreen trees on either side of her swayed from side to side. She could feel the breeze pushing at her back, helping her up the hill.

Simone laughed to herself as she got to the top of the slope. "Thanks for that, Gran. I needed a little boost up the hill tonight." She pulled out her stopwatch and read the time: seven minutes. Not bad for how long it had been since she'd run last.

As she walked down the slope toward the river again, the wind kicked up some dirt and blew it in the water's direction. She eyed it curiously, wondering if her gran was still trying to tell her something. Making her way through the trees on the side of the slope, she found herself back alongside the river. The orange moonlight deepened to a warmer shade of red around her. Enough light still shone down for her to see, but the trees created deeper shadows now, and she could tell the water had a darker depth to it here.

She knew if her gran was with her through the trees that her father would be with her where the land met the water. So, she continued walking until she heard splashing further upstream. She followed the edge of the water a few more steps before she stood over something knocking into a boulder. A large figure lay face down, floating among the ripples and stuck at the icy edge.

Simone froze in place. She felt the ice of the waters as if they were piercing her own skin. Yet, she was the voyeur watching from the side. She took a step closer as the reddening moonlight gave her a better glimpse of the body. Looking from side to side, she couldn't see anyone else around. She took a deep breath and channeled her ancestors' strength. Stepping back from the water's edge, she pulled out her phone to call the police. Her hands shook as she called, but soon someone was on the other line. As soon as she heard the voice, Simone began rambling.

"Yes, hello, this is Simone MacKinnon. I'm at the river trail near the hill by the old lumber mill, and I've found a body in the water. Please send someone quickly!"

"All right, ma'am. Just stay where you are, and we'll have officers there shortly. Is there anyone else with you?"

"No, it's just me out here, but I'm going to call my family while I wait." Simone listened to the voice respond on the other end of the phone and then ended the call.

Her heartbeat had slowed down only minimally from her run, and fear rose inside her as she sat alone in the dark with a dead body floating in front of her. Simone had never been afraid of the dark before. In fact, she'd embraced it. Yet, now, with the moonlight turning red and the surrounding sensation of death, her fearlessness wavered.

A few wet drops grazed the top of her hands and made her pause. She sensed the clouds forming overhead and the buildup of rain within them. It was coming from inside her. Simone sensed the fear taking hold, and she had to relax. She opened her hands and swayed them gently from side to side, whispering under her breath.

"Water within me, calm my emotions. Bring me into flow, without fear, only strength."

As she spoke the words and moved her hands, the rain slowed and the river waters calmed. She saw the body bob gently and hover against the edge. All she had to do was wait and breathe. So, Simone sat on the grass beside the water and focused on the rain easing.

Immediately as she sat, she felt her gran's presence beside her and the overwhelming feeling of a warm cup of tea soothing her. That was her gran, in life and now in passing.

"Thanks, Gran. I needed that and to know you're here with me." Simone exhaled and got the feeling that Autumn should be her next phone call. More than anyone else, Autumn always knew what to say. She found the number in her phone contacts and began dialing just as sirens blared in the distance.

"Autumn, it's already happened. I found the body." Simone rose off the ground and signaled the police approaching.

"Okay, Simone, I'm coming to you. Text me where you are, all right? And Sim . . ." Autumn paused for a moment to tap into what Simone needed. "Look for Ben."

Simone pulled the phone away from her ear and searched the trees as the officers came through. One by one, they rushed over to her with flashlights drawn and then to the river to find the body. When Simone glanced back in the trees and saw Officer Ben Walsh moving toward her, the rain finally stopped.

Ben scanned the darkness and found Simone, wet hair pulled back halfway and standing with her arms wrapped around her chest. He picked up his pace down the hill and went over to her. The other officers standing around her moved out of the way for him to put his hands on her shoulders and rub her arms to warm her up.

"Are you all right? I heard the emergency call, and I had to come myself."

Simone closed her eyes and nodded. "Yeah, no, I'm okay. I'm just a little shaken, I guess."

They both turned to face the officers pulling the body from the water.

"I couldn't tell who it was or anything. I just found the body lying face down."

"We'll figure it all out. You just relax, okay? Why don't you come sit down on this rock over here, and the paramedics can get you a warm blanket. You must be freezing now from the rain." Ben directed her toward a boulder on the edge of the trees, away from the officers at the water's edge. Just as he signaled the paramedics toward them, a yell came from the top of the hill.

"Simone!" Jo scurried through the trees and down the hill with Autumn close behind her.

A few officers tried to hold them off as they approached, but Ben intervened.

"It's okay. You can let them through. Ms. MacKinnon, Autumn, over here, please." Ben waved them toward the trees where Simone was sitting.

"Oh, thank goodness! I was so worried when you called Autumn!" Jo grabbed the blanket from a paramedic and wrapped her daughter in it with a big warm hug.

Simone gave Autumn the eye as her mother squeezed her tight. Autumn shrugged at her and smiled. "I didn't say anything. I was coming out here myself when—"

"Oh, you know nothing goes on without me sensing it. As soon as you phoned Autumn, I felt it was you and that something wasn't right. I wasn't going to let Autumn come without me."

"I'm fine, Mom, seriously. It just shook me a bit to find the body, and then . . ." Simone sighed. She touched her wet hair and looked from Autumn to her mother. They nodded, understanding where the rain had come from.

Autumn looked over at Ben beside Simone and smiled. "Ben, thanks for finding her so quickly and ensuring she was okay." Autumn knew there was something between Ben and Simone that they didn't completely admit to yet.

"I'm just doing my job." He met eyes with Simone as he continued. "But I wanted to personally make sure you were okay."

Autumn and Jo looked at one another once again, reading below the surface.

"Well, what now, Officer? Does Simone need to give a statement, or can we go home?" Jo asked while bundling up her coat more.

"Yes, we don't want to keep you out here anymore in the cold. I'll have Simone sit in the ambulance for a moment to write her statement and then you can take her home, all right?"

They all agreed, and Ben headed down to the water to talk with the other officers. Autumn and Jo helped Simone walk to the ambulance up the hill. They sat in silence for a moment, warming up in the heat and gathering their thoughts.

"I didn't expect this to all happen tonight. I'm sorry I came out here on my own." Simone looked at the two of them with guilt in her eyes.

"No, sweetheart, don't be silly. You couldn't have known, and honestly, the events were already set in motion. Your eyes were the ones that Sorcha saw through in her dream. It was always going to happen this way. We just didn't realize, and I'm sorry that it had to be you to find the poor man." Jo rubbed Simone's leg to give her daughter some comfort.

An officer came to the ambulance doors with a pen and paper in hand and lifted them toward Simone. "Ma'am, if I could just get you to write what happened."

Simone nodded and took them from the officer. He turned his back and stood next to the ambulance as she began writing.

"You know what? Tonight, let's just go home, make some of Gran's comfort tea, and snuggle up next to the fire. I brought home some of Eve's cinnamon sugar popovers for the morning, but we can dig into those tonight. How about it?" Autumn raised her eyebrows at Simone with a sideways smile.

Simone sighed. "I'll take anything Eve made right about now, and Gran's tea sounds amazing."

They nodded in agreement as a strong wind blew through, carrying with it the scent of iris flowers, the kind they'd planted in Gran's memory along the river's edge.

"I guess Gran agrees. Her comfort tea is the perfect choice." Autumn gave Simone a squeeze. "So it's settled. Tonight is for comfort. Tomorrow will be for sleuthing."

CHAPTER 5

Autumn pushed open the back door of the girls' shop, Parchment and Pine, and dropped Tavish onto the floor. Simone tumbled in behind her and lifted her round Lennon sunglasses over her head.

"What's all that noise out front? It's still too early for whatever's going on." Simone threw her vegan leather coat and bag down on the counter in the back and made her way to the front of the shop with Autumn.

Autumn flipped the sign over to "open" at the front door and peered out to see a couple police cars and officers hovering outside the flower shop next door. A few locals stood on the sidewalk out front, stretching their necks to see inside as well.

"Chief Ian Walsh is outside the flower shop with several of his police officers. Looks like a bunch of people are gathering as well." Autumn turned and squinted at Simone as she thought for a moment. "Oh my god." Autumn put her hands over her mouth as her eyes widened. Both girls stared at each other and intuitively came to the same conclusion.

"Mr. Leslie." They said the flower shop owner's name in unison, realizing the man held many similarities to the one found in the river last night.

"It was him. Oh my god, that was Mr. Leslie lying there in the river. I can feel it now. Why didn't I realize it last night?" Simone shook her hands at her sides as if trying to remove the uneasiness she felt.

"Yeah, it was him, but you couldn't have known. It was so dark last night, and his body was face down. There was no way to really tell." Autumn crossed her arms over her chest and watched the officers out the glass front door until she saw Chief Walsh heading over.

She propped the front door open for him and gave a tight-lipped smile. "Chief."

"Hello, Autumn. Simone, it's good to see you out this morning. How're you holding up?"

Simone shrugged and pushed her hands down into the tight pockets of her black skinny jeans. "As good as can be expected, I guess." She sighed and met the chief's eyes. "It was Tom Leslie from next door, wasn't it?"

The chief took off his hat and spun it in his hands. "I'm afraid so. We had his wife confirm it for us early this morning. Now we're just getting as much information as we can. You know the procedure." He reached out his arm toward Autumn to signify that she'd been in a similar situation with her gran.

"We understand. Is there anything we can do to help? I feel terrible, especially now knowing it was Tom from next door." Autumn rubbed her crossed arms with her hands and gave the chief a worried look.

"I'm sure Karen Leslie will need some consoling and possibly even some help with the shop if you're able. As far as I know, their children haven't been around much lately, and from the looks of it, she'll be running the shop by herself while things get sorted. I'm guessing she could use as much support as she can get right now." The chief nodded as he moved his gaze from Autumn to Simone.

"Yeah, definitely. We'll stop by later today and see what she needs." Simone stared at Autumn for confirmation as the chief turned to walk out the door. "Oh, but Chief?" Simone stopped as if the words got caught in her throat. "Does she know I found him?"

Chief Walsh gave her a saddened look. "No, she doesn't. All she's been told is that a runner found her husband late last night. I'll leave it up to you to decide if you wanna keep it that way or not." He placed his hat firmly on his head and walked out the door with a nod.

"What do you think? Should we tell her?" Autumn leaned one shoulder against the wall and watched the gatherers outside.

"We should. She has the right to know what happened. I would wanna know." Simone wandered back to the counter and plopped down on a stool behind the computer. She put her head in her hands and closed her eyes. "Another murder. This is too much drama even for me. I need more coffee and a good dose of some Fleetwood Mac this morning."

Autumn smiled and made her way to the back of the shop. "All right, let me get things going in here, and then I'll pop down to the Forest Brew for some drinks. I just need to get some pop-up cardstock trees and the paper lanterns on display. The Winter Solstice Night of Light event is in about two weeks, and I'm getting a little panicked that we won't be ready in time."

"Don't worry, we'll be fine. I've got all the designs ready to print and assemble, and we've got time before people come in to snatch up all the materials."

"I hope so. I know someone's going to come in early for these pop-up trees, though. They're meant for some kind of party, but that's all I know right now." While Autumn's clairvoyance had always been fairly keen, now that she'd assumed the role of the four-points witch, the air element had grown even stronger within her. It activated a world of intuitive knowledge that came to her at a moment's notice whenever she needed it.

Simone nodded as she set a Fleetwood Mac album to play over the sound system. "Got it. We'll make those the priority today, and I'll set the paper lanterns to print overnight. How about that?"

"That'll work." Autumn found Tavish pacing back and forth in the hearth room as he tried to find a warm spot to snuggle up. "Hey, Tav, let me start the fire for you, okay?" She crouched down and arranged the firewood before starting the fire. Yet, instead of the scent of burning firewood, she smelled sulfur in the air. She stood up immediately and moved her eyes around the shop. Sulfur was one of those smells her gran had taught her to always be cautious of.

"Look to where the wildflowers grow," the ancestors whispered in the air.

"Wildflowers," Autumn said under her breath. She heard something fall behind her and turned as Tavish scurried away from a few papers that had fallen off a side table. Autumn picked them up to find a brochure for the famous mountain region wildflowers stamped with approval from the flower shop next door.

"Hey, Sim, what's this brochure? Did you put this wildflower flyer in here?" Autumn held it up as she walked out of the archway from the hearth room.

Simone squinted at her to see what she was talking about. "Wildflowers? No, where did you get that?"

"It must have been lying on the side table in here. Tavish just knocked it over right after I heard the ancestors say something about looking for where the wildflowers grow."

"Huh, well, maybe a customer left it there. Who knows?" Simone typed a few things into the computer and then bent her head around the side of it to eye Autumn again. "The ancestors said something just now?"

"Yeah, the strangest thing." Autumn walked over to a shelf display full of scented candles and thumbed through them as she spoke. "I caught the scent of sulfur in the back room just as they whispered something about looking for where the wildflowers grow." She pulled a white lavender-scented pillar candle from the back of the shelf. "Here we go."

She made her way to the back room where she opened cabinets and found just the right ingredients. Autumn brought a glass bowl, a box of baking soda, and the pillar candle back to the counter. She poured the baking soda into the bowl and stood the candle upright in the middle of it before lighting it. Taking a deep breath in, she walked it back to the hearth room.

"Okay, that's much better! The scent is subsiding." Autumn grabbed the heavy curtains on either side of the hearth room archway and shook them to air out the smell. "But isn't that strange? Black magic smells of sulfur. Do you think this has something to do with those black specks in the water from Mrs. Allan's dream?"

"Now that you mention it, maybe there is a link, yeah."

"Did you notice anything strange about the river water last night?" Autumn walked back to the counter and brought out the cardstock trees she wanted to work on.

Simone sat back on her stool and folded her hands over her knee. "I don't remember anything strange. I mean, I kind of controlled the water a bit. It was moving quickly, but when I calmed myself down, the waters calmed down, too. That's all I really remember, though. I didn't see any weird specks or magic sparks like Mrs. Allan mentioned. Why? What're you thinking?"

"I'm thinking there's more going on than meets the eye. Maybe we can connect the dots somehow. I guess the water is our best option. If we can go back and try to connect with it, you may get some intuitive downloads this time. If you're feeling up to it." Autumn raised her eyebrows at her cousin.

"Yeah, I'm fine. I mean, I'm not looking forward to talking to Karen Leslie later today about what happened, but it's okay. I'm comfortable with the water even with this craziness happening."

"Okay, good." Autumn shook her head as she cut out a few cardstock pieces and made slits to slide them together. "And what about this strange wildflower message? We need to figure out where they grow."

"You mean besides our run-in with some wildflowers up on the mountaintop a little while back?" Simone tilted her head and gave Autumn the eye.

"Right, let's try to forget all about that for now."

"I have to say, though, that your memory-rearranging trick has been working brilliantly. I don't know how you came up with that one, but I love it. Maybe you can help me use that one on a few of my old boyfriends." Simone laughed under her breath and gave Autumn a nudge.

"To be honest, that just came to me in the moment. I never tried anything like it before, but it worked. I guess I need to keep that one in my back pocket in case anyone else needs help to remember things differently."

"Anyway, how about that coffee? Do you want to run down to the Forest Brew now?" Simone brought her palms together in a prayer position and batted her eyes at Autumn.

"Okay, okay. I'll get you some coffee." Autumn paused for a second to collect her thoughts. "Just do me a favor. Tell whoever comes into the shop while I'm gone that they don't need anything except that long flannel scarf over in the corner. That one has their name on it, but make it quick and don't give them anything else."

Simone tilted her head at Autumn and thinned her eyes. "Nothing else, huh? Okay . . . you got it." She made a saluting gesture and went back to finishing her designs on the computer as Autumn gathered her coat and bag to walk out the front door.

CHAPTER 6

Autumn pushed the door open to the Forest Brew and caught Eve's eye behind the counter. Autumn gave her a quick wave while her friend furiously filled orders for the long line of customers. Wading her way through the people packed into the coffee shop, Autumn heard whispers as she approached the front counter.

"I heard now that Tom Leslie is gone, Karen might have to sell the shop." Marion Bennett stood beside the counter, leaning in and chatting with another woman. Autumn shifted her eyes toward Marion and gave her a slight smile as she made her way toward the front of the line.

"Ah, Autumn! Lovely to see you this morning!" Mrs. Newbury ran the register of their family-owned coffee shop and bakery in the mornings. She always presented a friendly face no matter what was going on around town.

"It's busy in here! What's going on?" Autumn pulled her brown faux suede backpack off her shoulder and around the front of her body to retrieve her wallet.

"Oh yes, well, I'm sure you've heard about poor Tom Leslie. There must have been about a dozen police officers at the flower shop this morning, so it's no doubt you've seen something. And now everyone's in here this morning chatting about it and trying to get a closer look at what's going on." Mrs. Newbury sighed and shook her head. "It's been madness, but I can't complain about the business." She gave Autumn a brighter smile. "So what can I get for you?"

"I was actually stopping by for a cup of Simone's favorite cinnamon latte, a peppermint hot chocolate for me, and maybe a couple of Eve's special pastries." Autumn leaned in and lowered her voice. "Something calming, perhaps?" Autumn looked at Mrs. Newbury with a questioning smile.

Catherine Newbury raised her index finger in the air and nodded. "Ah, yes. I think I know what may do the trick. How about a couple chamomile honey cakes? I'll throw some in a box for you."

"That sounds wonderful! Thank you." Autumn pulled some money out and gave it to Mrs. Newbury.

"I'll just be a moment." Mrs. Newbury gathered up the drinks as Autumn moved around the counter to peer into the pastry case. The ladies who had been chatting at the counter now sat at a table behind Autumn and continued their conversation.

"I'm just curious what this means for the state of our downtown. If the flower shop is unstable, that means new developers will start looking again. We could see an influx!" Marion raised her voice for a moment and then seemed to rein herself back in, lowering it again. "I mean, I'd love to see some fresh development in this town, and this may be an opportunity for just that."

Autumn turned her head slightly at Marion but kept her back to the ladies. Marion cleared her throat and glanced at Autumn before continuing in a lower tone.

"I don't want to be heartless about this whole situation, but what's done is done. We may as well find a silver lining for the town. So our chamber of commerce will just have to address this and see what Karen Leslie plans on doing." Marion took a sip of her tea and went back to her scone for a moment.

Autumn popped her eyes up from the pastry display to see Mrs. Newbury coming at her with the drinks and bag of pastries.

"Here you are, dear. Tell Simone that the latte has a dash of caramel syrup just how she likes it. And I added an extra sprig of peppermint leaf to your hot chocolate." Mrs. Newbury winked at Autumn and handed her the bag.

"Thanks so much, Mrs. Newbury! Try not to work too hard." Autumn smiled at her and waved at Eve at the other end of the counter before heading out the door.

She walked down Main Street, wondering if what Marion Bennett had said was true. Now that Karen Leslie didn't have her husband to help with the shop, she might not be able to handle it on her own. Surely business was good enough to hire someone new. Autumn peeked inside the pastry bag in her hands as she walked. She could really use that calming honey cake right about now, but the aroma would have to do the trick until she settled in back at Parchment and Pine.

Autumn crossed the street, making her way onto the block with the girls' shop. The police officers had cleared out of the flower shop now, and only a couple people stood inside as she walked by. She moved past and walked into the Pine to hear someone grilling Simone at the back.

"Come on, I know you were there. It would be better to tell the story yourself than to have a bunch of rumors spread around town."

Tavish hissed at the woman from his perch on top of the counter while Simone handed her a shopping bag.

"Thanks for stopping in. Let's just keep it to the scarf for today. Enjoy." Simone gave the woman a tight-lipped smile as she grabbed the bag and turned around toward Autumn to head out.

Seeing her familiar face, Autumn instantly recognized her as Anabeth Greenwood, the prominent news reporter for *The Glenn Herald*. She was a few years ahead of the girls in school, so they didn't know each other well. Yet everyone in town knew Anabeth loved to find the feature stories for the front page of the newspaper.

Autumn, Simone, and Tavish all watched her walk out the front door.

"So I'm assuming she came in for the scarf and maybe an inside scoop?" Autumn unraveled her own scarf and placed it on the counter with the Forest Brew bag.

"Yep, thanks for the heads-up on that one. She came all sweetly and then tried to ease her questions in about finding the body in the river. I have no idea how she found out it was me who found Mr. Leslie, but this is stressing me out now." Simone plunked herself down on the stool behind the computer and sighed.

"Here, have a honey cake. Eve put a little extra something in it to help calm us down." Autumn pulled a pastry out of the Forest Brew bag and handed it over to Simone wrapped in a napkin.

Simone instantly took a bite out of it and rolled her eyes back. "Oh my god, this is amazing."

"I thought we could use some pastries to go with our drinks. Oh, and your latte has a little caramel mixed in as well."

"Thank you, Mrs. Newbury. She always gets it perfect. Every single time. I love the Forest Brew." Simone took a sip of her latte and savored it for a moment. "But honestly, how do you think the news found out so fast that I was the one who found the body?"

Autumn ran her hand over Tavish and gave him an ear scratch as she eyed Simone. "I saw a news van pull up at the scene last night as we headed out. I didn't want to say anything, but I'm sure they got a glimpse of us. Plus, odds are they heard someone mention your name on the police scanner. They monitor all of that to get the inside information, you know?"

Simone shook her head. "Great. I guess I better go over and talk with Karen Leslie before someone else tells her it was me, then."

Autumn popped a piece of Eve's honey cake into her mouth and took a swig of her hot chocolate. "Yeah, but before we go over there, I better tell you about the rumors I overheard at the Forest Brew. It got me a little concerned that maybe the flower shop won't be as stable now that it's just Karen running it."

"You mean, she'll be all alone to run it now? She could hire help." Simone shrugged as if it were no big deal.

"Maybe, but Marion Bennett made it sound like Karen probably couldn't afford help. And that could lead to more developers looking at this as an opportunity."

Simone rolled her eyes and got up from her stool to walk to the front window of the shop. She sighed and peered out, checking the foot traffic around Main Street.

"It's not dead around here by any means. Our town is thriving."

"You're right. We're doing well, and lots of other businesses are, too. So we'll just have to help Karen Leslie see she can keep the shop running herself and maybe even make it better than it's ever been before." Autumn thought for a moment as she spoke.

She went to the cabinet beside the back counter and pulled out a green pine-scented pillar candle. She carried it to the front of the shop and placed it in a tall black metal lantern in the front window display. Rubbing her palms together, she blew into them as she thought about her intention. A small flame rose in her right hand. Autumn used it to light the candle and closed the lantern door.

She whispered, "May this spark of change bring growth and prosperity to our town. As I say it, so shall it be." Tavish jumped up on the window display, and all three of them watched the candle flame as it stood unwavering and bright.

Autumn flipped the shop's front sign over to read "Closed" and locked it behind her. She tucked Tavish cozily down into a large flannel-lined canvas bag and followed Simone next door to the flower shop. The lights were still on inside, but they knew the Leslies liked to close up around that time.

Simone pulled open the door as the bell chimed above it. Karen Leslie looked up from sorting receipts at the back of the shop. She shook her salt-and-pepper bob away from her face and put on a soft smile.

"Oh, girls!" She lifted herself from the stool behind the counter and walked to the front of the shop to greet them.

Tavish poked his head out of Autumn's bag, and Mrs. Leslie moved closer to rub his head. "Tavish, I needed that cute little face of yours. It's so good to see you."

"Karen, how are you?" Autumn asked as Mrs. Leslie enveloped them both in a hug.

She swatted her hand through the air as if brushing something away while tears came to her eyes. "I just don't really know now that my poor Tom is gone." She looked at them with surprise. "Oh good heavens, I assume you heard around town and saw all the commotion."

The girls nodded and followed Karen to the back counter, where she began fussing with the receipts.

"We did. It's just awful, and we're so very sorry you're going through this." Autumn gave her a sympathetic look.

"Yeah, we know this was very sudden, and we feel terrible." Simone piggybacked on what Autumn had said and then gave her cousin a questioning look, not knowing how to breach the subject of finding the poor woman's husband.

Autumn tilted her head and pursed her lips at Simone, whose shoulders instantly fell at the thought of telling Mrs. Leslie.

Simone cleared her throat and tried to get Karen to meet her eyes before starting. "Uh, Karen, there's actually something we wanted to come over and talk with you about."

"Oh, all right." Karen lifted her eyes and fixed them on Simone now. "What is it, Simone? I've already had the life shaken out of me today, so I don't know what else would matter much. Go ahead."

"Well, I know the officers were here with you this morning, and they've relayed all they can, I'm sure. But they may not have told you it was actually me who found your husband last night." Simone pressed her hands down firmly into the pockets of her dark-wash jeans as she always did when she was nervous.

"You found my Tom? They said someone found him in the river after dark. How did you . . .?" Her voice trailed off as she spoke, and she grabbed for a tissue on the back counter before raising it to her nose and waiting for Simone to continue.

"Right, I ran along the river trail last night. I like to get some exercise under the moonlight. It helps me clear my head to sleep better, I guess. Anyway, I made my way up to the hill by the old lumber mill and veered off the path. While I was up there, I saw the body in the water and called emergency services." Simone shook her head back and forth with a pained look. "Karen, I'm so sorry. I had no idea it was Tom. We just found out this morning when we saw all the officers outside the flower shop."

"Oh, you poor thing! That must have been horrible for you!" Mrs. Leslie came around to the front of the counter and wrapped her arms around Simone. She looked back and forth from Simone to Autumn. "First your grandmother and now my Tom. I just can't believe this is happening. And the last thing I'd want is for you girls to go through all this again."

"No, Karen, don't you worry about us at all. You know, Simone is tough, and we've gotten through everything together. You'll do the same. I'm sure of it." Autumn put her hand on Mrs. Leslie's forearm to comfort her.

"Absolutely." Simone nodded and stood up taller now that she'd gotten it all out. "And we want you to know that we're here if you need anything at all."

"That's right. If you need some extra help while you figure things out, then we're here. I know it was just you and Tom running the shop, and your kids live somewhere else, so just tell us what we can do to help keep things going." Autumn grabbed a pen and paper from the counter and pulled it close to her.

"Well"—Mrs. Leslie glanced around the flower shop to take inventory—"I honestly have no idea at this point. I've only had today to process all of this, and my mind is just spinning. Of course, I'll have to tell the children, but I don't even know if they'll be able to come home at this point. This is all so sudden." She walked over to one of the table displays with tall red amaryllis flowers protruding from their pots. She stroked the petals as she thought. "This is a slow season for the shop, so that's one good thing. Of course, Tom always did the orders for the holiday parties and events in town, so I'll have to figure that out myself, I guess."

"Let us help you. I can come by tomorrow after work and sift through the orders with you. That'll free you up to do a few other things. How about that?" Autumn jotted the day and time down on the piece of paper in front of her, along with her name. "Here, how's six thirty tomorrow sound? Simone can close up our shop, and then we can see what else you may need, all right?" Autumn handed the paper to Mrs. Leslie, and Tavish gave an approving meow from his snuggle spot inside Autumn's tote bag.

"Tavish agrees with us, and you know we won't take no for an answer, anyway. So you better just say yes." Simone smiled and winked at her.

"I suppose I could use the help. That would be wonderful. Thank you both."

The girls nodded and headed for the shop door. "I'll see you tomorrow evening, then." Autumn stopped in the doorway to gather her thoughts and receive a downloaded message to offer. "Oh, and Karen," She looked back over her shoulder as she spoke. "Have a look at your wildflower inventory before then. Just a thought." Autumn smiled and waved at Mrs. Leslie as the girls made their way outside.

Simone walked back next door with Autumn and Tavish as she considered their visit. They pushed the door open but kept the sign flipped to closed for the night.

"Uh, Autumn." Simone stepped inside the shop and started rearranging some journals on one of the tables. "What made you mention the wildflowers just now? Did you hear the voices again?"

Autumn spun around and thought for a moment. "No, I just got one of my instinctive ideas that told me she needed to hear that. Why?"

"Well, funny you should say that"—Simone lifted her index finger in the air and tilted her head—"because Tom was there in the shop. I could feel his energy lingering around the vase of wildflowers on the counter. He was there the whole time, but of course, I didn't want to say anything to worry her even more."

"Huh, that is a little strange. I wonder what the connection with the wildflowers is all about, then. There must be something to it. Maybe I can find out a bit more when I go over there tomorrow night. What do you think?"

"Yeah, I think you better. His energy felt insistent and kept pulling me toward the wildflowers. Weird, but that's what it felt like."

"Okay, I'll check that out tomorrow, then. But . . . what would you say to going down to the water again tonight? You didn't really have time to connect with it and see if you could sense anything strange the other night. Maybe we could try at the river just behind your mom's house?" Autumn squinted her eyes and scrunched her face up in a pleading look just as Tavish popped out of the tote bag with his sweet kitten eyes.

Simone sighed and rubbed her face in her hands. "Yeah, all right. We can go over there tonight, and I'll see what I can sense."

Autumn scratched Tavish's head in approval of him taking her side. "I just keep coming back to the idea that the water wants to tell us something more, you know? And we need to find out sooner rather than later."

"Well, I'm still kind of creeped out after last night, but I need to get back to the water, anyway. It's my comfort zone, my gift, and . . . it's how I stay connected to my dad. I can't let anything take that away. So this'll give me a good excuse."

"Exactly, you need the water, and the water needs you." Autumn snatched up a few papers from the back counter and waved Simone to follow her out. "Come on, I can smell your mom's vegetable lasagna from miles away."

The girls walked out the back door of the shop and hopped into Simone's black Jeep SUV with Tavish snuggled nicely in the backseat. They cranked up the radio and let go of everything but the music and the aroma calling to their noses from the home-cooked meal that awaited them.

CHAPTER 7

Simone flopped down on the couch in the living room and put her hands on her belly. She lifted her chin slightly to call into the kitchen.

"Mom, that was the best vegetable lasagna you've ever made. I wish I could have eaten the whole pan, but my eyes were already bigger than my stomach."

Autumn laughed at Simone as she wandered into the room. "Hey, I called Eve to come join us, so she should be here in a few minutes."

"Good, I can sit here until then because I need some time to digest that amazing meal first." Simone groaned and closed her eyes for a moment.

"Geez, you're gonna give our mothers the impression that we never cook over at our house." Autumn sat at the end of the sofa by Simone's feet, and Tavish jumped up onto her lap to join them.

Penny shuffled in with a curious look. "I was wondering whether you two were getting along okay over there. Have you had time to cook or are you spending every moment at the shop and on this latest . . . situation?"

Simone chuckled under her breath. "Yeah, it's quite the situation. Autumn's got me going out to the river again tonight as soon as Eve gets here. We're gonna see if I can get any intuitive hits from the water." Simone opened her eyes and sprang upright. "It is pretty amazing, though. This whole idea that people started coming to us with these strange cases, and now we're knee-deep in some magical mystery. I'm kind of digging that." She lay back down with a smile and put her forearm over her eyes.

Autumn rolled her eyes at Simone as she stroked Tavish's fur. "What she's trying to say, Mom, is yes. We've been taking care of ourselves. Simone settled into my old bedroom, and I took Gran's. I did a little cooking last weekend and got some dinners ready for us ahead of time. So, we've been working our way through those. Plus, work is ramping up again with the Winter Solstice Night of Light festival coming. The town really depends on us for all the paper lanterns, so we've put in some extra hours to get the inventory up."

The doorbell rang, and Autumn lifted Tavish from her lap and onto the floor as she got up. She called over her shoulder while walking to the front door, "Simone is right, though. It feels strangely exciting to have this other side of what we do now. This mystery-solving side. Not that we want these terrible things to happen to people like Mr. Leslie, but I don't know. I like how people know they can depend on us to help."

Autumn opened the front door to Eve's bright smile. She stood on the porch, teeth chattering, wearing a toggle wool coat all bundled up and a chunky maroon hat with a pom at the top. A long bunch of dried rosemary stood in her hands like a bouquet. "Hey, Autumn. I brought these along since you mentioned a spell to remember things, and rosemary is amazing for that."

Autumn raised her chin as if understanding her. "Oh, okay. Come in. Simone is just relaxing before we head out back."

Aunt Jo made her way to the front hallway to greet their visitor. "Ah, Eve! It's so lovely to see you. How is your mother doing?"

"Hi, Ms. MacKinnon. She's doing well, thanks. She told me to tell you that if you want your usual Yule log cake this year, then be sure to come in this week and select the ingredients. That way she'll have them on hand before it gets too much later."

"Oh, right! Thank you, dear. Time has slipped away from me this year, and I just can't believe the solstice is right around the corner. I'll make a note to myself to come in. Are you girls heading out right away?"

Autumn waved Eve into the living room where Simone sat watching the fire that Penny had started in the fireplace.

"Yeah, I think we better head out now before it gets much later and colder." Autumn nudged Simone's shoulder and motioned for her to come grab her things.

Simone sighed and got up. "I'm coming. Hey, Eve, thanks for making it over here. It's getting chilly out there, huh?" Simone headed back to the front hallway with Autumn to retrieve their coats and boots.

"It's super chilly out there now. I couldn't believe it when I stepped out of the house tonight. It must have dropped at least twenty degrees since I closed up the Forest Brew."

"That's actually a good thing. The cold thins the energy veil and gives me better readings. I may get more out of the water tonight than we expected. Fingers crossed." Simone held up two twisted fingers poking out of her black quilted coat.

Autumn handed Simone her black knit beanie cap, and Autumn threw on her hand-knit white hat from Gran. "We won't be long," she called back to the living room. "Let's go through the back door, and I can grab a few other things we'll need."

Tavish circled Autumn's feet as she walked to the back door. "Aw, Tav, it's so cold tonight, cutie. Why don't you stay inside by the fire where it's warm, okay? You won't miss much. I promise." Autumn gave him a head scratch and made her way into the kitchen to grab a small cast-iron pot with a handle. She went over to the shelves opposite the kitchen island and glanced through an assortment of hand bells. One tarnished silver one stood out to her in particular, so she grabbed it. "All right, I'm all set. Sim, grab the metal lantern over there, and I'll light it for us."

Simone pulled a tall black metal lantern off the top of Jo's kitchen hutch. It was the same type of metal lantern Autumn used in her window display at Parchment and Pine to complement the girls' hanging paper lantern designs. The metal added a pleasing mix of materials and gave customers more ideas for incorporating everything into a cozy home.

Simone and Eve followed Autumn out the back door with the materials. As soon as Eve shut the door behind them, Autumn closed her eyes and started rubbing her palms together. She saw visions of herself levitating and drawing energy from the winds in her mind. With one big breath, she exhaled into her palms and felt the spark inside them. She opened her eyes and her hands to reveal a small flame in both hands.

Eve's eyes widened. "That's amazing! How did you do that?"

Autumn laughed and lifted her chin to signal Simone to open the lantern. Autumn used the flames from her hands to light the tall white pillar candle inside. "I've been practicing. Turns out, once you know how to activate the fire, it gets easier to draw on it when needed."

Autumn pressed her palms together tightly and merged the two small flames into one. She lifted her lit hand to chest height and turned toward the woods at the back of the garden. "Let's go."

The girls followed Autumn into the garden and through the trees that lined the back boundary. Autumn carefully moved around fallen branches and whispered under her breath as she went. "Land, sea, and sky, we walk this path to connect with your wisdom. Grant us a discourse with you tonight."

The wind picked up around them and pushed against their backs, carrying them closer to the river. The trees thinned, and in front of them sat the shimmering river trickling through the center and icy on the edges.

"We made it." Simone sighed and walked over to the water's edge, putting the lantern down beside it. "The rapids have slowed from the ice, so that will help. Plus, the moon is giving us some nice light tonight."

"Good, hopefully it'll all work in our favor, then." Autumn joined Simone at the water's edge, and Eve followed. Autumn kneeled and placed the cast-iron pot on the cold ground. She shivered and looked up at them. "Wow, the ground is pretty cold under me, and I'm keeping warm with the flame in my hand. We'll have to stay standing tonight. Eve, just hand me the rosemary, and I'll get it going."

Eve lengthened the rosemary stalks in her hands, snapped them in half once, and then again. She handed the pieces to Autumn, who placed them evenly in the pot. She inverted her fiery palm over the top of the rosemary and allowed it to catch the stalks on fire.

Coming to a standing position, Autumn blew a powerful breath into her hands and snuffed out the remaining flames in her palm. She reached out for the girls' hands, and they stood in a straight line along the river's edge with the cauldron blazing before them.

"Earth, air, fire, and water, we call on you for your memories. May we know the history kept in our waters. May we see its records of time. Seep the knowledge of the earth and the skies into these tides so that we may feel the imbalance and sense what needs to be done."

The flames of the cauldron rose and sparked into a brilliant orange, lighting up the surrounding area. The winds picked up, and Autumn's hair swirled furiously under her knit hat. She turned toward Simone. "It's your turn."

Simone smiled and rubbed her hands together to warm them up as she walked over to the icy water. She hesitated for a moment, exhaling deeply and gearing herself up for what she knew she had to do. She bent down to the water's edge and plunged her hands into a crack where the ice broke off. Holding them there a few seconds and then drawing them back up to her face, she let the water gently wash over her skin. She kept her eyes closed and did her best to concentrate on their intentions rather than the temperature of the water.

Eve and Autumn moved closer to Simone as she kept still, crouched over the icy edge. Simone slowed her breath and leaned down, placing her hands on the surface of the trickling water, barely reaching it. She let the cold ripples wash over her hands, and Autumn could see her body shivering in the moonlight.

"Sim, that's enough. You're gonna freeze." Autumn glanced at Eve with a worried look and back to Simone still leaning over the water. "Sim, that's good." Autumn tugged on Simone's shoulders and shook her out of her daze.

Simone leaned back on her heels and shook herself back to the present moment. She looked behind her at the girls and at the river bubbling in front of her. Slowly, the girls helped her to her feet. Autumn stared at her cousin, curious what had caught her attention so strongly.

"Come sit down on this rock while we close everything, okay?" Autumn took hold of one of Simone's arms while Eve got the other and guided her to the boulder beside them.

Autumn closed her eyes and lifted her palms at her sides. "Elements of earth, air, fire, and water, we thank you for your wisdom. May we honor this guidance by shifting the energies back into balance. As I say it, so shall it be." She opened her eyes and grabbed the flaming cauldron from the ground. Eve helped her walk it to the river and douse it with water. The girls turned back to Simone and sighed.

"Are you okay? Your hands were in those icy waters for several minutes." Eve crumpled her fingers up into a ball and covered her mouth with them as if watching nervously for something to unfold.

"Yeah, I'm good. I just . . . had some visions come to me, and I felt them so deeply. I felt the pain of the water and some kind of dark energy seeping into it, trying to take over and strangle all the good energy out. Almost like creeping vines under the surface. And the magic sparks that Mrs. Allan talked about, it's almost like the water is struggling to keep them from spreading, but it can't quite hold them back."

Autumn wrapped Simone's hands in hers and blew into them. "Let's get you back to the house, and then we can talk about this in front of the fire, okay? Eve, can you grab the materials for me, and I'll take the lantern?"

With a nod, Eve followed Autumn's instructions, and the girls made their way back through the trees together and up to Jo and Penny's house. Simone pushed the back door open, still feeling the chills coursing through her fingers as she recalled what she felt.

"Oh good heavens, you three were gone for quite a while. Simone, sweetheart, you look like you need to sit down. Penny!" Jo shuffled over to her daughter, wrapping her in a hug as she called to her sister for help.

Penny appeared in the kitchen doorway and stared at them all.

"Penny, get us some hot comfort tea, would you, dear? I have a feeling Simone has taken on an even greater burden tonight." Jo shook her head back and forth as she stroked Simone's hair. "One that I fear now, looking at her, we all may see come to light in the coming days."

Simone hoisted herself up onto a kitchen stool, and they all stared at Simone's chilled hands as she laid them flat, palm up, on the kitchen island, shaking and covered with tiny specks of shimmering black magic.

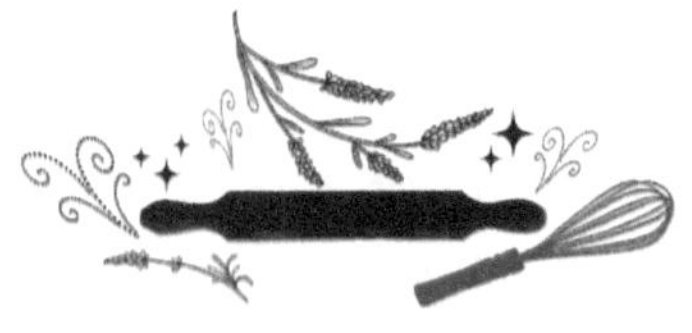

Eve's Amaretto Cream Tarts For Clarity

For the crust:

1 1/2 cups graham cracker crumbs , 12 full crackers

1/3 cup sugar

6 tablespoons unsalted butter , melted

Preheat oven to 350 degrees and grease a 9 inch tart pan.

Mix graham crackers, sugar, and melted butter in a medium sized bowl, then press into an even later in the prepared pie plate or springform pan.

Bake for ten minutes.

For the filling:

1 cup mascarpone cheese room temperature

3 Tablespoons amaretto or almond extract

1/3 cup powdered sugar

1 teaspoon vanilla extract

1/8 tsp lemon juice

1/2 cup heavy whipping cream

Mix on high speed while you whisper to the filling,

With each stir, I make things clear.

When the ingredients are well-combined, set aside. Then, in a separate bowl, whisk the whipping cream until light and fluffy. Fold the whipping cream into the mascarpone filling as you whisper,

One more fold for insights to appear.

Fill the tart crusts with the filling.

For the pears:

2 pears

1 stick of butter

2 tsp sugar

1 tsp almond extract

apricot jam

Slice pears into 1/8 inch slices. In a large skillet, melt butter over medium-high. Add pears, sugar, and almond extract. Cook on each side, swirling the pan gently, until caramelized on the surface, about 2 minutes. Remove pears to a plate to cool.

Once cool, top tarts with pear slices. Refrigerate the tarts for two hours and the smooth a thin layer of apricot jam over the top of the pear slices for a glazed finish. Enjoy.

CHAPTER 8

Autumn eased out the last of the lantern patterns from the paper-cutting machine in the back of the shop. She ran her hand over the perforated lines on the page and inspected the cleanness of the cuts. The girls had just finished a long day of printing lanterns for the solstice festival, and now Autumn planned to stack the pieces before heading over to the flower shop.

"Sim, I've got the last sheet out of the printer, so I'm gonna head over to help Karen. Will you be able to close up and meet me at home with Tavish?"

"Yeah, I'm all set, too. I'll just put out the fire in the hearth room and shut down the computer. Are you sure you don't want me to come over there, too, and then drive you home?"

Autumn made her way to the front of the shop and grabbed her coat and backpack from the wall hooks. "No, you go home with Tav and start warming up some of that sweet potato curry that's in the fridge. I've already messaged James and asked if he could pick me up on his way home from work. So I'll be fine. Besides, you need to rest more after the energy you took on last night. I was really worried about you with those black shimmers, but I'm thankful you know how to put an energy barrier around yourself and not absorb it."

"All right, I'll head home with Tav and rest. I can still feel the tingling on my skin, but you're right. It pays to do an energy barrier incantation every morning. Honestly, I don't think I could survive as a water energy without it. I'd be taking on all the energy around me and be super stressed all the time." Simone swatted her hand through the air. "Enough about me, promise me you won't try to walk home by yourself in the dark. This whole thing with the black magic specks freaked me out, and we should stick together until we figure out what's going on."

Autumn gave Simone a shocked look. "Wow, Simone MacKinnon not wanting to fly solo in everything she does. This is a first." Autumn laughed as she threw on her coat and bent down to give Tavish a head scratch.

Simone rolled her eyes at her cousin and came up to meet her at the front door. "Yeah, yeah. I like being a loner, but I'm being serious, okay? I don't want anything to happen to you, and something feels very off right now. So just do me a favor and get that ride home from James without giving me any more grief about it."

Autumn raised her right hand in the air. "Okay, okay. I promise. I'll call him to come get me as soon as I'm done helping Karen. But the same goes for you, too, you know. If I'm supposed to stick around other people, then I expect you to do the same. Practice what you preach." Autumn smirked at Simone and opened the shop door.

Simone sighed and grabbed the door from Autumn. "I'll see what I can do."

The girls smiled at each other, and Autumn walked next door, calling, "See you and Tav at home. Get some rest. I mean it."

Autumn pushed the door open to the flower shop and called to Mrs. Leslie. "Hey, Karen, it's Autumn."

Mrs. Leslie appeared out of the back with a large assorted bouquet of deep-cranberry-colored flowers and evergreens mixed within it. "Oh, hello, dear. I'm just making a few bouquets for the city hall Christmas party. The mayor's office wanted to fill the space with beautiful reds for the holiday season, so that's what they're getting."

"It's stunning. You did an amazing job, and I'm sure they'll be very pleased with it." Autumn couldn't help but admire the abundance of rich color and warmth in the shop for the winter season. Karen always had the best eye for making a space look lush and grand with natural colors and textures, and this year's display was no different.

"Plus, I have to say, you've done such a lovely job with this year's winter display. The colors feel so indulgent and perfect for the season. I absolutely love it, and I don't know how you blend it all together so beautifully."

Mrs. Leslie tilted her head at Autumn and gave her a warm smile. "Thank you, Autumn. I guess this is what I do best. You know I love flowers with all my heart, and they've just always been something beautiful that I could count on in my life besides Tom." Mrs. Leslie's eyes watered, and she choked up getting the last few words out.

"Oh, Karen, I know this must be hard. Here, come sit at the counter and tell me how I can help. Should we look through your orders for the day and get things organized?" Autumn guided Mrs. Leslie over to the counter and gave her a tissue.

She nodded at Autumn and opened up a spreadsheet on the computer. "I've been doing my best to log all our orders into this spreadsheet, but I may have fallen behind today. It's just been so overwhelming with it being just me in the shop. I've had to process orders, handle all the customers, work on the party requests, and that's not even all I have to do with getting our inventory on track." Mrs. Leslie waved her tissue in the air as she mentioned all she had to do.

Autumn gently rubbed her back. "Don't worry. It'll all be okay. Let's just start with inputting today's orders and making sure you've got everything in your system so you don't lose track of it, all right? Then, we'll work out the rest from there."

Mrs. Leslie nodded at Autumn and pointed to the spreadsheet columns on the screen. "Well, these are all the orders from the past few weeks. We log them in individually, and then we also note anything special about the payments and such. Tom always did this, though, while I prepared the flower arrangements. So I'm a little embarrassed to say I don't completely know his system."

Autumn nodded and glanced at the spreadsheet. "Why don't you wrap up a few more of your bouquets for the party, then, and I'll see if I can make sense of the spreadsheet. Just point me toward all your orders for the day, and I'll do my best to input them."

Mrs. Leslie stood up and slid a wooden tray over toward Autumn filled with invoices. "These are from the last couple of days, and I haven't looked at them carefully yet. It would be such a help if you could put them in for me!"

Autumn took off her coat and laid it on the back counter as she swapped places with Mrs. Leslie. "No problem. I'll get right to it."

Mrs. Leslie smiled and walked toward the back of the shop, picking out a few buckets of flowers from the refrigerator as she went. "I'll just be in the back if you need me."

Autumn pushed up the sleeves of her billowy teal knit sweater and scrolled through the page on the screen. She took the first invoice off the top of the tray and walked herself through the spreadsheet one column at a time. That one seemed to go fairly smoothly, so she took the next one out of the tray.

This time the order included a spray of wildflowers along with the bouquet, and it looked like Mrs. Leslie had written a note on the invoice to check the inventory. Autumn remembered her intuition suggesting to look at the wildflowers the other day, so she didn't want to dismiss the note. Mrs. Leslie would be far too busy to keep track of minor details right now, and Autumn wanted to ensure she and the flower shop got through this tough time unscathed.

"Uh, Karen?" Autumn called to the back, hoping not to interfere too much with Mrs. Leslie's bouquet-making.

"Yes, dear? Is something wrong with the spreadsheet?" Mrs. Leslie made her way to the counter and looked over Autumn's shoulder.

"No, it's not the spreadsheet. I wondered about the note on this invoice about the wildflowers. Did you check your inventory for those so you can process this order? Or is there a way I can do that for you?"

"Oh, the wildflowers! Yes, those are actually a special case." Mrs. Leslie nudged in toward the computer and took over to find another page for the shop inventory. "We grow most of our flowers on the farm on the outskirts of town, and some come in from different parts of this region. However, Tom always went foraging for the wildflowers himself."

Autumn looked at Mrs. Leslie with curiosity. "He did? I always wondered where they came from, but I didn't think we could pick the flowers from the local lands."

"It's true, you're not supposed to pick the flowers. As far as I know, Tom was one of only a couple people who had a permit to forage locally. It took us several years to convince the environmental department at city hall, but my Tom finally did." Mrs. Leslie leaned in closer. "It helped that we offered to give the city a discount on their special events. Still, it took a while for us to get approved for that permit. So Tom had a few areas around town where he could get the most beautiful wildflowers at certain times of the year."

"Like these you have here on display?" Autumn motioned to the overflowing yellow vines spilling out of a glass vase on the counter. The same ones that Simone noted Mr. Leslie's energy hovering around the last time the girls were in the shop.

"Yes, exactly. Tom found those winter jasmine near the river in town. He would go there regularly and watch the blossoms. When they were ready, he cut just enough for the next week's orders."

"I see. Do you think that's what he may have been doing the other night when he was at the river?" Autumn saw the worry seeping into Mrs. Leslie's mind.

"Probably, yes. I was at my knitting club that evening, but that's usually when he would go foraging. Let's check the inventory sheet and see if he made any notes." Mrs. Leslie scrolled through another spreadsheet as Autumn tried to follow it. "You can see the dates where Tom marked down the wildflowers he foraged, including the winter jasmine. They're listed here."

Autumn put her finger on the screen and pointed to a column toward the end where some items were marked with an asterisk. "What are these notes here?"

Mrs. Leslie moved away from the computer and started shuffling papers on the counter. "Yes, that. I don't know exactly, but I can guess." She crossed her arms at her chest and brought one hand up to cover her mouth. "Autumn, something was going on at the river. Tom had found out about it and got pretty upset. He started going down there so often to forage that he started noticing it regularly."

A lump formed in Autumn's throat. She wondered if there was a connection to the shimmering black specks in the water. "Go ahead, Karen. You can tell me anything."

Mrs. Leslie covered her eyes with her hand for a moment, and Autumn heard her holding back tears. She looked up at Autumn and nodded. "The lumber mill was polluting the water. Tom saw the runoff they allowed to spill into the river. It happened regularly to where Tom got so infuriated by the chemicals he saw. He wrote an email, confronting them for contaminating the water and saying how he would have to report it to the city."

Autumn considered the idea of chemicals polluting the waters. It would definitely offset the balance of the elements in the region and cause harm to the town's water supply, but that didn't account for any black magic. Maybe there was something more to the chemicals that Mrs. Leslie wasn't aware of entirely.

"So did Tom report the chemicals?"

"He told me the owner of the mill changed their policies and stopped the runoff, so there was no need to report them." Mrs.

Leslie tightened her arms around her chest, and Autumn tried to gauge what else she wasn't saying.

"You think there was more to it than that?" Autumn looked from Mrs. Leslie to the spreadsheet on the computer screen.

Mrs. Leslie sighed and pointed to the asterisks on the screen. "I think those asterisks were not only when he would go up to forage, but when he would meet with someone up at the mill. I can't be sure of it, but I think it's possible they may have bribed Tom to keep things quiet."

"So the pollution didn't just stop at the possibility of being reported. You think they were paying Tom off so they could keep doing it." Autumn stood up and paced around the shop, processing the information. "Why do you think there was a bribe involved?"

Mrs. Leslie sat on the stool behind the counter and folded her hands on the countertop with a sigh. "Because before he started inputting those asterisks, we were having a hard time making the rent payment. The orders just barely covered our costs, and every time he took the deposits to the bank, it looked quite light. The last several weeks, though, the asterisks had gotten more frequent, and I'd noticed him with a larger deposit envelope. Plus, he stopped complaining about the rent."

Autumn looked down at the floor as she paced, following the lines of tile with each step. "Okay, that's definitely peculiar, but that doesn't mean he was taking bribes. What about the asterisks? When did you notice those?"

"I noticed last weekend when I had to check the inventory for some of the upcoming bouquets. I pulled up the spreadsheet and asked Tom about the asterisks, and he mentioned he was double-checking on the pollution when he went foraging. When he said that, I knew there was something more to it, though. He's never been very good at hiding things from me, so I always knew when he wasn't saying something."

Autumn moved closer to the counter and stood next to the yellow wildflowers, trying to get some inspiration for what to do next. She breathed in deeply but couldn't pick up a scent from the flowers. So she concentrated on the air around them, allowing it to give her any knowledge that it could provide. Inhaling again, she took in bergamot, a recognizable scent for its correlation to abundance and wealth. She used to smell it in the air when Gran gave her an allowance for helping sell tea.

Autumn widened her eyes and looked at Mrs. Leslie. "We need to track the deposits. If Tom was being bribed, then maybe he took the money to the bank and put it in the shop account. That may be why the envelopes looked bigger than usual. Karen, if you want me to look into this, I can."

"Oh, Autumn, I'm so worried about what I may find, and yet, all I can think about is how this may have had something to do with my poor Tom's death. It's been keeping me up at night, and I don't know what to do." Mrs. Leslie turned off the computer screen and spun her body around to face away from it. "I just can't bear the thought that all this may have caused Tom's death."

"Have you said anything to the police about this?"

"No, I didn't mention it because they didn't say there was anything suspicious regarding the mill. I just don't know what to do."

"It's all right. Let's just see if there's anything to this first, and then we can notify the police if we need to. Would you like me to take your deposits down to the bank this week and see if I can find out anything more? I'm pretty good friends with Sarah there, so maybe I can get her to tell me whatever she knows."

"I don't want you to have any problems because of this, Autumn. It's bad enough Tom got himself involved in something."

Autumn walked around the counter to give Mrs. Leslie a hug. "Don't worry. I'll just take your deposit in as usual and see what comes up, okay? We don't have to take it any further than that if you don't want to."

Mrs. Leslie gave Autumn a hesitant nod. "All right, we make our deposits at the end of the week, so I've already taken it in for this week. I can tell the bank to expect you for next week, though, if you're all right doing this. I'll let you know in a few days when it needs to go in."

"Perfect. I'll be ready when you've got it all together." Autumn sighed and looked around the flower shop. "How about we call it a night for now? You need to go home and rest, and I'm expecting my ride in a few minutes."

"You're right, dear. I need a good night's sleep, and the shop will be closed tomorrow. So there's no sense in staying late tonight."

Autumn smiled and ran her hand across the long, yellow wildflower vines one more time. A low humming noise slowly grew in her ears, and she heard the whisper of the ancestors.

"Gather the elements. Reveal the vine."

She curiously eyed the streaming flower strands as the humming slowed. "Reveal the vine," Autumn whispered under her breath.

"What was that, dear?" Mrs. Leslie questioned.

"Oh, nothing." Autumn shook her head and turned to see the headlights of James's black truck outside at the curb. "That's my ride. I hope I helped tonight." Autumn gathered up her coat and bag and gave Mrs. Leslie another warm hug.

"Yes, dear. I always appreciate your help. Thank you."

"Will you be able to close up and get home all right?"

"Oh, I'm fine. I'll close up as soon as you leave and head right home. I'll see you early next week, then?"

Autumn nodded and waved as she walked out the front door, nervously trying to shake off the feeling that more danger lay ahead, not just with the water but for the town as well.

CHAPTER 9

Autumn stumbled out of her bedroom, rubbing her eyes while Tavish excitedly circled her feet.

"Someone's hungry this morning." She went straight to the kitchen to put the teakettle on, start the coffeepot, and get Tavish started on his breakfast.

Simone peeked out from behind her bedroom door and squinted. "You're up already? It's too early to get up. We don't even have to open the shop today."

Autumn swiveled her head over her shoulder. "I know, but our moms are coming over for breakfast. Plus, last night I invited James over, so I need to throw some clothes on before he gets here. I was hoping we could all talk about the things I found out last night."

Simone perked up and scurried into the kitchen in her lipstick-red cozy socks. "All right, I'm awake. Sounds like you found out something good last night, huh?"

Autumn poured a cup of coffee for Simone and grabbed herself a tea mug out of the cabinet. "I don't know about good, but yeah, I did. Tom was involved in something, and I'm worried that it may have led to his death. Let's wait until everybody gets here, though. I need to get dressed." Autumn dunked a readymade tea bag of rooibos into her cup and hurried back into her bedroom. Tavish looked up from his food for a second to see her whirl by and then stuck his head back down into his bowl.

Simone slid onto a kitchen stool and warmed her hands with her coffee mug. "Great. Get me all excited to hear what's going on and then ditch me." She sighed and looked into her mug. "At least I have coffee."

Autumn leaned her head out the bedroom doorway as she pulled her hair into a low side braid. "Relax, I'll give you all the details in just a minute, but I want to look somewhat presentable when James gets here." Autumn fumbled around in her bedroom to pull on a pair of stretchy black fleece leggings and an oatmeal-colored tunic sweater. She threw on some tinted moisturizer and mascara and came out into the hallway.

"How's this? Casual for a Sunday morning but still cute enough?" Autumn posed in the hallway long enough for Simone to glance over and give her a thumbs-up.

"You're good, but you know you don't even need to try with James. He's completely smitten with you already." Simone walked to the front window with her coffee mug as she heard a car pull up outside. "Our moms are here."

"Oh, good! I'm starving, and they said they'd bring break-fast." Autumn opened the front door for the two ladies to walk straight in carrying paper bags and jugs of drinks.

"Morning, girls. How did you both sleep?" Jo went directly to the kitchen to drop everything on the island. "We seem to have brought the whole Forest Brew pastry counter with us this morning."

"Did you stop and get all of this just now?" Simone made her way in to see the selection while Autumn greeted her mother trailing in at the door.

"Yes, we brought the juice, fruit salad, and an oatmeal bake from home, but we had to stop for some fresh pastries at the coffee shop. I saw Eve making them yesterday, and I knew I couldn't resist them for long." Penny dropped her coat by the front door and brought the bags inside.

"Thanks for coming over this morning. I figured this would be the best time to talk, and James is coming by as well." Autumn unloaded the pastry bags and put the muffins and coffee cake rolls onto a large platter while Simone pulled out more tea mugs.

"Oh, is James bringing his mother along as well?" Jo looked up curiously.

"I don't really know, but I'd guess it'll just be him. I think Mrs. Allan has been staying home and keeping to herself the last few days. From what James mentioned, this last dream really shook her." Autumn took a sip of her rooibos and closed her eyes to savor it.

"You're right. I went over to check on her the other day, and she's been resting. The dreams always take a lot out of her, and this one made her feel so worried and even vulnerable. I took her some of my special anxiety-calming bath salts to help relieve her concern. Hopefully, she's taking advantage of them." Jo set a stack of plates on the kitchen island and took one off the top for a coffee cake roll.

Tavish let out a big meow and trotted to the front door just as the bell rang. He sat beside the door, looking at everyone in the kitchen as if they should have known someone was there.

"Tav, how do you always know? I'm glad I keep you around." Autumn scooped up the cat and pulled the window curtain back on the door to reveal James standing there. She opened it up and stood back to let him inside.

"Long time no see." James grinned and looked at her with his warm brown eyes.

Autumn let out a soft laugh and closed the door. "I really appreciate you bringing me home last night. It was good to see you at the end of a long day."

James rubbed Tavish's ears as the cat purred. "Yeah, I felt the same way. You calmed me down after a rough day at work."

The three women eyed each other with curiosity in the kitchen as they watched Autumn and James.

"James, come inside and have something to eat. We've got lots of wonderful pastries and fruit. Help yourself." Jo waved him in as she poured him a cup of orange juice.

They made their way into the kitchen to join everyone, and James gratefully took the juice from Jo.

"Tell us how your mother is doing. Is she taking care of herself?" Penny inquired as she dished out a few items onto a plate for him.

"She's actually slowly getting back into things, and she was very grateful for the bath salts. Thank you for those, Ms. MacKinnon." James nodded at Jo.

"Oh, call me Jo, please. You've been around enough now to be part of the family. It's just Jo to the family." She gave him a wink and took a bite of her coffee cake.

"All right, Jo. Thank you. Yes, Mom has been sleeping better now that the dream passed, and she's cooking again, which is good for her." James dug into a slice of the oatmeal bake. "Mmm, this is amazing."

"Oh, thank you." Penny smiled at him. "I put a few comforting spices into this batch since I knew we could all use some of that."

"Speaking of needing some comfort, I wanted you all to come over this morning because I found out a few things we should discuss." Autumn sipped on her tea and then sat it down on the kitchen island to start into her speech. "Simone closed up the shop last night so I could go over and help Karen Leslie at the flower shop. I mentioned this to James on our drive home, but I was worried about her after some rumors I heard at the Forest Brew."

"Rumors? What rumors?" Jo perked up from her plate.

"Marion Bennett spoke to someone else from the chamber of commerce about how Karen Leslie may have to sell to a developer now that she's the only one to run the shop. Marion seemed to think the shop wouldn't survive with just Karen to run it, and that made me really concerned. So Simone and I talked about it and decided to help Karen with a few things while she got her bearings." Autumn played with her tea mug as she spoke and glanced over at Simone.

"You found something out while you were over there. What was it?" Simone pressed her elbows down onto the counter and leaned in to hear.

"While I input some orders into the computer for Karen, I needed to look through their inventory. So she opened the spreadsheets and showed me some marks Tom made in the books on certain days."

"He was keeping track of something in their inventory? Like what?" Jo seemed confused.

Simone sat straight up and eyed Autumn. "Wildflowers."

Autumn nodded in agreement with her intuitive cousin. "Yeah, wildflowers. Turns out, Tom was one of only a select few people who have a local foraging permit. He went down to the river occasionally and foraged for their wildflowers, only he saw things he wasn't supposed to see."

"Like strange magic in the water?" Simone tried to put the pieces together. "Like what was on my hands the other night and in Mrs. Allan's dream?"

"No, it wasn't. I'm still not sure how that fits in here, but he found out that the old lumber mill has been allowing chemicals to run off into the river water. Apparently, he confronted them about it and told Karen they intended to stop. She didn't think that actually happened, though."

"She thinks he lied to her? They've been married for years and have been very happy together. I wonder what would make him lie to her." Penny topped up everyone's drinks as she listened.

"Karen thinks they were paying him off. Bribing him to keep quiet about it, and he possibly met them on the days when he foraged up there by the river." Autumn nodded in thanks to her mother for the tea.

"But why on earth would he take bribe money? He's always been so conscious of the environment and a huge proponent of keeping our lands protected. He would have been pretty desperate to take bribes and look the other way about damage to our water system." Jo shook her head in disbelief.

"It sounds like the desperation came from wanting to keep the flower shop afloat. Karen mentioned having a hard time paying the rent until he started taking thicker deposit envelopes to the bank. That's when she noticed the marks in the inventory log."

Jo raised her hand to her mouth. "Oh my, so the flower shop was in trouble."

"I think it was, and possibly even more so now that Tom is gone. Karen is all alone to run it, and most likely these bribes will stop now that Tom is dead. She's really worried that it's all connected, but she hasn't gone to the police yet."

"Well, why on earth not? They need to investigate," Penny interjected with frustration in her voice.

"She's just making assumptions, and I think she's afraid of what the police are going to dig up." Autumn moved over to her plate and took a few bites of the coffee cake roll.

James shook his head and looked around the room. "So how do we help? Where do we need to start?"

"I think I know where." Autumn turned to her aunt, Jo. "I heard the voices again in the flower shop last night. They mentioned something about gathering the elements to reveal the vine, and I keep thinking about the founding families."

"Of course, the founding families exist precisely for this purpose. James, your family is one of them, so you're probably familiar with the responsibilities." Jo moved into the living room and stood in front of Gran's heirloom wardrobe on the side wall behind the front door. She ran her hand along the wardrobe doors. "The five founding families—plus our own ancestral bloodline that activated the elements—are bound together and to these lands to protect its energy and maintain the balance. If necessary, the families must come together and activate their gifts as one to shield from further harm."

"And each of the families have different elemental gifts to bring together," Simone chimed in as she walked toward her mother in the living room.

"That's right." Jo nodded and looked at the wardrobe. "Inside our family Book of Spells, we hold a cleansing spell that requires activation from the founding families. It's a spell for when the lands are in real danger, just as they were when our ancestor bestowed gifts on each family."

"So we need to gather the founding families and determine whether the cleansing spell is necessary now." Penny stood beside her sister at the wardrobe and placed her hand on the doors as well. "It's time to open the cabinet." She turned her head toward Autumn as she felt the energy vibrating from inside the wardrobe.

"That's been playing in my mind, yeah." Autumn walked over to the wardrobe with Tavish and James close behind her. "What do we need to open the cabinet?"

"The right intention. Everyone come close and gather hands. James, you as well." Jo reached her hands out to them, and they all locked hands in a circle. "Close your eyes and repeat after me." Jo cleared her throat and breathed deeply. "Ancestors of these lands, we come to you for support in resetting the balance and reclaiming our waters. With my words, allow us to retrieve the spells you've chosen for us to use. Bound by the elements, we seek balance together. Bound by the elements, we seek balance together."

The rest of them joined in with Jo as she spoke and repeated the saying several more times. Autumn felt a tinge of heat at her chest from her gran's locket. She opened her eyes and lifted her hand to pull it out from under her tunic. Penny opened her eyes to glance at Autumn and gasped as a brilliant green light emanated out of the locket's edges.

Autumn opened the locket as James, Simone, and Jo turned to her as well. "Here's the key." Autumn removed a tiny antique key from inside the locket and held it up to show everyone.

"Wonderful." Jo smiled and raised a hand to signal Autumn to open the wardrobe.

She twisted the tiny key into the lock and pulled the doors open to reveal a large wooden box on the bottom of the wardrobe floor. The edges glowed with the same green light shining from her locket. Autumn bent down and opened the lid on the box to pull out an old hardbound antique book.

"Wow, that looks incredible," James whispered under his breath.

"Our family Book of Spells." Jo took the book from Autumn and brought it over to the coffee table in the living room. She knelt next to the table, and the book pages began fanning themselves out until the right page lay open in front of her. Jo read the page aloud. "'Cleansing Harmful Energies Through Interconnection.'"

"Interconnection? What does that mean exactly?" Simone peered at the book over her mother's shoulder.

"It means we need to be one. We need to gather the families." Jo ran her finger down the page, reading through the spell as she spoke.

"But how do we gather everyone together and figure out if we really need the spell?" Autumn knelt beside Jo and glanced at the book with her.

Jo brought her eyes up to meet Autumn's and sat quietly for a moment, receiving guidance from her intuition. She smiled and patted Autumn's hand with her own. "We hold an enchanting dinner party."

Penny clapped her hands together and raised them to her mouth as her mind began processing the idea. "Yes! An evening of interconnection, discourse around the imbalances, and . . ."—she thought for a moment before continuing—"a demonstration at the river's edge to reveal the direness of the situation."

"That'll definitely be an evening to remember." Simone widened her eyes and gave Autumn a questioning look.

"They're right. It's the best way forward." Autumn shrugged.

"All right, then, I guess we're hosting a dinner party." Simone put her hands on her hips and felt the energy of relief swirling its way up from the Book of Spells and into the room.

CHAPTER 10

Autumn pulled a stack of cream linen envelopes from her soft faux suede backpack and untied the twine strand that held them together. She ran her hand along the front of the top envelope, admiring her work. She and Simone had made the invitations for most of the day yesterday, giving them an old-world feel to signify the long-standing connections of each founding family. They calligraphed the names in dark-black ink on the front and melted a red wax seal on the back. Autumn saw the seal regularly as a child in the region, and it was one that her gran familiarized her with the older she became. Yet, until this point, she hadn't realized that the symbol unified the elements and the families who protected them.

The Celtic quaternary knot of four infinitely connected corners stood in the center of the seal. It represented the elements of earth, air, fire, and water joining. The founding families used the symbol to communicate with one another about important matters, and Aunt Jo recommended the girls use it on the invitations. It would be a clear sign to the families that the dinner was an urgent matter.

Autumn stood in the back room of the Forest Brew, waving goodnight to some preservation committee members while holding the invitations close to her chest. As chair of the committee, Autumn made sure this evening's meeting remained a quick one. The Winter Solstice Night of Light was the biggest thing on the calendar right now, and the preparations were mostly done. Other than that, the downtown revitalization project continued to be well underway. The Allan family's construction company had already refurbished the old wishing fountain, and a small section of the cobblestone streets had been repaired. After the lantern festival, they would discuss the river walk renovations further. For now, though, there was a lull in activity, which was good since Autumn intended to focus on solving this recent death and the energy imbalance.

She waved to Mr. Lachlan as he put his coat on to head out the door. "Oh, Mr. Lachlan, I have something for you." Autumn handed him an envelope and paused for a moment as he looked it over. He flipped the invitation over to reveal the wax seal on the back and raised his eyes to meet hers with seriousness.

"Your presence is requested this Wednesday. My family hopes you can attend." She lifted her pointer finger in the air.

"But there is something that I'd actually like to ask if you have a moment."

"Of course, Autumn. Anything." Bryce Lachlan guided Autumn's arm over to the side to get them both out of the way of all the committee members heading out.

"I was wondering if you've noticed anything strange about the reservoir lately. Anything out of the ordinary or maybe . . . a different energy than usual. I figured you'd be the one to notice since you run the marina and maintain those waterways." She gave him an inquisitive look.

Bryce ran his hand over his chin as he thought. "Now that you mention it, the water has been murky lately. I haven't put much stock into it, though, since winter's here and everything's freezing over. I imagine we'll see the waters run clearer once the snow and ice melt next spring. Does this have something to do with Tom Leslie being found in the river?"

"Nothing's really clear right now, but there are some things my family needs to discuss with all the founding members. Please, just think about it and join us on Wednesday, all right?"

"Yes, of course. I'll plan to be there. Thanks, Autumn." Bryce nodded and headed out the door.

Autumn continued waving over a few other members as they gathered their things to leave. She motioned to James's uncle, Dillon Ross, and Mayor Halpin. "Gentlemen, I have something for you both." Autumn handed them each an invitation with their family names on the front. The two men looked at each other and then at Autumn. "I'm sure you're both aware of some recent events around the river, and considering things that have transpired, my family requests your presence on Wednesday evening."

"Right, yes, we best be there, then." Mayor Halpin flapped the invitation against one hand and nodded in agreement.

"Yes, ma'am. If you and the mayor say we need to be there, then be there I shall." Dillon patted the mayor's shoulder and gave him a firm smile. He tipped his head to Autumn, waved back at James in the corner, and headed out for the night.

"Autumn, anything you want to give me a heads-up about before Wednesday?" The mayor squinted his eyes.

"We have some suspicions about the water in town being . . . polluted. Possibly with chemicals and other things even more dangerous. There's a chance it connects to Mr. Leslie's death."

Mayor Halpin gasped and ran his hand over his mouth. "I see. If that's the case, then this definitely calls for a gathering." The mayor shuffled the invitation back and forth in his hand while he thought for a moment. He waved goodnight to a few other committee members as they both stood together to the side of the doorway. "Let's keep this as quiet as we can for now, okay? Once we get the other members involved and figure out what we're dealing with, then we'll see how far we need to go to make things right."

"I agree. Thank you, Mayor." Autumn shook his hand with a hesitant smile.

"Good, and don't worry yourself over it all now. You just have a good night and rest, you hear?" He raised his eyebrows at her and threw his wool trench coat over his arm to walk out.

James approached Autumn at the door as the last of the committee members walked out. Other than the Newburys and the waitstaff cleaning up, Autumn and James were the only ones there.

"Walk me back to the shop after I talk to the Newburys?"

"Of course. There's something I wanted to talk with you about, anyway." James stared at her with his warm brown eyes.

"Uh oh, whenever you start a conversation like that, it never leads to anything good."

James tilted his head to his shoulder and widened his eyes. "Well, I wouldn't say that. It's not always something bad, but I guess it's not usually good, huh? I'll have to fix that in the future."

Autumn nodded and smiled. "Yeah, you definitely will. Maybe try something like asking me to dinner or talking to me about an amazing new project you have going on or something. You know, something other than doom and gloom." Autumn sighed. "Now I'm officially stressed about whatever it is you want to tell me."

James waved his hand back and forth to dismiss his comments. "No, it's okay. Just focus on the Newburys right now, and then we can go back to the Pine, okay?"

Autumn tightened her lips and stared at him for a moment, gauging how serious he looked. "Okay, yeah. Just give me a minute, and we can head out."

Autumn turned and headed over to Mr. Newbury, who was tidying things up on one of the back tables. "Mr. Newbury, I have something for you."

He turned to find Autumn standing behind him with an invitation in hand. "Oh, what's this?" He took the envelope from her and inspected it.

"An invitation. My family requests your presence on Wednesday evening for dinner and . . . a demonstration." Mr. Newbury flipped the envelope over to reveal the wax seal. He lifted his head in surprise and waved his wife over. "Catherine."

Catherine Newbury stopped wiping the tables and walked over to them. Her husband raised the envelope so she could see the seal as well.

"Oh my! Something's happened?" She tucked the dish towel into her apron and took the envelope from her husband. Mrs. Newbury read the front of the envelope aloud. "The Newbury Family." She shook her head, looking back and forth between Autumn and her husband before opening the invitation and scanning it. "The presence of your founding family is requested on Wednesday evening for dinner at the MacKinnon residence. To be kept in confidence, as always." Catherine gripped Autumn's hand. "Oh, dear. It's been quite a while since I've seen the seal used. We had better drop everything and be at dinner, then."

Autumn gave Catherine a hug. "We'll expect at least one of you there, but you're welcome to both come. And we could use Eve's help as well." Autumn turned to see Eve coming into the back room to gather up some dishes. "She's quickly becoming an invaluable part of our little threesome."

Eve's parents squeezed one another tight, and Catherine stared at their daughter for a moment. "I had an inkling she'd fit in nicely when the time came. Eve has always had the strongest connection of us to the earth."

Eve walked over to her parents and Autumn. "What's up?"

Autumn raised her eyebrows at Eve's question. "We were just saying how much we appreciate you coming around lately. And my family's invited you all to dinner this week, so you have to come."

"Oh, okay, is it just dinner or is this about the black magic?" Eve glanced around at them all as she blurted it out.

"Black magic? Oh my word!" Catherine Newbury covered her mouth with her hands.

"Oh, should I not have said something? I'm sorry, Autumn. I just thought . . ." Eve gave Autumn an apologetic look.

"No, it's fine. You're right." Autumn put her hands on Eve's arm, trying to calm her worry. "It is about the magic, but we haven't pieced everything together yet." She locked eyes with Mr. Newbury now, speaking directly and in a tone that offered a new perspective on her authority. "We'll be discussing the latest events and the possibility of some harmful energy in our town. If you all would be so kind as to attend, then you'll find out more about how you can do your part to help."

Mr. Newbury nodded in agreement. "Right. We'll do our part."

"Thank you both so much. Eve, I'll see you Wednesday, but just try to keep things under wraps for now." Autumn smiled warmly at Eve and turned to gather up her things.

James held out Autumn's coat for her as she slipped her arms into the sleeves. He reached for her hand and led her out of the Forest Brew and onto the dark Main Street to head for Parchment and Pine.

The moment the cool night air hit her skin, Autumn took a deep breath and looked into James's eyes. "So are you gonna start talking now?"

A large grin spread across his face. "You don't forget anything, do you?"

"Nope, not really." Autumn laughed as they strolled down the street under the tall lights. "So let's hear it. I know it's not about a picnic under the stars or some other dreamy thing. You better just pull the Band-Aid off and tell me whatever it is."

The streetlight changed, and they stopped at the corner to wait for it. James angled toward Autumn and rubbed her arms with his hands. "How am I ever supposed to get anything past you?"

"You're not, and that's how I like it."

"Uh huh, okay." James looked around them under the streetlights. Only a couple other people strolled along the other side of Main Street. He sighed and looked at her. "I had a dream. This one felt dark and close to me somehow."

The light changed, and Autumn grabbed his hand to continue walking the block with Parchment and Pine. "Well, that doesn't sound very good. Let's get into the shop and start a fire in the hearth while I hang some lanterns. You can tell me more and reassure me that everything's gonna be okay." Autumn smiled at him as they reached the shop door.

James stopped and pulled Autumn closer to him before she could pull her keys out of her backpack pocket. He ran his hand along her cheek and leaned in. "Everything's going to be okay."

He pressed his lips against hers, and she could feel the warmth enveloping her even as the winds intensified around them. The awning fabric on the storefront window flew up with force, flapping loudly in the wind. The two of them remained unperturbed, standing in each other's arms in the doorway.

"How can I argue with that? You always seem to comfort me when I need it most." Autumn pulled out her keys and let them both inside. As they walked in, she pulled him close to kiss him again and breathe in the roasted-chestnut scent that warmed her heart.

CHAPTER 11

J ames stoked the fire in the hearth room of Parchment and Pine while Autumn pulled out a few paper lanterns to hang throughout the shop.

"Don't make the fire too big. I need to get home to Simone and Tavish soon, but I need to hang a few lanterns to show the customers coming in for festival orders. Plus, you need to tell me about this dream of yours." Autumn strung a navy piece of raffia ribbon through the top of a white rectangular paper lantern. She placed it on the floor in a group of several lanterns sitting beside a ladder.

"Here, let me hang these up for you." James came out of the hearth room, grabbed a lantern, and climbed the ladder. "Are you sure the fire inspector is okay with you hanging all these from the ceiling?"

"Oh, yeah." Autumn waved her hand through the air like it was no big deal. "He knows we have our own way of putting things out, no modern technology needed. So he basically lets us do what we please."

"He knows, huh?" James gave her a curious eye as he tied up the lantern.

"Yeah, the fire chief is the mayor's brother, so they're a founding family. They know what we're capable of." Autumn tilted her shoulder up to her chin slyly.

James laughed and climbed down the ladder. "Well, I know what you're capable of, too, and I think we're all in trouble."

Autumn punched his shoulder gently. "Hey, you better watch it. There may come a day when you really need me."

James nodded and sighed. "Don't I know it. It worries me you're in the middle of all this again, but I know you're meant to rebalance things. So I just want to be here to help, but I'm afraid I make things worse by sharing these dreams."

"No, your dreams are important. Yours and your mother's dreams have allowed us to see things coming. Otherwise, this stuff would have blindsided us. So I really appreciate you trusting me enough to share them. And speaking of dreams, tell me more about the most recent one."

James moved the ladder over a few feet and grabbed another lantern to hang. "This one felt intense. Someone was in the water, reaching above their head, flailing their arms around, but they were far below the surface, looking for someone to help them. I could feel their fear and panic, as if I were in the water with them."

Autumn looked up at him on the ladder. "Your mom said she could feel the fear of being at the river in her dream as well."

"Yes, but she felt like she was watching in the dream. In mine, I'm looking at the person in the water, but it almost feels like an extension of me. Like I have some kind of connection with the person desperately trying to be rescued. Yet, the person was distinctly separate from me. I've never had that type of connection to a dream experience before. When I woke up from it, my lungs felt like they were burning, and I couldn't control my breath."

Autumn felt a warm sensation on her chest as she listened to James. She tucked her hand into her sweater collar and felt Gran's necklace resting on her skin. She knew it must be glowing under her sweater, which usually meant she should pay attention to something.

"Was this the first time that ever happened?"

The warmth of the necklace subsided as Autumn smelled a powerful aroma of vanilla wafting through the air. It reminded her of the closeness of their family evenings when Gran and Aunt Jo baked together. She wondered if perhaps there was something familial about James's dream, but she let it go for the time being.

He came down from the ladder, sighed, and brushed his hands together to signify the job was complete. "Yeah, this is new. I've never experienced anything like it. But I don't really know how far off the dream might be, because the water seemed normal. It wasn't completely iced over like everything is becoming now. So that makes me think this is a long way from actually happening. And yet, my dreams rarely come that far in advance. I'm not sure what to make of it."

"All right, well, let's go sit in the hearth room for a few minutes and try to process it. We've gotta wait for the fire to die down before leaving, anyway. I'll make some tea."

Autumn scooped up the materials left on the ground, and James pulled the ladder closed before bringing it to the back. She started the electric teakettle in the back room as she called over her shoulder, "You know, I really like spending all this time with you, but I feel like I'm the one getting the better end of the stick. I mean, you gave me a ride the other night, and now I have a beautiful hanging lantern display to show off."

James propped the ladder up beside the back door of the shop and made his way to Autumn. "I guess I'm gonna have to cash in my chips, huh? We need a proper dinner or something."

"Speaking of which, are you coming to the house on Wednesday for the dinner party?" She handed him a mug of peppermint tea, and they walked over to the chairs in the hearth room.

"That depends if you want me there. I'm sure my uncle, Dillon, will attend, but I wasn't sure if you needed anyone else from our family." He took a sip of the tea and wrinkled up his forehead. "This is good. Peppermint?"

Autumn nodded and smiled. "Yeah, sometimes I like to end the day with peppermint tea. Gran used to make it to help me relax and calm my nerves. Plus, it's good for any headaches from the day."

James leaned back in the chair and let himself sink into it. "It has been a long few days, so this is much needed." He looked over at her as she crossed her legs into her chair and wrapped her hands around the tea mug. "You know, this has been really good for me, too. Spending time with you and getting to know you better. I feel like I finally have someone to talk to openly, and that's nice."

She smiled at him and nodded in agreement. "Good, I'm glad. Because before you came along, it was always Simone with her tell-it-like-it-is comments and Aunt Jo's wind-in-her-hair, breezy nature. Of course, my gran was a voice of reason, but now that she's gone, I needed someone to talk to as well. So maybe we came into each other's lives at the perfect time."

"I think we did." He took another sip of his tea and pointed to the fire. "The embers died down. We can probably wrap up."

"Okay, but I want to hear more about this dream on the way home. I can expect a ride again, right?" Autumn stood up and took the tea mug from him to rinse it in the back sink.

"I wouldn't leave you here to walk home alone. Come on, I'm parked out front. You can analyze my dream once we get going."

She threw her knit scarf around her neck and wrapped it a couple times before grabbing her coat and bag. They double-checked everything around the shop one last time and made their way to the front of the shop to turn out the lights. Autumn still smelled vanilla lingering there. As they walked out the front door, the scent swirled around them and into the street, hovering around James's truck all the way home.

CHAPTER 12

Autumn rearranged the remainder of Gran's tea jars on the green hand-painted hutch inside Parchment and Pine. She gathered the black teas together into straight lines and made a large opening in the center of the hutch shelf.

"Why are you reorganizing? The jars were fine the way they were. Besides, we don't have anything new to put there." Simone came up beside Autumn and stared at the hutch inquisitively.

"Not yet, but something will go here soon. I just know it." Autumn pulled out a dust cloth and wiped down the shelf. "I wanted it to be ready for whatever's coming."

The bell at the front door chimed, and both girls turned to see Penny walking through the door. She carried a basket on her arm and placed it down on the ground in order to remove her hooded down coat. She always had been a practical one.

"Morning, girls." From the basket, Penny pulled out a few small brown kraft paper bags folded over at the tops.

"Hi, Mom. What have you got?" Autumn peered into the basket.

"Oh, I thought I'd get some ideas for something I'm considering. But I don't want to get too far ahead of myself. It's just a thought." Penny handed one of the brown bags to Autumn. "Open it up."

Autumn peeled back the round white sticker that kept the top folded down. She eyed the inside and then held it up to her nose to sniff. Lifting her head in surprise, she turned around to find Simone hovering behind her. So, she handed the bag to Simone to smell.

"Turmeric and ginger." A slight smile crept over Autumn's face.

"A healing tea?" Simone handed the bag back to her aunt, Penny, who placed it down in the basket.

Penny walked further into the shop, wringing her hands. "I know I'm not your gran. She had a beautiful gift with her teas, and no one can ever replace her. But I hoped to reinvigorate her tea line into something more . . . healing and restorative instead of problem-solving, as she liked to do." She lifted her hands as if to calm any assumptions. "Of course, this is all just an idea, and it doesn't have to go anywhere if you both don't want it to." Penny eyed them both with hesitation.

"So, you're saying that you want to put your earth energy to use here in Hollow's Glenn? To reinvent Gran's tea line?" Autumn bent down to grab the basket and rummage through the bags of tea. She smelled the herbs trying to contain themselves within the little bags, but they each were bursting at the seams with incredible scents.

"I know quite a bit about herbs and how to use them to heal. That is what I've been doing all these years in the mountains. But I found myself looking for a way to stay and be present with you now, and this could be the answer to that. If you want me to stay, of course, and if you feel I could do your gran's tea justice." Penny fidgeted with the hematite crystal bracelet on her wrist as she waited for the girls to respond.

Autumn walked over to the hand-painted hutch she had just cleaned off moments before and started laying out the brown bags of teas in the empty space.

"Mom, I don't just think you can do Gran's tea justice. I think you can create an incredible new collection that not only honors our roots but also supports renewal in people's lives. That's what you really do. You heal the person holistically in mind, body, and soul, and I think it's high time you did that here." Autumn stood back to look at the teas she had laid out on display. "I mean, the teas are already bursting at the seams with healing magic. I can smell each one of them melding together and trying desperately to be let out of the bags. We may as well sell them as a proper collection."

Penny hugged her daughter and stared at the lovely rows of tea bags Autumn had aligned on the hutch shelf.

"Autumn's right, Penny. There's a green aura around these bags similar to your own. You've infused them with your healing spirit, and that's gonna be incredibly powerful. I mean, Gran's teas were amazing, but these . . . these look like they're on a whole new level." Simone threw her hands up in the air. "When can we sell them?"

Tears formed in Penny's eyes as she nodded. "Oh my goodness, how about in the next few weeks after we get into the new year?"

"Sounds like you have yourself a new job and your very first order." Autumn smiled and took another whiff of a tea bag.

"I guess I do, don't I?" Penny pulled a few more tea bags out of the basket for the girls to smell.

Just as they sorted through the teas, the bell chimed again.

"Good morning, ladies," a strong voice called from behind them. They turned to see Ben Walsh standing in the shop with a sheepish smile on his face.

"Ben, hi. What are you doing here?" Simone suddenly felt butterflies swirl in her stomach.

"Oh, well, I, uh . . . I came to check on you and see how you've been doing after what happened. How are you holding up?"

Autumn and Penny exchanged looks and then glanced between Simone and Ben. A connection definitely existed between them, but Autumn wasn't sure if Simone had let herself believe it yet.

"I'm good. You don't need to check up on me. I mean, I'm glad you came, but seriously, I'm fine." Simone stuck her thumbs in her back jeans pockets as she spoke.

"Okay, well, I thought you might want to get some fresh air. I know it's getting chilly out there, but I actually find this to be one of the best times of the year for a motorcycle ride. The air is so crisp, and the landscape is beautiful right now. And I'm on my lunch break, so I figured I'd come check on you and ask if you'd like to take a ride, too."

Unsure of what to reply, Simone dropped her mouth open and hesitated. She turned toward Autumn for a little help.

"Sim, why don't you go? It'll do you some good to get out for a bit. You can both grab some lunch while you're out, too." Autumn widened her eyes at Simone and tried to tell her telepathically she'd be crazy to pass this up.

"Yeah, okay." Simone shrugged. "But I thought you needed to go down to the bank soon to take in a deposit. Did you forget?"

"Right . . . the deposit." Autumn had completely forgotten she was supposed to take the flower shop deposit down to the bank today. This was her chance to find out more about the thicker envelopes Mrs. Leslie had seen her husband taking to the bank.

"I can stay here for a while. You girls both do what you need to do. I'll tend to the customers and start planning for a new tea display, all right?" Penny started shooing them both away.

"Mom, are you sure? I won't be gone too long, and I can bring us both back some lunch from the Forest Brew. Would that work?" Autumn really wanted to see what she could find out from her friend at the bank, and this would be one of her only chances to get over there.

"Absolutely. Simone, don't worry about being back by a certain time. We'll take care of everything. And Autumn, you just help Karen and bring back something tasty for me."

"If you're both fine with it, then yeah, I guess I'll go for that ride." Simone smiled at Ben. "Let me just grab my coat from the back."

Simone jogged to the back of the shop, threw her black quilted coat over her black V-neck sweater, pulled a pair of vegan leather gloves on, and crammed her phone into her jeans pocket. "Okay, I'm ready." She came back up to meet Ben and waved to Autumn and Penny.

"See you both soon. I've got my phone if you need me." She tapped her pocket and followed Ben out the door to his motorcycle parked on the street.

Autumn and Penny moved closer to the front window to watch them speed away.

Penny put her hands on her hips and shook her head. "Well, isn't that interesting? Simone's actually letting someone into that shell of hers."

"She's selective in all the right ways. But he seems good for her, and something tells me he's gonna be around for a while." Autumn headed to the hooks by the front door and pulled down her scarf. "Once I get the deposit from Karen, I'll just be a few minutes at the bank. I'm gonna try to talk with my friend Sarah Marshall. She works there now, and maybe she'll be more inclined to tell me what she knows."

"Just be careful who hears you. We don't know what's happening yet, so it's better to keep things quiet. This town is full of busybodies, not to mention whoever did this to Tom Leslie is still out there. I don't want you getting hurt." Penny moved away from the front window and toward the door to see Autumn out.

"I'll be discreet, don't worry. The last thing I want is to stir up more trouble. Although, I have an idea more is coming whether we're ready or not."

Autumn gave her mother a hug and walked out the shop door, grasping her gran's necklace around her neck and hoping her ancestors were coming along with her to ask some questions.

CHAPTER 13

The flower shop was full of customers when Autumn stepped inside. She waded through the people choosing their favorite stems from large buckets on the display tables and found Mrs. Leslie at the counter.

"Oh, Autumn, there you are! I worried you had forgotten." Mrs. Leslie rang up a customer and grabbed an envelope from underneath the counter. "Here, this is all ready for you, and the bank knows you're coming."

"Perfect!" Autumn looked around at the buzz in the shop. "What's all this about? Are you running a special?"

Mrs. Leslie sighed and ran her hand over her forehead, looking exasperated. "I'm beginning to think it has something to do with the article that ran in the paper this weekend about my Tom. It was that Anabeth Greenwood woman who wrote it, and I think the whole town has been in now. Probably to snoop around and see what's happening for themselves."

Autumn tilted her head in contemplation. "I didn't see the article, but I know she was in our shop, asking questions of Simone. Simone didn't tell her anything, but it sounds like Anabeth just took what she had and ran with it. I'm sorry, Karen. I know this is a lot." Autumn leaned in closer to whisper. "But on the plus side, you have a lot of customers, and that always helps."

Mrs. Leslie put her hands on her hips and whispered back to Autumn, "True. I need the business. And yet, I have no idea how I'm going to get these orders filled with it being just me. I'm going to have to come up with an idea." She waved her hand in the air to dismiss it. "Oh, but don't worry about that. It would help so much if you would take this down to the bank and see if you . . . hear anything. Like we discussed."

Autumn nodded and took the envelope from Mrs. Leslie. "Of course. I'm heading there right now, and I'll let you know how it goes." She tucked the envelope into her backpack and made her way through the crowd to the door.

Autumn didn't know what to make of the flower shop or the fact that the newspaper had run an article. She had to get her hands on the latest paper and see it for herself. She made her way down Main Street and pulled her gray wool coat tighter around her. The temperature dropped, as it was now the last month of the year and only about a week away from the solstice.

She took a few moments to admire the shop windows along the street. Each one displayed beautiful greenery and garlands.

String lights wrapped the trees that lined the street, and Autumn hoped the festive atmosphere would be enough to keep people coming and supporting the town. Just the thought of developers sweeping in to take over the historic charm made her want to defend Hollow's Glenn at all costs. She had to help the flower shop stay afloat and keep the Leslie family there. Yet, Autumn knew the influx of customers from the article wouldn't last, not to mention if there had been any bribe money. She hoped that by some chance the flower shop had just had a few great weeks of extra cash flow, but she knew somehow that wasn't true.

Autumn crossed her fingers and made her way past city hall and into the bank. She walked a little way into the lobby when someone called her name.

"Autumn!" Her friend Sarah waved her hand in the air from her desk on the side. "I'll help you over here."

Autumn smiled gratefully and headed over to Sarah's desk. "Hey, Sarah. How's everything going?" She sat down on a chair and pulled the envelope out of her bag.

"Things have been great. I've been busy with work and spending time with Dave. In fact, we've gotten pretty serious lately." Sarah slid her hand over the top of her desk so that Autumn could see it closer.

Autumn gasped when she saw a large diamond ring sitting atop Sarah's finger. "You're engaged! Oh, Sarah, I'm so happy for you. Congratulations!"

"Thanks, Autumn. I'm so excited, but we're going to take a while to plan the wedding. With all that's been going on in town lately, we want to make sure things settle down first."

"Right. Dave must be so busy at the town-planning office now. I completely forgot that he worked there until now."

Sarah shuffled some papers and took the envelope from Autumn as she lowered her voice. "Yeah, the recent situation at the river has all of city hall up in arms about security concerns in town and even access to the river at night. And the article that just posted this weekend created such a stir."

"Right, the article." Autumn wondered what must have been going around. She had to get her hands on that article.

"Poor Mrs. Leslie. She said you were helping her get things sorted out when she called earlier. Something about helping with the books." Sarah stopped what she was doing for a moment and looked at Autumn to confirm.

Autumn shook herself out of her daze and confirmed. "That's right. Since she's right next door to the Pine, I figured we should help her out as much as possible. It's only her right now, and she mentioned that Tom always did the books. In fact, she got confused about when to actually bring in the deposits and how much because there were some weeks that seemed to be much higher than others."

Sarah pursed her lips and looked around them to check if anyone was listening. "There were some weeks when Mr. Leslie would come in with a much larger deposit than usual. These last few weeks in particular. It made me curious, but he always equated it to having a big offer going at the store. So, I just brushed it off. This is the first deposit since he . . ." She cleared her throat and paused for a moment. "Well, since he died. And this one looks much more in line with what the shop normally deposits."

"Okay, so it's lighter again." Autumn squinted at Sarah and tried to gauge what she was thinking.

"Oh, definitely. At least a few thousand lighter than the last few." Sarah nodded vigorously and continued inputting numbers into her computer. "I'm just gonna take this over to the counter so they can confirm my count. I'll be right back." She slid her chair back and got up with the envelope Autumn had brought.

Autumn watched Sarah walk away and crossed her arms over Sarah's desk. She casually leaned over it to get a better view of the computer screen. Sarah had left the Leslies' account open, and Autumn scanned it to find any hints at the figures Sarah had talked about. She noticed the deposits labeled in green with a plus sign, and the last several listed were in the tens of thousands. The one she had just brought in, though, sat around six thousand. There was definitely a disparity between the numbers of the last few weeks and the typical deposits.

Autumn heard Sarah's footsteps heading back to the desk, and she leaned back into her seat again.

"Okay, all set. Here's your receipt for today's deposit. Please give that to Mrs. Leslie for her records and let her know that she's welcome to come in anytime to review the shop account.

And if she'd like you to help more often, then we can add you to the account access list." Sarah handed Autumn the receipt as she gathered up her things.

"Thank you so much, Sarah. I really appreciate your help." Autumn smiled and pointed to Sarah's finger. "Oh, and give my best to Dave. You make a really lovely couple, and you should tell him I said he's a lucky man."

"Autumn, you're the sweetest. I love seeing you. Give my condolences to Mrs. Leslie, will you?" Sarah already started typing on her computer and waved another customer over to her desk as Autumn put on her coat.

"I will, thanks." Autumn headed toward the door and put all this aside for a moment to think about her lunch order. She was starving now, and she'd promised her mother she would return with lunch. She pushed open the bank door and made her way down Main Street, headed for the Forest Brew on the next block.

As she stopped for the streetlight to turn, the wind picked up furiously and sent the smell of Gran's honesty tea wafting through. Autumn hadn't smelled that tea for several months, since right before Gran died when she made it for a local couple. Yet now, it was as if she was in the kitchen with Gran steeping a big pot of the tea.

An idea popped into Autumn's head as she crossed the street toward the coffee shop. She pulled out her phone and stopped in front of the shop to call her mother. Her mother answered the shop phone right away.

"Hey, Mom, I'm actually just down the street about to walk into the coffee shop, but I had a question for you. What were the ingredients to Gran's honesty tea?"

"Oh my, let me see if I can remember." Penny paused for a moment on the phone. "It definitely had geranium leaves and myrrh oil in it. Those were the essential ingredients. But I believe almond extract added a twist that was all her own. Your aunt Jo used to comment about it being like amaretto cookies, and I just loved that idea."

Autumn knew her mother was smiling to herself with nostalgia on the other end of the phone. "Okay, so it's the almond that brings it all together, interestingly. Thanks, Mom. I'll be back with lunch soon." Autumn hung up the phone and went into the Forest Brew.

Eve immediately waved at her from behind the counter. "Autumn, I can help you over here."

She walked around the line of customers at the cash register and sat at one of the pastry counter bar stools. "Thanks, Eve. I appreciate it. Hey, are you and your family going to make it tomorrow evening to the dinner party?"

"Yes!" Eve clasped her hands together with a dish towel between them at her chest. "I wouldn't miss it!" She covered her mouth for a moment. "Oh, I'm sorry if I'm being too loud. I know we're supposed to keep it under wraps."

Autumn laughed. "It's okay. We're having guests for dinner and a lovely evening, right?"

Eve nodded and winked. "Right. Exactly. So what can I get for you? I just put together a new recipe for amaretto cream tarts. Would you like to try them?"

Autumn's jaw dropped open, and her eyes flashed over to the pastry counter beside her. She searched through the overflowing baked goods to find the tarts. They looked sumptuous with their sprinkle of cocoa powder and crystalized sugar on top.

"Those are actually just what I was looking for. But for tomorrow night, though. Could you make a couple dozen for the party?"

"Yeah, absolutely. Anything for my favorite dabbling besties." Eve slid the case open to pull out a tart. "Here, have a taste and let me know how this will accompany the dinner."

Autumn took a bite and closed her eyes. The luscious cream melted in her mouth, and the graham cracker crust gave it a substantial finish. "This is amazing." Autumn tried to speak through her mouthful of food.

Eve shrugged her shoulders up and bounced on her tiptoes. "Oh, I can't wait to make more."

"Good, I'll take the order for those, and I'll place a lunch order for today. My mom's waiting at the Pine, and I promised something warm and filling. Let me just go grab a menu at the front, and then I'll let you know what I decide."

Eve nodded, and Autumn headed to the register to find a menu, when something else caught her eye. On a table sat *The Glenn Herald* newspaper. She glanced at the headline article titled "Local Man Found Dead In River." Autumn squinted her eyes and scanned the article for a moment. It mentioned a man being found by a runner in the evening and the possibility of foul play. She startled herself back into the moment as she heard someone clearing their throat behind her. Autumn turned and stepped aside to find Vera Cunningham standing there.

"Oh, Autumn, hello. I didn't recognize you from behind." Mrs. Cunningham pulled out a chair and sat down. "Is everything all right? Are you looking for something?"

"No, I'm sorry. I didn't mean to be standing over your table. It's just that I saw the paper, and it caught my eye." Autumn pointed to the front page.

Mrs. Cunningham put her hand on Autumn's wrist. "Isn't it awful? Another death in Hollow's Glenn. The family lives down the street from us on the outskirts of town, you know. I drive by their flower farm every day that I come into town."

"I didn't know you lived on the edge of town as well." Autumn turned to face her now, and Mrs. Cunningham lifted her hand to offer her a seat. Autumn graciously accepted in order to learn more about Mrs. Cunningham's connection with the Leslies.

"Yes, we've lived there for about twenty years now. Your grandmother used to come to the house occasionally and deliver her tea. It's such a lovely area of town to live in, but honestly now, I'm not so sure. I have my suspicions, you know." Mrs. Cunningham nodded and took a sip of her tea.

"Really? Was there something going on in the neighborhood?" Autumn acted as casually as she could, even though she wanted to know every detail.

"Well, Tom Leslie always felt he knew how to handle the land better than anyone. I mean, he was a wonderful flower farmer, but he was so serious about it. So it came as no surprise when I heard of the dispute between him and the Fergusons over their farmland." Mrs. Cunningham leaned in over the table toward Autumn. "Something about the property line not being drawn correctly and it entitling the Leslies to more land. I heard they served papers to the Fergusons and got ready to take them to court."

"So the Leslies asked that more land be theirs? That's interesting." Autumn sat back in the chair and folded her arms over her chest.

Mrs. Cunningham nodded and sliced off a small corner of her coffee cake. "Tom Leslie was a polite man, always doing what he could to help. But with the land, he was adamant about what he thought was best. Even here in town, I've heard he's made a few complaints over the years about some environmental concerns." She raised her eyebrows as she took a bite of her coffee cake.

"I had no idea he felt that strongly about the farm and the environment."

"Oh yes, but recently it sounded like more than just taking care of his land. Almost like they needed that extra land to stay afloat. And if I know Grant Ferguson, he wasn't going to let anyone take that land away from him. He meant to hand it down to his son and their new grandchildren for their family home. You don't interfere with a man's family, or there might be consequences." She took another bite of her coffee cake and wiped her mouth. "Well, I really need to be on my way, but it was nice to see you again, Autumn."

"You as well, Mrs. Cunningham." Autumn got up from the table as Mrs. Cunningham put her coat on.

"Oh, you know, I meant to tell you how much I've been enjoying that calendar you gave us. And Bill recently put in some holly bushes for me, inspired by that calendar. I just couldn't be more thrilled." She snatched up her purse and left a tip on the table.

"I'm very glad to hear it."

"You know, if you have any more of your gran's tea at all, I'd love to have some for comfort on these dreary winter days coming. Stop by if there's any chance you might have a batch." Mrs. Cunningham patted Autumn's arm and nodded as she walked away.

Autumn took a deep breath, trying to process all that she'd said. If the land dispute was true, then Grant Ferguson could be another potential person to want Tom Leslie dead. Perhaps she could do a little investigating of her own out at the Leslies' farm and bring some of Gran's tea along as an excuse. For now, though, her stomach told her she needed to get lunch for her and her mother and get back to the Pine.

The kitchen doors popped open at the back of the coffee shop, and Autumn looked up to see Eve holding a piping hot chicken pot pie in her hands. Autumn's expression melted as she saw it, and she lifted her finger to tell Eve she'd be taking the whole thing to go.

CHAPTER 14

Simone stood shivering on a stepladder in Jo and Penny's garden, stringing paper lanterns up in a large maple tree. The lanterns created an enchanting ambience for this evening's dinner besides showing off Autumn and Simone's new collection ahead of the solstice festival.

"Pull it up a little higher." Autumn directed her cousin as she supervised the display.

"How's this?" Simone tugged on the twine carrying the lantern to lift it into the tree branches.

Autumn put her palms out in front of her to signal Simone to stop. "That's good. You can tie it there."

"Girls, this looks absolutely lovely!" Penny walked out the back door of the house and into the garden, carrying a stack of cranberry-colored flannel linens. "I'm going to lay the table while you finish that up. Autumn, we're going to need you to start the bonfires and warm the air a bit before the guests arrive, but it wouldn't be a bad idea if you could warm things up for us while we get ready, too. Would you mind, darling?" Penny gave her daughter a sympathetic look as she threw the flannel tablecloth over the large wooden barn table.

"Of course, Mom. Just give me a minute." Autumn closed her eyes to pay attention to the wind blowing through the garden. The chill bit through her, but she tried to calm her breath and encourage the fire energy within her to come forward. She began whispering under her breath.

"Winds of these lands, merge with the fire energy within me. Flow with warmth and comfort to surround this garden and those on this land tonight with the pleasantness of a spring day. Flow with warmth. Flow with comfort." Autumn repeated the last few words a couple more times and felt the heat rising within her arms. She lifted them up in front of her, and immediately the wind raged around in a swirling motion.

Autumn opened her eyes as the wind died down. She felt the settled air warm on her face and smiled as she looked around the garden.

"Oh, that's much better. Thank you!" Penny called as she pulled her scarf off from around her neck. "It must have warmed up at least twenty degrees! Autumn, my darling girl, you're quite the wonder." Penny shook her head and smiled with pride as she continued placing evergreen boughs along the centerline of the table.

"I'll say you are. Can you do that on the nights it gets into the single digits this winter? I love the cold, but it'd be nice to skip the bitterness altogether. Just a suggestion." Simone pulled her black fleece neck gaiter off over her head and sighed with relief.

Autumn shook her head at her cousin and helped her mother place glass candle holders along the table. "I'll see what I can do."

"You know, Simone"—Penny glanced over at her niece with sly eyes just as Jo pushed through the back door with a large wooden bowl full of sage bundles and clear quartz crystals wrapped within them—"I haven't heard how your motorcycle ride went with Ben yesterday. Did you have a good time?"

"What's this?" Jo turned her head toward her daughter with a look of surprise on her face. "Ben Walsh took you on a motorcycle ride?" Jo smirked with interest as she placed a sage bundle at each place at the table.

Simone sighed and walked over to the table to help the three of them finish the place settings. "He just stopped by the shop to check on me after all that's happened, and he suggested we get some fresh air. That's all." She shrugged and placed a few pinecones atop plates, trying not to blush.

"He likes you. A lot, judging from that kiss he gave you the other night at the river. And I know you like him, too." Autumn threw her hands up in defense as Simone shot her a glaring look. "Don't deny it. You're really cute together. Or would you rather I say he counterbalances you?"

"I don't need anyone to balance me out. I'm perfectly capable of balancing myself, thank you very much." Simone tilted her head to the side, thinking for a moment as she pulled napkins through round circles of rosemary. "Although, I will admit I do like spending time with him. He appreciates my independence and, yes, my rebellious nature. But he also looks out for me, which is endearing. I don't know. I guess I just wanna give him a chance."

"The Walsh family is full of good men. He'll definitely watch out for you." Jo stopped setting the table and gave her daughter a hug.

Simone eyed her mother curiously. "Said the woman secretly in love with Chief Walsh all these years."

"Oh, stop." Jo waved her hand through the air to dismiss the comment. "There may be a connection between us, but it's no longer time for us. It's your time, and I'm glad to see you're taking advantage of it." Jo perked her head up and looked around the garden. "Now, what's happened to the chill? Autumn, have you already changed the weather?"

Autumn nodded. "Oh yeah, I did. We were freezing out here getting everything ready, so Mom suggested I get a head start on the spell. I don't know if we could have stayed out here all this time otherwise, but it looks like we're wrapping up now."

"Yes, this all looks wonderful! Thank you so much for this beautiful display! Now, I've got to finish dinner and consider how we're going to present all the news to the founders. Girls, why don't you get yourselves ready and then head down to light the bonfires and the luminarias along the path to the river, all right?" Jo swatted at the air to signal them to go inside.

Autumn started for the door when she remembered something. "Oh, one thing before I get ready. I asked Eve to bring a batch of her amaretto cream tarts for dessert."

"Those sound lovely." Jo gave her niece a questioning look while feeling as though there was something more to it than just dessert. "But they're not just to complement dinner, are they? The tarts give something special to our guests tonight?" The three women looked at Autumn, searching for an answer.

"I smelled Gran's honesty tea in the air just as I headed into the Forest Brew yesterday. When I called Mom to confirm the ingredients, I immediately knew I was supposed to order the almond dessert that Eve had prepared."

"That's interesting. I had no idea when I spoke to you it had to do with the dinner tonight. The almond brings increased mental clarity and connection with a higher plane. It should heighten openness and connection tonight," Penny said while walking over to a small, bare bush sitting beside the back door.

She bent down and ran her hands along the branches of the bush in a caretaking way. Just as she moved her fingers over a thin branch, a couple tiny green leaves and a small white flower grew right in front of her. Penny plucked the flower and placed it in her palm to walk over to the three of them. She pulled the petals open to reveal a small almond inside.

They all looked at her in amazement. "Almonds are a beautiful expression of magic. Give the tarts to as many of our guests as possible tonight. They'll aid in our ability to decipher what's going on and to heal it." With that, Penny handed the almond flower to her daughter, patted her on the shoulder, and headed to the garden perimeter to put a shielding spell around the space.

CHAPTER 15

Autumn heard the doorbell ring downstairs as she put her clear quartz drop earrings on and fastened Gran's locket around her neck. Stretching his legs and yawning, Tavish stood up from his warm spot on the guest bed Autumn used occasionally.

"Come on, Tav. We need to get downstairs and start the evening. You can sleep more after we're done tonight, I promise." Autumn gave the cat a head scratch and checked her slimming burgundy turtleneck sweater dress in the mirror one last time. Tavish meowed, and Autumn tilted her head to look at the cat in the mirror behind her. He stood with his front paws on her tall black faux leather boots that lay on the bed.

"I guess I need those, too, huh?" She smiled and grabbed the boots to tug them on. "Good, now we're ready. Let's go."

She walked out the guest bedroom door as Tavish sauntered behind her down the stairs. A flood of people came through the front door as she made her way down. When she got to the last few steps, Autumn looked up to see Aunt Jo welcoming in James and his mother.

James caught Autumn's eye and smiled warmly. She had never seen him look so dapper before in a layered plaid jacket with a navy-blue cardigan, collared shirt, and tie underneath. He walked over to her as she took the last steps on the stairs.

"Hello, stranger." James grabbed her hand and kissed it while Tavish circled his feet. "And hello to you, too, Tav."

"You look very put together this evening." Autumn slung her arm in his and walked with him through the house to the back door as his mother continued chatting with Aunt Jo.

"I was going to say the same thing about you, although you're much more . . . spellbinding than anything." He gave her a wink and continued to escort her to the back garden quickly filling with guests.

"Spellbinding. Hmm, I'll take that as a compliment." Autumn released James's arm and caught Simone's eye. She raised her pointer finger to signal to her cousin that she needed one minute. "James, I need to light the fires. Give me a moment, and I'll find you soon."

He nodded, and she made her way over to one of the large cauldrons sitting on the stone patio. Simone joined her and nudged her shoulder.

"James is looking rather handsome this evening." Simone raised her chin toward him.

"He is, you're right. But let's focus on what we're here for tonight, okay?" Autumn said, pushing up her sweater sleeves and shaking her head.

"Okay, fine. I'm just making an observation that maybe I'm not the only one who's interested in someone right now." Simone smirked and moved in close to her cousin. "What do you need me to do?"

"Looks like my mom already put all the logs into the cauldrons. I'll get the fires going if you can pour the waters around the outer channel of the cauldrons. She left some pitchers of water out right there." Autumn pointed to the corner of the house.

"Got it. You get started." Simone tapped Autumn's shoulder and went over to the house to grab the pitchers.

Autumn took a deep breath and focused her energy. She envisioned the fire within her igniting at her solar plexus and fanning out through her body and into her hands. Rubbing her palms together, she whispered to herself.

"Fire energy within me, ignite the cauldrons of our garden and light up the night as we come together to restore the balance of energy." Autumn brought her hands to her mouth and exhaled deeply into them. As she moved her hands in front of her, small flames ignited in each palm and grew larger as she moved them toward a cauldron. "Bring forth the light. Bring forth the light. Bring forth the light."

She placed her hands down on a log in the cauldron and ignited the entire bowl. One by one, each of the other cauldrons around the garden sparked with their own flames that grew large enough to light the entire space.

Simone walked back over to her cousin with two large pitchers of water. "Ready for me?"

Autumn nodded as she breathed into her palms to snuff out the flames. "Yeah, go ahead."

Simone bent down to the cauldron in front of her and poured the water from the pitcher into a channel running along the outer rim of the bowl. The water flowed around the entire cauldron, showing the reflection of the flames within the rippling surface.

"I'll do the other ones as well. Why don't you help our moms?" Simone headed to the next fire bowl while Autumn found Aunt Jo walking into the garden from the porch that wrapped around the opposite side of the house.

"Welcome, dear friends and respected guests. As you may have noticed, our garden is warmer this evening than the air from the surrounding town. We've not only prepared our dinner space to keep us comfortable for our discussion, but we've also cloaked the garden from prying ears and eyes. This evening will be enchantingly private. Now, please place your coats on the benches provided and enjoy some refreshments before we begin shortly."

Jo met the girls in the center of the garden. "Well done, girls. The bonfires look beautiful, and it feels wonderfully warm out here. Thank you."

Penny appeared next to them with Eve and her mother. "I'll get the food from the kitchen in a moment, but I wanted to bring Eve and Catherine over for a quick chat."

"The garden looks lovely, Josephine. Really, I don't know what the evening has in store for us, but I'm thankful we'll get to enjoy your garden for a while." Mrs. Newbury gave Aunt Jo a gentle hug and nodded in approval.

"Thank you so much, Catherine. We need to have you over more often, but we have been appreciating Eve coming around." Jo smiled and winked at Eve.

"Yes, that's what I'd like to discuss with you all." Penny met eyes with each of them. "As you know, I am an earth witch and have been deeply connected to the lands here to do my healing work. I clearly see Eve has the propensity to be an incredible earth witch herself. I mean, she's already doing well with her spells. You've done well with her, Catherine." Penny touched Catherine Newbury's arm in approval.

"Yes, my Eve always has had the strongest inclinations in the family. We're so thrilled that she's been able to practice more with Autumn and Simone. Sweetheart, we really are proud of you." Mrs. Newbury put her hand over her heart and turned toward her daughter.

"Thanks, Mom." Eve blushed and looked down at the ground sheepishly.

"That's actually what I was wondering about." Penny shifted between Eve and Catherine. "I'd like to work with Eve a bit and teach her a few healing spells, if that's acceptable. I know she puts her magic into her food, but food can be an incredible healing tool. So, she may actually have strength in healing properties as well. If you'd both be okay with it, I can take her under my wing. But I don't want to step on anyone's toes." Penny waited expectantly for Catherine to reply.

Eve stood there with her lips tightly clamped together as she stared at her mother.

"I've done my best to teach her what I know throughout the years, but I'm afraid she's surpassing my gifts. Eve, if you're ready to take on more, then it's your decision." Catherine raised her eyebrows at her daughter. "Would you like that?"

"Oh my goodness, would I ever! Yes, Ms. MacKinnon, thank you. I would love to learn as much as I can." Eve flailed her arms around so much as she spoke that the water glass in her hands sloshed around and overflowed.

Penny laughed. "Well, let's start by calling me Penny. If I'm going to teach you and you're going to be part of the girls' coven, then we better be on a first name basis. Anyone who's over at our home practically every evening should call me Penny."

They all smiled and exchanged glances. Autumn knew this meant a lot to Eve, and she leaned across their circle to hug her.

"You're going to be amazing at this," Autumn whispered in Eve's ear.

Eve pulled away and whispered back, "Thank you. For everything."

"Now, we need to start dinner and the discussion before it gets much later. Girls, will you help Penny bring out the food while I get everyone to the table?" Jo lifted her arms to suggest they all get moving.

"We'll get it all, Mom. You just get started." Simone led the way into the kitchen to bring out the enormous platters of lamb, roasted brussels sprouts and cranberries, brown sugar sweet potatoes, and more. They all grabbed something to bring to the feasting table and to place in the center for all to enjoy.

Jo clapped her hands and spun herself around to view the entire garden. "Everyone, dinner is served. Please make your way to the table, and we'll get started." She walked to the head of the table, poured herself a glass of mulled wine, and smoothed the bottom of her vintage green velvet dress with her hands.

"Now, as you all know, we haven't called a meeting of the founding families in close to a decade. We've been able to maintain the balance of our land, sea, and sky for quite some time. But the moment has come when we need to be proactive in order to protect that balance. First, we must acknowledge each of the families and call the elements. Whoever holds the amulet for your family, please hold it up now." Jo paused and looked down the line at the table.

One by one, each representative of their founding family pulled out a large antique brass quaternary knot symbol on the end of a chain necklace from underneath their clothes. They each held them up high to face one another at the table and allow everyone to see.

"We have the five founding families starting with the Halpin family." Jo lifted her arm to present Mayor Halpin as he rose from his seat and nodded. "The Newburys, the Rosses, the Lachlans, and the Carmichaels." As Jo said each name, the corresponding family representative carrying the quaternary knot stood. "And now, the original MacKinnon clan from the ancestral bloodline." Jo welcomed Autumn to stand up from her seat right next to Jo at the table.

Autumn rose and ran her hand over Gran's locket necklace as she stood. An emerald-green light glowed vibrantly along the edge of the locket, and everyone around the table gasped.

"You may know that we have been without a four-points witch to connect all of our elements together for many years. My mother, Lorna MacKinnon, held our traditions together while we waited for the next to take over. As of recently, we found that witch, Autumn MacKinnon." Jo clapped, and everyone followed suit in awe of this recent development.

"Autumn will lead us this evening in calling to the elements, and after tonight, she will be the one to oversee the founding families. Under Penny's guidance and mine, we will support her in understanding our traditions and rituals." Jo sat down and looked up at her niece to begin.

Autumn cleared her throat and moved her eyes around the table, trying to disregard the nervousness she felt. "Thank you, Aunt Jo. And thank you all for being here tonight on short notice." She exhaled and found James at the table to ground herself. He gave her a nod and softened his eyes as he kept them fixed on her. She felt her muscles relax and continued to speak.

"I'm honored to lead you as we call in the support of the elements. If you'll close your eyes with me now . . ." Autumn closed her own eyes and focused on the air around her. She smelled the smokiness of the bonfires and the earthiness of the feast in front of them. She sensed herself embodying the elements now in every breath.

"Elements of earth, air, fire, and water, we call to you now. Support us as we seek balance in the coming days and reset the energies of our region once more. Surround us with your wisdom so that we may embody the strength of many mountains, many winds, many flames, and many oceans. As I say it, so shall it be." Autumn opened her eyes to find the warmth and light of the locket dissipating around her neck. She bowed her head graciously to everyone and sat back down.

"Thank you, Autumn." Jo raised her glass. "Now, help yourself to the feast, and our discussion and demonstration will take place once everyone has eaten. Enjoy!" Jo placed her napkin in her lap and took a large platter of vegetables from Autumn.

Penny leaned across the table toward Mr. and Mrs. Lachlan seated on the other side of Jo. "Cornelia, tell me, how are things with your family?"

"We're doing fine, Penny. Our son, Cory, finally came home, and I'm glad to have him back where he belongs. He'll be helping Bryce at the marina while he's here, and we're hoping he'll come to his senses and continue the family responsibilities once and for all." Cornelia Lachlan took a bite of her meal and closed her eyes for a moment to savor how good it was.

"Has he not been home in some time, then? I know it's hard to be away for so long." Penny rubbed Autumn's shoulder next to her and gave her an apologetic look.

"It's been almost three years since he's been back. Off gallivanting on the coast for some time, and we've had quite the time getting him to accept that our family has certain obligations here. He never did like being attached to Hollow's Glenn." Cornelia continued cutting up her dinner and spoke very matter-of-factly. "But he's here now, and I'm going to make the most of it. In fact, I need to stop into the girls' shop and order some invitations for a homecoming party. I want him to know how important it is to us now that he's here."

"We'd be glad to help you with whatever you need for the party. Just come in, and Simone and I will get things sorted for you." Autumn smiled at Mrs. Lachlan but felt a sudden warmth from her necklace as she said the words aloud. She glanced over at Simone, who had been listening on the other side of Penny, and gave her a curious look.

When everyone finished their meal, Jo stood up to start the conversation.

"I hope everyone has enjoyed their dinner. For those of you unaware of why we called this gathering, I'll get right to the point. The balance here in Hollow's Glenn has been disturbed, substantially, I'm afraid. I'm sure you've all seen the recent events of Tom Leslie's death at the river." Jo paused to confirm with head nods around the table. "That death was predicted by Dillon Ross's sister, Sorcha Ross Allan. She's in attendance here tonight, along with her son, James, and her brother, Dillon." Jo raised a hand in Sorcha's direction.

"Sorcha's dreamwork showed the death before it occurred. I'm sorry to say that Simone discovered the body when it was already too late. But some elements of Sorcha's dream bothered us greatly. Shimmering sparkles of black magic spreading through the river and damaging not only the water but the lands as well." Jo began pacing around the table as the guests all exchanged looks of concern.

"Thanks to Autumn, Simone, and Eve, we recently confirmed that the water is in fact holding some type of black magic within it, and it's attempting to spread." Jo stopped pacing behind Simone and put her hands on her daughter's shoulders.

"How do you know this? Did you see it with your own eyes?" Mayor Halpin propped his elbows up onto the table and leaned into his hands.

Simone nodded and spoke up. "Yes, we did. I connected with the river water the other night to see what I could gather. I sensed the vines creeping through the waters and the intensity of the damage. When I removed my hands from the water, shimmering sparks remained all over them for a while.

My hands felt like ice all night, and I had an overwhelming sensation of harm and pain."

"Oh, you poor girl! When did this happen?" Mrs. Carmichael chimed in.

"Just a couple days ago, and we gathered everyone together as quickly as we could, considering the circumstances." Penny wanted to keep everyone as calm as possible. "It doesn't seem to have spread extensively yet, but we don't know where the black magic came from or why it's there."

Autumn stood up at the head of the table to continue with what she knew. "We know, however, that on top of the black magic, there is also pollution in our waters. The lumber mill allowed runoff into the river, and that runoff most likely caused damage to our waterways as well. It's hard to say if the two are related, but we know for sure that both together substantially harm our lands."

"So this does have to do with Tom Leslie, then. He always had a bone to pick with anyone not taking the environment around here seriously. I bet he caused a commotion up there at the lumber mill about the pollution. Poking his nose in where it didn't belong just like he was doing over at our marina, right, Cornelia?" Mr. Lachlan nudged his wife, but she stayed silent beside him.

Autumn wrinkled her forehead at him. "Mr. Leslie had some issues with the marina as well?"

"He filed for a conservation easement right alongside my marina! Told the city some wildflowers grew there that needed to be preserved, and that put a stop to my permit request to expand the marina into a restaurant and whatnot."

The mayor swatted his hand through the air. "Oh, Bryce, you know as well as I do he wasn't the only reason the planning department needed more time with your request. Besides, if we will not be good stewards of our lands, then who will? That's the whole point of being the founders." Mayor Halpin threw his hands up in the air and then crossed his arms over his chest.

Bryce Lachlan leaned his head back behind the long row of chairs to see the mayor more clearly. "All I'm saying is maybe a connection exists in all of this. I don't know about this black magic part, which of course needs to be taken care of. But maybe that lumber mill is the problem."

"Let's not get ahead of ourselves here." Autumn swallowed hard and focused on James as more insight came to her. "The black magic is our primary concern right now, which is why all of you are here. We can't suppress it unless we all put our energy together. That much is obvious now. So that is our intention tonight."

Jo nodded and joined Autumn at the head of the table. "That's right. If you would all follow us down to the river, we need to show you exactly what's going on." Jo waved Penny forward with a tray full of Eve's amaretto tarts. "First, please grab your coats, as the air will be chillier once we leave the garden. And be sure to take one of Eve's amaretto cream tarts for the walk. They're a special blend to give us some extra awareness this evening. The more insight we all have the better."

The guests rose from their chairs and moved toward the side benches to gather their coats as instructed. They each took a tart from the tray and bit into it graciously. With just one bite, the garden colors, scents, and sounds grew more vivid and pronounced. Autumn looked at Eve and smiled.

"The tarts are working their magic," Autumn whispered as she watched the guests move around in amazement.

Eve crossed her fingers and smiled at Autumn. "That's a good start."

Autumn knew what was waiting for them at the river, and she sensed the butterflies in her stomach as the guests readied themselves for the demonstration. She hoped the elements could give them another solid hour of support. Then, just maybe, they could hold off the black magic from doing more damage than they even realized possible.

CHAPTER 16

Penny pointed to some lantern lights on the dinner tables. "Gentlemen, if you would, please carry a lantern light from the table along with you." Penny then gestured to Autumn, Simone, and Eve. "Girls, lead the way."

Eve raised her eyebrows at Penny and placed her fingers on her chest to ask if she really meant for her to lead as well. Penny nodded at Eve with a serious look to show her confidence.

The girls made their way through the garden and down the path through the trees, which Simone had lit previously with luminarias on either side. Everyone followed closely behind them until they reached the river. The girls placed the lantern lights down on the ground and stood in a straight line at the river's edge.

"Girls, please proceed." Jo nodded and the girls all got into position. The guests huddled in as closely as possible and watched intently.

Autumn and Eve bent down by the icy water's edge and put their hands on the earth together.

"Mountain lands, we call on you to be the foundation of strength tonight. Fire within, we activate you to guide the way." Autumn felt the warmth starting in her palms as they lay on the ground. She looked up at Eve tracing several circles in front of her. Autumn lifted her palms to reveal the small flames growing within them. She moved them closer to the circles Eve had drawn and allowed the flames to spread into the circles, forming several small bonfires on the edge of the river.

Autumn stood up again and brought her hands to her mouth to snuff out the flames. She joined hands with Eve and Simone again. "Winds of our ancestors, give us the clarity to see what lies beneath the surface. Waters that flow through our lands, reveal your secrets."

Autumn saw the guests whispering to each other as they watched. She'd never shared her magic so openly before and felt vulnerable, but Simone and Eve stood by her side and this demonstration was important. The founding families had to see for themselves the harm being done. She looked at her cousin and gave her a nod to continue.

Simone turned and bent down to the icy water. She hesitantly placed her hands over the icy edge the same way she had done a few days prior. Nervous about taking on the same black magic energy again, Simone told herself the others surrounded her with support and strength from the elements.

"Everyone, please reveal your amulet necklace in the open and then join hands. Focus your energy on the river." Jo guided them in as she went down the line, helping each guest to do as instructed.

Simone called to the water and felt its forceful energy pushing back at her against the ice. "Bring forth what lies beneath. Bring forth what lies beneath. Bring forth what lies beneath."

As she spoke the words, tendrils of dark glowing light showed underneath the water still flowing in the center of the river. It spread out under the ice and faintly appeared as black sparks of magic trying to edge its way to the land. The entire river looked like a network of black veins intertwined and pushing their way further out from the center.

"Oh my word." Mrs. Newbury couldn't believe the sight before her. "Eve told me it was dire, but I had no idea."

Simone pulled her hands from the waters and stood up, shaking a bit. Autumn grabbed Simone's hands to warm them inside of hers.

Mayor Halpin turned to Aunt Jo. "Josephine, you're right. We can't allow this to continue. It needs to be stopped right away."

Jo nodded in agreement. "That's right. If the black magic continues until the river freezes completely, then it will most likely seep into the earth as well. The earth and water will no longer sustain us, and these lands will undoubtedly suffer just as they once did. We cannot let that happen. Therefore, tonight, we must perform a cleansing spell to remove as much of the black vines as possible." Jo pulled the MacKinnon Book of Spells out of a large worn sachet case she'd brought with her.

Penny dropped hands with those next to her and stepped forward. "This will require each family to tap into their gifts and allow them to converge with the rest of our energies. We have to pool our strength in order for Simone to cleanse the waters."

"I haven't used any fire energy in quite some time. I'm rusty in wielding it. Is that all right?" The mayor gave Penny a worried look.

Penny put her hand on the mayor's shoulder to reassure him. "That's all right, Stephen. Your intention matters most, and that will guide the energy within you to where it needs to go. Simone will do the rest."

"We just need to give permission for Simone to use our energy. Come and gather closer to the water." Jo stepped forward a few paces with the book, and the others followed. "Focus on your breathing and center yourself on that."

The founding families clasped their hands together and kept their eyes on Josephine. She demonstrated a few deep breaths and then nodded to the girls.

"Eve is going to hand each of you a sage bundle. We'll clear the energy here before performing the spell." Autumn grabbed the large basket of sage that the girls had brought down earlier and handed it to Eve.

Going down the line of founders, Eve handed them all out, and Autumn followed behind, blowing warm air on each sage bundle to set it alight. After all the bundles began smoking, Autumn returned to face them all.

"Please swirl the sage sticks in a clockwise motion in the air as I say the words." Autumn closed her eyes and lifted her arms to the side. "As the air is pure, so is our intention. As the air is pure, so is our intention. As the air is pure, so is our intention." She exhaled strongly and opened her eyes with a smile. "Now we can begin. Please lay your sage down on the dirt in front of you and join hands."

Autumn, Simone, and Eve turned toward the river and opened their palms at their sides. Jo moved toward Simone and lifted the Book of Spells so her daughter could see the words of the spell in front of her. Simone began moving her body from side to side in a serpent-like motion. Her arms swayed, and she whispered under her breath.

"Push against the dark, force away the harm with your rapids, and cleanse the way through these lands." With Simone's words, the waters changed in the center of the river. Rapids formed and pushed upstream toward the black shimmers underneath. Every time Simone moved her arms across her body, the rapids got stronger and crashed against the tightly wound vines. The water built up higher and higher with each crash, as only a small portion of the shimmering vines dissipated in the rapids.

"Clear your minds. Move your energy toward the water with each breath you take." Josephine squinted her eyes and strained with everything she had while instructing the group. "This one chance could stave off the poison that lies within."

"I feel it pulling at me." Dillon Ross struggled to keep his balance in the line.

"I feel it, too. It's like a magnet drawing us in and grasping for our energy." Sorcha Allan did her best to speak as James clenched his mother's hand.

Simone pressed her palms straight out in front of her now like there was an invisible boulder she tried to shove through the air. "The vines are slowly dissolving. I see them cracking and floating away under the surface, but it's happening too slowly. I can only push against the magnetism so much."

Simone made one last forceful exhale and threw her entire body weight into her arms as they pushed across the air. Autumn saw a few vines crack and melt away just as Simone stumbled to the ground. Autumn and Eve both hurried to catch her as she fell, but Simone had completely drained her energy.

Jo bent down beside her daughter. Brushing back the dark strands of hair from Simone's face, Jo gave her a comforting smile and nodded to Autumn to continue.

Autumn stood and looked around at the founders, the trees hovering above, and the bonfires on either side of her. "These vines are strong, but we are stronger. We've melted a few of them away tonight and cleared some shimmers from spreading in the water. But this does not end things. More black magic will appear, especially until we find the root cause." Autumn glanced at James with concern. His soothing face encouraged her to keep going. "Hopefully with this clearing spell, we've held it off long enough to find a more permanent solution. But now you all can see the urgency we face."

Mayor Halpin walked to the front near Autumn. "I'll speak to the city council and institute restrictions around the river. We'll cordon it off until we determine what's happening. James, why don't you speak to your father about getting some samples of the water tested? Maybe we can find out what we're dealing with that way, even if it just helps us with the pollution aspect of things."

"Yes, Mr. Mayor. We'd be glad to help." James drew closer and wrapped his arm around his mother as he spoke.

"Bryce, can you do some water patrols down at the marina? See if there's anything strange going on down there that you can tell."

"I'm on it. I know those waterways like the back of my hand, and I'll be able to tell if anything seems off." Autumn caught Bryce giving his wife a serious look, and she knew instantly they were keeping something quiet.

"All right, then, Autumn, we have our marching orders. How can we wrap up for tonight?" The mayor waved her forward to speak.

She felt a lump forming in her throat and tried to swallow hard to push it down. As she moved her eyes over each one of them, Autumn saw a glimpse of heartbreak coming but knew resiliency would carry them through. She looked intently into each one of their eyes and stood a little taller.

"Each one of you carries these waters inside you. Whether or not you have water as a gift, you are still bound by every element. And no matter what happens from now on, the water within us stays resilient and impassible if need be. We must find that inside ourselves now because we're being called to challenge a darker magic than we've encountered in some time. Stay connected, be aware, and above all, please trust your gifts. They will allow us to overcome this and restore the balance together."

Penny walked over to give her daughter a squeeze. "Thank you all for participating this evening. I'll lead you back to the garden where you can gather your things and take a rosemary circle home with you. One sits at each place on the table, and they'll bring you protection, balance, and energy cleansing after this evening's affair."

Penny grabbed a lantern from the ground and walked everyone back up to the house as the girls put out the bonfires along the river. James stayed back to help Autumn lift Simone from the ground and hold her steady as they made their way up to the garden.

When Simone settled in the garden, Autumn led James to the wraparound porch and grabbed his hands for a moment. They stopped and looked at each other under the porch lights as everyone walked past them toward the front.

"You're getting stronger." He moved his eyes from her hands to her face.

Autumn shifted and looked away for a moment, coming back to him with appreciation. "Maybe, but I still feel unsure that I can do this. Lead everyone and be the energy that holds all this together." Autumn sighed and moved in a little closer. "But then, I look at you and that all somehow melts away. And I just say what I need to say or do what I need to do without thinking about all the rest."

"Well, as much as I'd like to be the thing that gives you strength, something tells me you're making the shift yourself. You're opening up to who you really are and possibly even seeing that person for the first time." James pulled Autumn's hands up to his chest and held them over his heart. "I'm just glad I get to be a small part of that."

"You're becoming much more than a small part." She smelled the cherry cordial seeping from his pores and enveloping her in comfort. "It's like you're a whole new foundation for me to stand on."

He leaned down and pressed his lips against hers, and as he kissed her, Autumn felt the intentions of her head and her heart merge into one. Even though they hadn't succeeded in fully clearing the river that night, she now felt clearer than ever about who she was meant to be.

CHAPTER 17

Autumn stoked the fire in the hearth room at Parchment and Pine as Tavish snuggled his tail tighter around his body. She laughed at the cat.

"Honestly, Tav, I don't know how you could be any cozier right now." Autumn rubbed his head and walked out the curtained archway into the main area of the shop.

"Are you heading out for lunch?" Simone called from the front as she organized their latest batch of winter wrapping papers on a tall wooden ladder against the wall.

"Yeah, I'm headed to the library and then to city hall. I'm going to see what I can find out about the lumber mill owner and that conservation easement over at the marina. Why? Are you planning lunch?" Autumn raised her eyebrows at Simone a couple times in hopes she'd say yes.

Simone shrugged. "I guess if you're gonna do all that, then I can go grab something and take it over to my mom's shop. Do you want to meet me there when you're done?"

"That sounds good. We can close the Pine for a couple hours today. It's been slow, anyway." Autumn went to the back room to gather her things. "Get me a bread bowl with broccoli and cheese soup, would you? I think that's the special at the Forest Brew today. Oh! And a pomegranate iced tea. Eve started making a new recipe for the holidays." Autumn shoved her arms into her gray wool coat and bundled up.

"Pomegranate, huh? I might have to get one of those, too." Simone pulled her phone out of the back pocket of her skinny jeans and typed in the order. "Got it. Are you sure you don't need any help at the library?"

"No, I'm good. It'll be quick." Autumn sensed her cousin glaring at her and imagining hurricane winds stirring up over there. "No strong winds, I promise." Autumn raised her right hand in the air. "I'm doing better at keeping the elements in check, so no matter what I find, I'll keep things locked down, okay?"

"Uh huh, sure. As long as I don't see clouds billowing overhead when I'm trying to get lunch." Simone shook her head.

"Hey, that's your department. I'm not the one who makes it rain when I'm upset." Autumn pulled the front door open. "I already fed Tavish, so he should be cozy for a while. I'll see you in a bit." Autumn walked out the door and started down Main Street.

The library sat a few blocks down, so she'd get some fresh air while she walked. Autumn strolled past the shops on her block and made it to the corner just as a couple women bumped into each other, knocking their bags to the ground in front of her.

Autumn jogged up to help them retrieve the various bottles of bath salts and soaps that lay strewn on the sidewalk, obviously from Aunt Jo's bath shop across the street. "Let me help you both."

"Oh, Autumn, dear, thank you." Mrs. Leslie looked up to give her a warm smile. Then, with a glaring frown, she glanced over at the woman who had knocked into her.

Surprised at Karen Leslie's expression, Autumn moved her eyes to the other woman and realized it was none other than Anabeth Greenwood. She'd written the news article about Karen's husband being found in the river. No wonder this was an awkward situation.

"Mrs. Leslie, I'm sorry to bump into you like that. I must have had my head down with my phone." Anabeth's mouth dropped open like she wanted to say something more, but Autumn shook her head in disapproval. They picked up the rest of the bottles and returned them to Mrs. Leslie's bags. "Right, listen, about the article."

"There's nothing for you to say about it. I know you'll report your story no matter what it takes, and it's clear that the real people behind the story don't actually matter to you." Mrs. Leslie stood up and lifted her chin at Anabeth.

"Well, that's harsh. I care about this town, and that's why I write about what's happening. People need to be connected and aware of their surroundings. It keeps us all safer and more knowledgeable." Anabeth gave Autumn a desperate look.

"Aware of their surroundings, you say? Like you were just now?" Mrs. Leslie rolled her eyes and adjusted her bag on her hip.

"I think Anabeth is just saying she hopes to keep everyone informed." Autumn shrugged and nodded, but Mrs. Leslie appeared frustrated.

"Well, call it whatever you'd like. I read the article, and you didn't need to include all the details and speculations. Not everyone needs to know our business. Now, if you'll excuse me, I have to get back to the flower shop. Autumn, dear, it was nice to see you." Mrs. Leslie strode away as they both watched her.

"Geez, I just did my job. Why don't people understand that?" Anabeth flopped her arms at her sides and shook her head.

"It's hard having your personal life out in the open like that, especially when it's something so tragic as losing your husband, you know?" Autumn wanted to make sure Anabeth actually understood where Mrs. Leslie was coming from.

"I understand. I really do, but it's important people know what's happening around them. Like, take you, for example. I've heard you're quite the sleuth and that you're a big part of bringing your gran's killer to justice."

Autumn sighed and started walking away. "Bye, Anabeth."

"Wait! I'm serious." Anabeth ran to catch up with Autumn as she crossed the street. "You're looking into the Leslie murder, too, aren't you?"

Autumn stopped and looked straight at Anabeth before realizing she stood right in the middle of the road. She quickly started walking again and shook her head.

"Come on, I bet you have some leads you're following that you haven't let anybody else in on yet. Am I right?" Anabeth tried to keep pace as Autumn quickened her steps. "What if I told you I knew a thing or two as well?"

Autumn stopped walking again and squinted her eyes at Anabeth as she adjusted her backpack on her shoulders. "What do you know?"

Anabeth shrugged and looked around them, checking to make sure no one was listening. "Oh, just that there's been a lot of paperwork filed in relation to the Leslies. A recent lawsuit about some land and some environmental complaints and whatnot. Seems like Mr. Lesliehad gotten on a lot of people's bad sides."

"Yeah, well, none of that means anything. They're probably just typical disputes." Autumn kept walking and crossed Havensbrook Place, stopping in front of the library. "If you'll excuse me, I have some things to do."

Anabeth glanced up at the university extension library to the right of them and then back at Autumn. "Right. I'll leave you to it, then. But if anything comes up, or if you need an extra set of eyes on something, I'm here to help. And I've got great researching skills." Anabeth smiled at Autumn and then headed in the opposite direction.

Autumn laughed under her breath and headed into the library. She went straight to the back and asked the circulation desk to call her friend Becca Winsome from the genealogy department. Becca had helped so much when Autumn's gran had passed, and Autumn knew she'd help her sort through some archival documents again.

Before long, Autumn saw a slender woman making her way through the heavy doors at the back of the library. Becca popped through in a knee-length pleated skirt and a white blouse that tied at the neck.

"Hey, Autumn, it's nice to see you. What can I help you with?"

"Hi, Becca, I actually need to get into the archives downstairs. Can you help me?" Autumn squinted hopefully at her.

"Sure, just follow me." Becca led the way through the heavy doors and down a spiral staircase to the lower level of the library. They walked through the long hallway lined with wall sconces toward the genealogy department that was funded by a large endowment at the regional university.

"Are you looking for more family information?"

"Yes and no. This time I'm looking into the old lumber mill in town, but I'm interested in the family who owns it. Do you know where to start?"

Becca nodded and thought for a moment. "Yeah, you want the Campbell family. I believe Emily Campbell owns it now."

She turned to the arched wooden doorway behind them and typed a code into the keypad on the lock. She pushed the door open, and the two of them found themselves in the archives room. "You're familiar with how we organize the documents in this room now, right?"

Autumn nodded. "I think so, mostly. But do I start with the family name? Campbell?"

"You could, yes. I don't know if they have a relation to any of the founding families, but you can try it and see. I think they've been here in the mountain regions for decades, so the name might lead to something." Becca lifted her finger to her chin and spun around in a circle. "As a matter of fact, I have some newspaper clippings from when the Campbells initially developed the mill. Let's see if I can pull those up."

Becca went over to a large floor-to-ceiling drawer cabinet on the side wall. She thumbed through several newspaper and magazine clippings in the drawers until she pulled one out of a drawer labeled "land development."

"Here it is. I remember seeing this one." Becca handed it over to Autumn and waited.

Autumn read the headline on the page aloud. "Wealthy Family Invests In Long-Term Growth." She took the page over to one of the large square tables in the center of the room to peruse. "It says here the Campbells originally came from Canada and then worked their way down here for the lumber business."

Autumn gasped and pointed to a photo a little further down on the page. "Ross." She moved in closer to the page to get a better look at the details in the photo. She stared at the woman in the photo beside a taller, well-presented man with a beard. "Silvia Ross, wife of Edmund Campbell, and their son, Bernard Campbell, stand on their newly acquired lands on the north end of Hollow's Glenn."

Becca shrugged. "Does the name Ross mean something to you?"

"Yeah, it does." Autumn tapped her finger on the picture. "Becca, I'd like to look at the history of the Ross family. Are they in the same founders documents as the MacKinnons over there under the window?" She lifted her chin toward the drawing cabinets underneath the half-circle window on the far side of the room.

"Yes, they should be there if it's a founding family. Look toward the bottom drawers for Ross, and you'll probably find the family tree, along with any family crests, deed information, and anything else that ties them to the town. I need to get back to my desk and finish some work, but you know where to find me across the hall if you need anything." Becca put her hand on Autumn's shoulder and stepped past her toward the door.

"Thanks, as always, Becca. I appreciate it." Autumn headed toward the window wall.

"That's what I'm here for." Becca smiled and closed the door behind her.

Autumn pulled open a couple of drawers at the bottom of the cabinet and flipped through pages. She found documents pertaining to the other founding families, including the Halpins and the Newburys. Then, inside the second-to-last drawer from the bottom, Autumn found a large yellowed packet of parchment bound with a string. It carried a Celtic symbol of a raven sitting on a crescent moon on the cover.

She pulled out the packet and ran her hand over the cover. Soft embossed letters at the bottom of the front page read "Ross, The Prophecy Keepers." She quickly flipped open the pages and wondered if this manuscript tied everything together about James, his mother, and their gifts, not to mention this connection to the Campbells.

The lights flickered above her, and Autumn felt a rush of energy course through her body. The surrounding air changed to a teal blue color like the depths of the ocean, and the page in front of her swam in her vision. She blinked a few times and took a deep breath, feeling a strange urge to close the booklet but pressing forward anyway.

On the next page, she found the Ross family tree. James's name sat toward the bottom of the tree, along with his mother and Uncle Dillon. Closer to the top, Autumn found Silvia Ross. The woman appeared to be a great, great aunt of James, but her union with Edmund Campbell was undocumented on this parchment. It did, however, list the dates of her birth and death.

Autumn nodded to herself, confirming that this must be the same Silvia Ross. The dates matched with the dated newspaper article. She flipped through a few more pages and then came back to the family tree. The page still appeared fuzzy in her vision, but she drew her eyes closer to look at the line with James's name on it.

To the side of his name, where a partner's would sit, a very faint symbol of an owl atop the Celtic quaternary knot lightly skimmed the surface of the paper. Autumn had never seen the symbol used in that way before, but yet it felt very familiar. The lights flickered once again, and she heard the faint whisper of her ancestors.

"Time reveals to the mind what the heart already knows."

Autumn looked up at the ceiling to find the lights perfectly steady again. She closed the parchment booklet, placed it back into the bottom drawer of the cabinet, and made her way out the door.

She stopped to knock on the door on the other side of the hallway and peeked her head in. "Becca, I'm all set for today, thanks." Autumn gave her a wave and hurried back up to the spiral staircase and up through the library.

Throwing the front doors open onto Havensbrook Place, she closed her eyes and took a deep breath. Her heart raced, but she had no idea why. The air felt crisp and pure in her lungs, and she took in as much of it as she could.

Autumn opened her eyes, repeating to herself what she'd found in the library. "Silvia Ross. Bloodline relative." She gazed down the street toward the downtown square for a moment and thought of James working on the riverfront revitalization project. "The heart already knows."

Across the street, the bells at city hall chimed atop the tower out front, and Autumn started moving toward them. They represented a familiar sound that always drew her in, even though she had never actually seen the bells themselves.

"Shake it off, Autumn," she said to herself. "One more stop."

She crossed at the streetlight and for the first time, Autumn saw the bells dip back and forth in rhythm, revealing the Celtic quaternary knot emblazoned on the body of the bell.

CHAPTER 18

Autumn pulled the double glass doors open to the mayor's office just as he strolled out of a meeting room. She caught eyes with him and waved. The mayor shook a few people's hands and then made his way over to her.

"Autumn! What a pleasant surprise! What brings you to city hall today?"

"Hello, Mr. Mayor. I just finished at the library and thought I'd stop in to learn more about the conservation easement near the marina." Autumn looked at the mayor with a serious look, hinting at the connection to Tom Leslie that he already knew as a founder. "Could you point me to the right person for that?"

"Right, yes." The mayor looked back at the people coming out of the meeting and flagged someone down. "Autumn, you know Dave Stewart, I presume." The mayor welcomed Dave into their conversation.

"Yes, Dave, hi. I actually just talked to your fiancée, Sarah, at the bank. She mentioned you worked here now." Autumn shook his hand and gave him a friendly smile.

"That's right. I've been overseeing the planning department for about a year now, and it's keeping me very busy so far." Dave and the mayor both nodded in agreement.

"Dave, Autumn needs some information about the conservation easement proposed down by the marina. You remember that one coming up for approval?" The mayor looked at him quizzically.

"Yeah, that one is still pending, as it caused quite a stir with the town council. Apparently several council members wanted to keep options open for development around the reservoir. It could be a potential area for real growth and investment. However, a strong case could be made for preservation of the wild lands there as well. So, we have tabled it for now, as far as I know. Why, is there some reason for it to come up now?" Dave eyed them both and crossed his arms at his chest.

"Oh, uh . . ." Autumn hesitated to answer as she considered how much to divulge.

"Autumn has some due diligence to do as she gets up to speed. She's now the chair of the preservation committee, you know." The mayor nodded at Autumn to get her to follow along.

"That's right. I recently took over the position from my grandmother, and I wanted to make sure I'm aware of everything affecting preservation and development matters. I'll probably be gathering lots more information as I get around to looking at town requests and things." Autumn nodded vigorously to show that was exactly what she meant.

"Oh, right, I think I remember seeing something about you taking over the preservation committee." Dave threw his hands up in the air. "Well, if that's the case, then I'm sure I'll see you more often. You'll probably need lots of information from the planning department to carry out your committee meetings."

"You're right. I'll have to get to know everyone in your office more, seeing as how I'll probably work with them regularly." Autumn smiled and looked at the mayor to search for what might come next.

"Yes, well, Dave, I imagine you can give Autumn any details of the easement request, like any dates she needs or whatnot. It may even be good to connect her with someone in the environmental office so she has a contact there as well." Mayor Halpin touched Dave's shoulder and shook his hand. "I really must get to another meeting, but I'm sure Dave will take care of you from here, Autumn. It was good seeing you." He waved and walked away as the two of them smiled.

"Okay, you can walk with me to the planning office if you'd like, and we can pull up the specifics of the easement." Dave lifted his hand to point the way and let Autumn go first.

"Thanks, that would be great. I appreciate any information you have to get me started. I really need to know the reasoning behind the complaint filed and how the request began." Autumn walked alongside Dave as they made their way out of the mayor's office and back through the lobby of city hall.

Further into the main area, Autumn noticed a familiar figure across the way.

She paused and turned to Dave. "Actually, would you mind if I met up with you in a moment? I need to stop and speak with someone, but I can find my way to the planning department."

"Of course, take your time. Whenever you're ready, I'll have the file pulled for you to peruse, okay?"

Autumn nodded as Dave walked away. She made her way across the lobby as the woman turned to face her. Standing across the echoing heights in the city hall entrance stood her distant cousin, Lainy. She had her dark-brown hair pulled halfway up and wore a tailored black blazer over a white crew neck and fitted camel-colored pants. As soon as she spotted Autumn, her cheeks went rosy.

"Autumn, hey." Lainy tilted her head at her. "What are you doing here?"

Autumn took a few more steps and met Lainy while laughing under her breath. "I could ask the same thing of you. I'm just here to get some information, but you look like you're staying awhile." Autumn moved her hand up and down to point out Lainy's outfit.

Lainy looked at her clothes and smiled. "Well, I didn't want to say anything quite yet, but I interviewed for the job of event manager here at city hall. Turns out, they wanted me to start as soon as possible. I hadn't really thought too far past that yet, but things have been going well here, and I just thought . . ." Lainy's voice trailed off as she spoke. She wrinkled her forehead, unsure of what Autumn might think.

Autumn placed her hand on Lainy's forearm to reassure her. "Lainy, that's amazing, and you don't have to keep anything to yourself. We're all glad you're here, and we want you to stay."

"You do?" Lainy turned her head to the side.

"Yes, we do. In fact, I think you should come by the house tonight. Everyone should be there, including Eve, I think. It'll be nice to have you again as well, and then you can tell everyone your news, okay? I won't take no for an answer." Autumn pulled her phone out of her backpack and started typing. "I'm sending you the address for our house. We'll all be there around seven."

Lainy's face brightened, and she pulled her phone out of her blazer pocket to see the message from Autumn. "Okay, seven it is."

"Good. And bring a warm coat in case we go outside for a bit."

Lainy squinted at Autumn, curious about why they'd be outside when it was so close to freezing. "Right . . . I'll dress warm."

Autumn hugged her softly and then turned to head back to the planning department with a hopeful feeling. Something told her their fourth coven spot no longer remained open.

CHAPTER 19

Autumn pulled the sweet potatoes out of the oven for a winter buddha bowl dinner when the doorbell rang. She threw the pair of potholders she'd been wearing down on the kitchen island and jogged to the front door.

"I'll grab it if you can scoop up the potatoes." Autumn yelled back to the kitchen as Simone saluted.

Autumn opened the front door to a packed porch. "Wow, I didn't expect everyone all at once! Come on in!"

"Oh, thank goodness! It's dreadfully cold out here, and I need something warm in my belly before we head out again." Jo scooted inside and shimmied out of her vintage coat.

Penny kissed her daughter on either cheek and held her shoulders. "Hello, sweetheart. How was the day?"

Autumn sighed and tilted her head back and forth. "Uh, so-so, I guess. I have a lot to discuss with everyone, though, so come inside and get cozy." She moved aside so her mother could make her way in. "Hey, Eve! Did you finish up early at the coffee shop tonight?"

"I did! My mom said she'd wrap things up so I could be here on time. Hope that's okay!" Eve looked at Autumn hesitantly.

"Of course it's okay. We invited you for dinner and spells. Plus, you're always welcome. You know that."

Eve smiled shyly and removed her beret and toggle coat. "Okay, good, because I brought some freshly baked cornbread to go along with dinner." She pulled a brown Forest Brew bag from behind her back and presented it to Autumn with a look of pride.

Autumn took the bag and peeked inside. She closed her eyes and took a deep inhale of the comforting aroma of bread. "This smells amazing! Did I mention that you're welcome anytime?" Autumn gave her a big smile and wrapped her arm around Eve's shoulders to bring her into the kitchen, when another knock sounded at the front door.

Penny went over and opened it again to find Lainy on the other side. "Lainy! I was just thinking about how lovely it would be if you joined us this evening."

"Hello, Penny. Autumn invited me tonight." Lainy slid inside the entryway and glanced around the room. She opened up her long-handled camel-colored tote bag and pulled out a bottle. "And I brought wine."

Penny put her hand to her chest and gasped. "Oh, that sounds wonderful! This will be just the thing to ground us before doing some earth work. Thank you!"

Everyone followed each other into the kitchen as the smell of roasted pumpkin seeds wafted out.

"We've got everything ready for our buddha bowls. Just fill your bowl with all the ingredients, and we can eat here in the kitchen. There's kale, sweet potatoes, pomegranate, farro, apples, pumpkin seeds, and dressing. Help yourself." Simone pointed to each of the ingredients lined up on the island in ceramic bowls.

Jo eyed the spread as Autumn and Penny put the cornbread and wine out as well. "Oh, girls, you've been doing wonderfully with your cooking. Your gran would be so proud to see you using her kitchen like this."

"I just came up with the concept of the plate." Simone pointed at her chest. "Autumn did most of the cooking. She knew exactly how to work with the ingredients and cook them to perfection. She coaxed the flavor out of everything."

"Mmm, so that earth energy I handed down to you presents itself now and then." Penny grabbed a plate and smirked as she loaded up on farro and kale.

Autumn shrugged. "The earth keeps me steady. It's always there lingering under the surface, and it naturally presents itself in daily life. Almost like it pulls me back down to reality and calms my nerves, if that makes sense."

Eve nodded and chimed in. "That totally makes sense to me. Baking soothes me, and when I work with herbs and spices, I don't feel clumsy and all over the place like I usually do."

Lainy raised her eyebrows at Eve. "Good to know. I'll remember that when I put in my next order at the Forest Brew." They all laughed and looked at Eve with sympathy.

"No, I'm being serious." Eve sighed and slipped onto one of the kitchen stools. "I always feel out of place and uncomfortable unless I'm working in the kitchen."

Autumn wrapped her arm around Eve and squeezed her. "Well, you're not out of place here. In fact, you fit in perfectly." Eve's face warmed with Autumn's words, and she lifted her gaze to Penny, who nodded in agreement.

"That's one reason we're here tonight. I'd like to teach Eve a healing spell with you girls as elemental support." Penny spooned a mouthful of her dinner.

"I prepped the clearing in the woods for us. So, we can head out after dinner. Lainy, I was hoping you'd join us for a spell or two, if that's okay with you." Autumn poured a glass of wine and handed it to Lainy while waiting for a response.

She grabbed the wine glass and nodded. "I'd like that, but it sounds like you're working with more earth energy tonight. Do you really need me?"

"What are you talking about, do we need you? Autumn invited you for a reason, and as far as I can tell, we could always use more fire energy around here. There's way too much of everything else." Simone went over to the tea cabinet and bent down to the bottom shelf. She pulled out a small wooden box, unlatched it, and grabbed a few sticks of palo santo to bring back to the kitchen island. "Here. You should be in charge of lighting the smudge sticks tonight."

Lainy agreed. "I can do that."

"And besides her fire energy, Lainy has something more to share with us tonight. Right?" Autumn turned to Lainy and prodded her to open up.

She took a sip of her wine and looked around the kitchen at all of them. "I do, actually. Since you've all been so gracious in welcoming me here, I thought I might consider staying longer. So, I took a job at city hall as an event manager." Lainy put down her glass and bit her lip as she waited to see everyone's response.

Eve blurted out, "Congratulations! I'm so excited to hear about all the amazing events you'll be planning!"

When no one else spoke up, Lainy got a little concerned. "Of course, I'll just be trying it out, and nothing's set in stone."

Jo teared up, and Penny walked over to her sister to grab her hand.

"Lainy, we've waited a long time for our family to round out again." Penny looked directly at Lainy and spoke from her heart. "I know from experience how hard it's been to feel separated and distant. But we're coming back together now, and there's nothing we'd all love more than to have you stay permanently if that's what you want as well."

Lainy swallowed hard and contemplated Penny's words. She'd never felt at home anywhere before, but somehow with the MacKinnons, she knew she'd always have a place.

"I would, thank you." Lainy exhaled deeply, and Autumn came over to give her a hug.

"All right, then, let's talk about what I've been finding out before we head into the woods." Autumn put her bowl down and brushed her hands together. "I'm definitely concerned about the environmental complaints Tom Leslie made, particularly the ones for the river and the marina lands."

"The marina lands? You mean the waters that go into the reservoir?" Penny wasn't sure if this related to the river being polluted or something more.

"No, actually. This has to do with the lands surrounding the marina. Bryce Lachlan mentioned being upset about it the other night, and I followed up with it at city hall this afternoon. Turns out, there's a dispute going on over developing the lands around the marina. I think you can guess what side of that debate Tom Leslie was on."

"Oh my, the wildflowers! Yes, that's why Bryce was in such a tailspin about it at dinner." Jo put her hand over her mouth in realization.

"Yep, Tom didn't want anything developed over those lands where the wildflowers grow, and there's a large patch of flowers right next to the marina. So . . ." Autumn looked around the room at all of them. "That puts Bryce Lachlan on the list for potential suspects unhappy with Tom Leslie and who had a motive to have him gone."

"Wow, we're racking up a list here! That's interesting considering Mr. Lachlan was a founding family member." Simone widened her eyes and gave her mother a look.

"I know. We need to be careful about looking into the founding families." Autumn knew she bordered on a sensitive territory with this theory.

"Especially when the founders have abilities and positions of power in the community. But . . ." Jo paused and looked around the island. "Our family oversees the founders. If anyone needs to be held accountable, then it's our responsibility to do that." She smoothed her skirt over her legs as she spoke.

"And there's something else that I came across today." Autumn paced the kitchen. "The Campbell family, who owns the lumber mill, relates directly to another family we know."

Jo eyed Autumn for a moment, trying to receive some intuitive insight into what she was about to say. She gasped and leaned back on her stool. "The Ross family."

Autumn nodded. "Yes. The Ross family."

"Sorcha Allan's family?" Simone asked with confusion.

"That's right. Sorcha Ross Allan, her brother, Dillon, and of course, her son, James." Penny began putting the pieces together out loud. "That means the Campbells, who were intentionally polluting the river, may also have access to magic from their bloodline."

"Precisely. Which puts Emily Campbell even higher on our list of suspects." Autumn stopped pacing and leaned into one of the kitchen cabinets. "Plus . . . when I found this out at the library earlier, I also came across a strange symbol in a blank space on their family tree." Autumn didn't mention that the space sat next to James's name. "It was an owl atop the quaternary knot."

"Well, the owl represents the wisdom of the air element. You know that. And the unity knot symbolizes our connection with the elements, but the Ross family has the gift of dream-work that accompanies water. The unseen things that lie below the surface. So, I'm not sure why the owl fell on their family tree." Jo fidgeted with the rings on her fingers as she considered this.

"Not to mention the pages were swimming when I tried to read them, as if they didn't want me to see what was written." Autumn pulled her hair back and wrapped a few strands around the rest until it was all in a loose ponytail.

"Things better left unseen." Penny remarked as she poured herself a glass of wine. "Sounds like the documents foretell something that your eyes are not yet ready to know. But perhaps they will in time." Penny sighed. "Maybe we should focus on our spells for this evening. Something we can control right now. Come now, finish your meals. The woods await us."

They all finished their bowls, and Autumn collected everything into the sink as Simone handed out their coats. Tavish wandered out from the back bedroom and stretched his legs just as they were all heading to the door. Autumn smiled and grabbed the cat after throwing on her green cape.

"Hey, Tav. Wanna come to the woods with us?" She rubbed his head as the cat purred, and the warmth of his fur sent hot sensations through her hands and arms. She thought to herself as she took the cat out the door. Something told her the sensations were a primer for what was to come. Earth energy wouldn't be the only thing needed soon. Her fire connection would be tested as well, and Lainy's presence played a necessary part in making it work.

CHAPTER 20

Tavish jumped to the ground from Autumn's arms as they took the last step off the porch. He hopped onto the trail leading into the woods while the five of them huddled together, waiting for Autumn.

"Autumn, dear, light the way for us, please," Jo requested with a shiver in her voice.

"Of course." Autumn squeezed beside Simone in their circle and rubbed her hands together. She closed her eyes and summoned the elements. The winds howled around them, and the women drew in closer to keep the chill at bay. Autumn pulled her hands to her mouth and blew a breath into them that ignited two flames.

"There. That'll do." Autumn opened her palms at her sides with the flames rising from their centers. She led the way through the woods with Tavish by her side and her long cape trailing behind her.

When they reached the clearing in the center of the tall pine and aspen trees, Autumn made a circle in the dirt with her foot while Tavish found a large log to lie down on. Jo and Penny placed a few logs inside the dirt circle, and Autumn knelt to light them with her hands before putting out her own flames.

"Now, Eve, I'd like to go over at least one healing spell with you this evening. I don't know which you'd prefer. I have a healing salve made from pine tree sap, a recovery incantation using the energy of the earth, and a mint leaf poison removal concoction. Which one sounds good?" Penny walked the perimeter of the clearing to look for ingredients as she waited for Eve to reply.

Autumn stopped for a moment beside Eve. She turned to look into her eyes.

"Uh, just a minute, Penny. Is everything okay, Autumn?" Eve squinted her eyes to see her better in the dark.

Autumn stood still as a chill ran through her body. "The tree sap. Choose the tree sap."

"Okay . . ." Eve stared at Autumn curiously as she yelled over her shoulder without taking her eyes off Autumn. "Penny, we can do the tree sap." Eve hesitated, still watching Autumn. "Seriously, are you all right?"

Simone walked over and put her hand on her cousin's shoulder. "What's up? You okay?"

Autumn nodded and shook herself out of the daze. "Yeah, I'm fine. I just . . . got really cold suddenly, and then I had this insight about what Eve needed to learn tonight. Like if she didn't choose the tree sap, then I might never warm up. It was really strange, that's all."

"Well, I chose the tree sap!" Eve hoped Autumn would perk up a bit, but she still seemed off.

Simone wrapped her arms around Autumn and brought her back toward the bonfire. "Let's just call the elements and get started. Lainy, do you have the palo santo?"

Lainy emerged with the small wooden sticks in her hands. "Got 'em." She splayed out a few sticks in the fingers of one hand and snapped her fingers on the other. A flame rose out of her thumb as she snapped, and she held it to each of the palo santo sticks to light them.

"You can do it, too?" Simone stared at Lainy.

She nodded her head as she handed out the sticks to each person. "Yes, I've been practicing since I was a child. It's one of the first things I realized I could do besides making the fire dance to my will."

"Wow, are you serious?" Eve's mouth dropped open as she took a smudge stick and blew out the flame.

Lainy laughed and handed the last stick to Autumn. "Yeah, I never really got over how cool it is. But connecting to the fire gives me direction and focus, if that makes sense. Otherwise, things feel too scattered and chaotic to me. The fire brings order and a method to all the madness."

"I can understand that." Autumn nodded and stood along the circle. "For me, the flames ignite when I have an intensity building up inside me. Yet, once they activate, the flames feel very deliberate and focused. They know their way and nothing stands in their path."

"Exactly. Fire has a will, and earth, air, and water can either fuel or bind it. So it must be diligent in its purpose." Lainy blew out her smudge stick flame and swirled it around the top of her head and across the front of her in the air. The others followed her lead.

"That's why I've kept the flames at bay and control them lately. I've bound them with my intention and use of the air element. Makes sense now when you put it like that." Autumn moved the smudge smoke in front of her face and peered at the bonfire through the smoke.

"Girls, let's get you into the proper positions. Penny and I will stand to the southeast and southwest so as not to distract from where you naturally belong. Now, in an ideal world, you would have another here to claim the air position so Autumn could be the fifth point to oversee them all. She'll have to do for your air element right now." Jo grabbed Autumn's shoulders and guided her to stand at the east end of the circle. She waved Simone over to the west.

"Eve, stand at the north. That is the position of the earth in our tradition." Penny lifted her chin to signal her to move to the top of the circle. "Exactly."

"And of course, Lainy, that means fire is to the south. If you'd like to walk the circle starting at the north first and make your way around, smudging the circle as Autumn calls the corners, then that would be wonderful." Jo made her suggestions and then took her spot at the southwest corner. "There you go, dear. Well done."

Lainy lifted the palo santo in the air and walked behind each of them along the perimeter of the circle as Autumn raised her hands at her sides.

"Elements of earth, air, fire, and water, we call you tonight. Guide us in our magical workings to protect and support us throughout our practice. As I say it, so shall it be." Autumn dropped her arms as Lainy made her way back to her place to the south.

"Wonderful. Now, I've collected some of the sap from a few surrounding trees. It's not much, but I'll demonstrate how to do the healing spell, and then Eve can try it. Does anyone have a minor cut or scrape that we can try this on?" Penny scanned the circle hopefully.

"I do." Simone lifted her pant leg to reveal a lengthy burn mark. They all looked at her with surprise, and she shrugged. "It was from the exhaust pipe on Ben's motorcycle. I accidentally pressed my leg on it and got a burn, but the ride was worth it." Simone smiled to herself, recalling the fun she'd had with Ben that afternoon.

"Must have been some ride." Lainy nodded in approval.

Penny brought over a wooden bowl with a small amount of pine tree sap inside and a flat wooden spatula. She placed her thumb and index finger into the sap mixture and pulled it up between her fingers before closing her eyes and whispering,

"Medicine of the earth, undo the wounds that run deep. Make them strong once more."

She immersed all the fingers of one hand fully into the sap as she placed the other hand firmly on the earth. Penny began chanting softly. "Laaammmm . . . laaaammmm." The sound hummed from her throat and hung in the surrounding air.

The girls all peered over the lip of the bowl to see the mixture inside sparkling with beautiful shimmers of red and green, almost like a brilliant Christmas tree. Penny nodded and brushed her fingers together to remove the traces of sap.

"Eve, would you hand me those large aspen leaves over there?" Penny pointed to the leaves on the ground, and Eve complied.

Penny patted the ground for Simone to come sit beside her. She positioned Simone's leg so she could properly get to the burn. Penny scooped the sap onto the wooden spatula and gently rubbed it onto an aspen leaf. She placed the leaf firmly onto Simone's burn and repeated the chant.

"Laaammm . . ." She motioned to Eve to repeat the process with more sap and another aspen leaf until she covered the wound completely. "While that does its job, Lainy and Autumn, why don't you both attempt to work with the fire together?" Penny smiled at the girls and sat up straight as if waiting expectantly.

"What do you mean?" Autumn gave her mother a curious look.

Jo stepped in with some encouragement. "Autumn, remember, you are the linchpin of all the elements. You intensify the others and give them power. Together, you can work in alignment to create incredible magic. Try it."

Autumn and Lainy stepped closer to the fire and made their way to either side. They faced each other across the flames. Tavish hopped down from his tree log and came to sit beside Autumn for support.

She and Lainy opened their palms and stared into the flames. The fire rose higher into the night sky, and the heat intensified enough that the women on one end of the circle felt significant warmth. The flames danced as Lainy moved her eyes around the bonfire, and the flames followed her eye movement.

Autumn brought all her frustrations to mind and sent them into the flames. Sparks mounted into fireworks across the sky and swirled in patterns that resembled vines. She felt her head pound and stepped back for a moment, pressing her fingers into her temples. A raging wind blew through the air all at once, snuffing out the high flames and bringing them back down to only small embers at the base of the bonfire.

Lainy rushed over to Autumn on the other side of the fire circle and grabbed her to keep her steady. "Are you okay? I felt the fire pulling away from us."

"What just happened? Did you hear voices, cuz?" Simone tried to move closer while keeping her leg steady with the leaf bandage in place.

Autumn shook her head. "No voices, but I saw the vines in the fire, which means they're intensifying and trying to spread to more than just the water. And I know whoever's behind this is only getting started."

The women squeezed in closer to Autumn as the last embers of the fire went dark. Tavish wrapped himself around Autumn's legs, and Lainy snapped her fingers to make a spark of light for them to see each other again.

"I think I'd better get more serious about uncovering what's really going on." Autumn pulled the hood of her cape up over her head and lifted Tavish up to eye level. He placed his wet nose onto hers, and his soothing energy made the intensity of her headache disappear.

CHAPTER 21

Tavish ran up to the front door of Parchment and Pine. Autumn looked at him curiously.

"What are you doing, cutie? Nothing ever gets you to move from your place by the fire except maybe some magic." Autumn crossed the shop floor and peered out the front window to see James strolling through the door.

She smiled as he came inside. "Oh, now I see. Tavish knew his favorite person was arriving. He didn't want to miss you."

James scooped up the cat into his arms and made his way over to Autumn. "I'm at least second in line for his favorite, but I can't argue with that." He brushed the hair away from Autumn's eyes and looked at her deeply. "Hi."

She could stand there and stare into his warm eyes all day. "Hi, yourself." Autumn kissed his lips softly and laughed at Tavish. "Thanks for coming. I know you've been busy wrapping up the downtown development project before the holi-days."

"No, it's fine. I had a break today since they finished the cobblestones. So, we won't have the final inspection until to-morrow." He followed her to the back of the shop and waved at Simone coming out of the back room. "Hey, Simone."

"Oh, hey, I didn't hear you come in. Autumn says you're gonna take her to do some sleuthing today." Simone raised her eyebrows up and down at him.

"Oh, she does, does she?" James turned to Autumn with a questioning look.

Her mouth dropped open while she found the right words. "I just need to . . . gather some information, and I was hoping you'd accompany me."

"Well, I'm glad you called instead of going out by your-self. Where exactly are we headed?" James leaned on the shop counter and stared at her.

"To the edge of town by your place, actually. The flower farm the Leslies own sits out there. Apparently, there's a dis-pute going on between them and their neighbor regarding who owns some property. I thought we'd go check it out, and I can bring Mrs. Cunningham some tea she requested, too. It's a good excuse to be out there." Autumn held up a kraft paper bag with one of her gran's tea labels on the front.

"I see. So, we're going to be trespassing, then?" James nod-ded as he thought about it.

"Not trespassing. Just doing a bit of surveying. For Mrs. Leslie's sake and for the town. We need to figure out what's going on around here before the water gets much worse. Things are getting serious, and if we're gonna restore the energy balance, we need to act fast." Autumn looked at him with puppy dog eyes.

James sighed and looked down at Tavish at his feet. "She knows how to get me, doesn't she?"

Simone laughed while giving him a sideways glance from behind the computer. "I've got the store for the rest of the day. Just find out whatever you can."

"And you've got me." James gave Autumn a sideways smile. "I'll take you over there. But I should get something out of this deal, too." James stood up and followed Autumn to get her coat and bag.

"You get to hang out with me. That should be payment enough." She wrapped her oversized dark-gray knit infinity scarf around her neck and pulled her hair out from under it. Her wool coat hung over her arm, along with her backpack, inside of which she placed the bag of Gran's tea. Autumn grabbed James's arm with her other hand and started across the shop.

"True, but I could always use more." James walked Autumn to the front door and opened it.

"I'll probably see you and Tavish at home after you close up the shop, okay? Thanks for staying!" Autumn waved to Simone and headed out the door with James.

He opened his truck door for her out at the curb, and they drove away toward the edge of town. The flower farm sat at the end of Hollow's Glenn just before Ivansedge, the next town over.

"If we have time, we could stop and see your mom," Autumn suggested.

"No, she's out today with her sister-in-law. They usually get together once a week. Thanks for suggesting it, though." He turned and gave her a smile.

"Yeah, of course. I just wanna make sure she's okay with everything that's happening."

"She's stronger than she lets on. These dreams have been a constant in her life since she was young, same as me. I think she's come to terms with them, even though they take a lot out of her."

They drove past the edge of the aspen trees on the outskirts of town and onto a skinny gravel road running through farm fields. James slowed down the truck and leaned toward Autumn a bit.

"What did you say the address was again?" He looked down at the map she had open on her phone.

"Uh, it's 2045. That's it right up there." Autumn pointed straight ahead at a black mailbox sitting on the side of the road.

"Okay, then. I guess we're here." James pulled into the long driveway on the other side of the mailbox and parked close to the road. "Where do you want to start?"

"Well, it seems like the house numbers get bigger the further out they go. So, the neighbor on the far side over there must be the one in the dispute. Let's hop out and walk the property to see where the lines may be."

"No one's here. You sure we shouldn't stop at Mrs. Leslie's house?" James opened the door and came around the front of the truck.

"Karen Leslie's at the flower shop today, and she doesn't have anyone else living with her. It should just be us out here." Autumn started walking through the fields mostly covered with straw for the winter.

A few little sprouts of green appeared on the far edge of the field. Autumn followed the lines in the straw, walking through where flower bulbs had most likely been planted for the next spring season.

"Autumn, wait. What do you see?" James jogged to catch up.

"Over there in the far corner. There are little sprouts." She raised her chin to show him where she was going.

They made their way to the back edge of the property close to where the Leslie home sat. James crouched down and gently brushed his hand over the tiny sprouts.

"They look like the beginnings of winter pansies." He raised his head to look at her and then noticed someone trudging through the adjoining field toward them. James stood up instantly and opened his mouth to speak.

"Who are you and what are you doing here?" a man shouted from behind Autumn. He wore a large flannel jacket over a T-shirt and jeans.

James lifted his right hand as if to signal they weren't there to cause trouble. "Sorry, sir. We're friends of the Leslies."

"Yes, I'm Autumn. I've been helping Karen Leslie since her husband passed. We were just here checking on things."

The man pointed his finger to a dirt line across the ground where the straw stopped a couple feet behind James and Autumn. "Well, that's where the Leslie land stops. So, you're on my land now. These here are my bulbs sprouting."

Autumn's eyes moved to the pansy sprouts in surprise. "Oh, I didn't realize. I thought the flowers were all on the Leslies' land."

The man let out a huff. "That's where they'd like them to be. All on their land and nothing for the rest of us. Seems they think they can take whatever land suits them, but that's the line." He pointed back to the dirt strip again.

"So there's some kind of dispute about it, then?" James questioned the man in a calm, understanding manner.

"No, thanks to Tom Leslie! He went and sued us to take over a larger strip of my property, saying something about the lines being drawn wrong or something. But I'm telling you right now that this is my family's land, and we intend to keep it. Our flowers are just as important as theirs, and I know they're jealous that this strip always bears the most beautiful blooms every single year."

The man bent down to check on the pansies, and Autumn saw the care he took in tending to them. Her instinct told her he had deep ancestral connections to that land and that his energy was tied to it.

"You have quite a connection to the land. I don't blame you for trying to protect it. When we hold something dear, it's second nature to defend it." Autumn knelt beside the man to see the sprouts.

James stepped to the side so he could observe them both. He knew Autumn had a keen awareness for what people needed. But in that moment, the way she communicated appeared to speak genuinely to the man's heart.

"Well, you're quite right." The man shook his head at Autumn. "Generations of Fergusons have tended to this land. I'm proud to be one of them, and there's no way I would let anyone take it away."

"I see that, and I know it can be hard when someone threatens what's important to you. I've experienced that myself." Autumn stood up with Mr. Ferguson. His eyes carried pain in them, and he looked as if he wanted to bare his soul to her.

"Yes, well, life has a way of bringing pain. It comes to us all." The man stirred himself out of Autumn's captive attention and moved his eyes over to James. "Now, why was it you said you were out here?"

"Oh, well . . ." Autumn glanced at James.

"We wanted to check on things for Mrs. Leslie. We heard the weather might take a turn today, so it was the least we could do to come out and check on things." James nodded in hopes the man would relent his questioning.

"Yes, and I also have a batch of tea for the Cunninghams. Do you know which house is theirs?" Autumn warmed her face as she asked.

"Oh, the Cunninghams. Yeah, they live on the other side of our place. We're in between them and the Leslies."

Autumn raised her arms to show some surprise. "Great! We can head over there now and deliver the tea. Thank you so much for chatting with us today, Mr. Ferguson. It was lovely to hear about your family's connection to the land." Autumn grabbed for his hand and shook it while the man looked bewildered.

"Well, all right, then. Just be careful walking back through the fields. You don't wanna twist an ankle out here." The man gave James a salute and watched them head back to James's truck.

James climbed in and started the engine as Autumn situated herself on the other side. They both waved out the truck windows as Mr. Ferguson stood there until they drove down to the Cunninghams.

"I don't know how you did that, but you put him at ease enough that I honestly thought he might tell you his entire life story if we stayed long enough." James parked the truck in the Cunninghams' driveway and shook his head at her.

Autumn shrugged. "Sometimes I just know exactly what people need to hear, and it comforts them talking to me."

James looked at the Cunninghams' house for a moment and thought. "So, what do we think about Mr. Ferguson, then? He has a bone to pick with the Leslies."

"Yeah, he does. And I could tell he would do whatever it took to keep the land for his family. I mean, that land is something that's potentially been their entire family's livelihood for generations. Messing with that would definitely give someone cause to harm."

Vera Cunningham peeked out the front door to see who had parked in her driveway. She wiped her hands on a dish towel and moved onto the porch as she squinted at them. As soon as she saw Autumn in the truck, she waved.

Autumn and James got out and headed for the porch. "Hi, Mrs. Cunningham. I wanted to stop over with the tea I promised you."

"Yes, that's right. The tea!" Vera got very excited and threw her hands up in the air. "Come inside. It's freezing out here, and I've got a nice warm apple crumble that I just made."

The two of them followed her inside to the kitchen, where they sat at a small four-person table. Mrs. Cunningham served them up a warm bowl of the crumble and placed a container of vanilla ice cream on the table as well.

"Did you come all this way just to give me the tea?" She sat beside them and watched them eat.

"Oh, I wanted to check on Mrs. Leslie's place since she's all alone these days." Autumn met Vera's eyes with a sympathetic look.

"I know, it's just awful. I brought her some stew the other night, but she seems so lonely over there by herself. She mentioned talking to her daughter recently, though. Maybe she'll actually come home for the funeral and all." Vera nodded and smiled at them.

"Oh, I didn't realize. Karen does need more help with the shop, too." Autumn wondered if Karen's daughter would stay long enough to help, or if she'd check the box in being here and then leave again.

"Her daughter, Quinn, can be overbearing. She's got some high-powered job in the city. When she makes it home, the girl usually directs her parents about all they need to change. From what I've heard, she would love nothing more than for her mother to pack things up and head to the city where Quinn can keep a closer eye on her."

"Hmm . . . I guess I remember Quinn being type A, but I hadn't heard about wanting her parents to move away from Hollow's Glenn." Autumn ate another spoonful of the apple crumble and gave James a face about how good it was.

"Oh, they've been going back and forth about it for years." Vera swished her hand through the air as if it were nothing. "But enough about the Leslies, what do you two lovebirds have planned for the weekend? It is Friday, after all."

James and Autumn stared at each other blankly and smiled sheepishly.

"Well, we hadn't made any plans. I just wanted to help Autumn with the tea delivery." James pushed aside his empty crumble bowl. "I should probably get her back home before the weather shifts."

"Nonsense! You know, they just opened the skating rink over at the reservoir. You both go down there and take a spin around the lake. It's just a few minutes away. If the snow starts, that would make for quite a romantic afternoon." She flowed her words together with a hopeful tone.

"Ice skating, huh? That would be fun if I could convince someone else to go." James smirked and eyed Autumn.

She sighed and looked back and forth between the two of them prodding her. "Well, I have some time this afternoon, and it's been a while since I've skated."

Vera cleaned up their dishes and waved them up. "There you go! Enjoy some time together. The lake is beautiful this time of year."

Autumn hugged Mrs. Cunningham, and they walked through the house back to the front porch. "Please let me know how you like the tea. It should give you that comforting feeling you were looking for."

"Oh, I'll put a pot on this evening when Bill comes home. He's quite receptive to those teas now, thanks to you." Vera winked at her as they headed to James's truck.

They slid into the truck seats, and he locked eyes with Autumn. "You're finally gonna make good and take me out on a proper date?"

Autumn dropped her mouth open and smiled at him. "I guess I am. As long as you don't make fun of me for how badly I skate."

He tilted his head at her. "Please, I don't buy that for a second. You're good at absolutely everything you do, and I don't think skating is any different. We'll just have to see if you can keep up with me."

Autumn laughed and thought about how good it felt to spend time with someone so right for her. She looked out the truck window as the Ross family tree from the library popped into her head. It wouldn't be so bad to maybe one day be part of it.

CHAPTER 22

James laced up his hockey skates next to Autumn on the wooden bench at the edge of the reservoir. Dozens of friends, couples, and families dotted the ice in front of them to enjoy the first skate of the season.

James pointed to someone out on the ice. "Hey, look, there are my uncle Dillon and aunt Abigail. I wouldn't have expected to see them out here today."

"Yeah, there sure are lots of people out here. There's even that reporter from the newspaper, Anabeth Greenwood." Autumn raised her chin in Anabeth's direction and locked eyes with her. Anabeth gave Autumn a wave and nudged the photographer next to her to get a photo.

Autumn thought it surprising that the start of skating season would rate so highly on Anabeth's radar, but it must be an otherwise quiet week after the eventful recent murder. While she got caught in thought for a moment, someone nudged Autumn from behind.

"Hey there, long time no see." Lainy came around to the front of Autumn and smiled. "I didn't expect to see you out here."

"Oh, hey! Yeah, we made a last-minute decision to come. How did you get off work so early from city hall?" Autumn finished lacing up her skates and stood up alongside Lainy and James.

"They actually planned an office event here today. Apparently, it's some morale-boosting program that city hall is trying out. They invited everyone to leave early and get some fresh air before the snow comes tonight." Lainy tied her belted coat and stood her collar up to button around her neck. "Anyway, I'll see you out there." Lainy stepped away carefully until she got to the ice and skated away to find her coworkers.

"My aunt must have gotten out early, then. She works in the city hall human resources department. I'm guessing my uncle canceled his therapy clients for the day to be with her." James put his hand out to Autumn, and she grabbed it.

They walked out onto the ice together and skated on the edge of the pond. Seasonal music played quietly in the background, and Autumn couldn't help but feel content. She tightened her fingers around James's and focused on the breeze blowing across her skin as she skated around the pond.

"Jo mentioned that your uncle Dillon helped her do some more cleansing at the river. I think they've gone once or twice since the founders dinner, but the progress has been very minor." Autumn watched James's aunt and uncle skating hand in hand around the curve ahead. They looked like a middle-aged couple still very much in love with each other.

"My mother mentioned something about it the other day. Dillon is very emotionally attuned to people and things. While my mother and I have the gift of dreamwork, he received the gifts of empathy and emotional receptivity. Probably a blessing and a curse for someone who's a therapist. It makes him incredibly perceptive, though, and able to understand things that usually go unseen or unsaid."

Autumn nodded, trying to process the information. "That must be why Aunt Jo wanted his help, then. He could perceive what was truly going on with the water."

As they did another lap around the ice, clouds grew menacingly overhead. Autumn felt an intense shift in the air as the winds picked up strongly. She took a deep breath in and smelled a developing scent of sulfur mixed with the familiar hints of vanilla. Her stomach dropped at the scent as they slowed to a stop near the skating booth at the edge of the pond.

"I didn't expect the snow to start for another couple hours, but those clouds look pretty intense." James eyed the huge gray clouds above them.

Autumn tried clearing her throat and turning to the side to breathe into her arm, but the sulfur smell kept getting stronger. She felt the deepening heat of the locket on her chest and put her hand over the top of her sweater where the locket sat underneath.

"Are you okay? Is something wrong?" James put his hand on her arm and wrinkled his forehead as he watched Autumn struggle.

"I'm fine. But the air . . ." Autumn scanned the ground while she tried to focus, but a piercing scream disturbed her thought.

"Help! Someone, please help!" The cry came from across the pond.

James squinted his eyes and noticed his aunt Abigail kneeling on what appeared to be broken ice. He steadied Autumn, made sure she was okay, and then took off across the pond. Autumn did her best to follow him.

When they reached Abigail, a couple other people stood beside her, peering down into the ice.

"Dillon fell into the ice! I don't know what happened. One minute the ice was solid, and the next it cracked under our feet." Abigail gripped James's arm as he bent down beside her, and she gave him a terrified look.

"Sir, call emergency services right now." James pointed to someone beside his aunt. He looked to the side and pointed to the next person. "I need you to move everyone back several feet."

The man nodded with understanding and lifted his arms to push everyone away from the gaping hole getting larger in the ice. James lay on his belly and searched inside the hole. The waters looked so dark with nothing visible underneath.

Autumn saw a crack slowly getting larger. When she narrowed her eyes to see where it began, she spotted hints of shimmering dark lines below the surface of the water. They crept along underneath the ice and sparkled with black magic.

"James! Be careful. Those aren't ordinary cracks." Autumn pointed to the one getting larger. She pulled her necklace out from under her coat to show him it was glowing intensely with emerald-green light.

He looked at the necklace and then at Autumn with a grave expression. "We need to get him out of this water before he drowns or freezes to death."

Autumn exhaled and lay beside him on the ice. Abigail covered her mouth with her shaking hands while scanning the waters.

A security guard scurried across the ice to them and put his hand on James's shoulder. "I've radioed for help. What can I do?"

Autumn looked at him and then at James. "Hold on." Both men stared at her in confusion, but James realized Autumn must be getting some insight. "Lainy and Anabeth. Run and get them over in the crowd. Just Lainy and Anabeth." She spoke as matter-of-factly as she could.

As the security guard scurried back across the ice as fast as he could, James turned to Autumn. "What's the plan?"

"We're going to heat the ice and crack it even more so that we can find Dillon in the water." Autumn swallowed hard and looked at Abigail. "Mrs. Ross, I need you to move way back toward the edge of the pond where everyone else is standing. Can you do that for me?" Autumn's tone seemed hurried but adamant.

"I'm not leaving! My husband is in that water!"

James took hold of his aunt and gave her a quick shake. "Abigail, we will find him, but I need you to move away from here. It's not safe. Go back to the edge of the pond for now."

Abigail stared at Autumn for a moment, searching her face for some kind of affirmation, and then nodded at James hesitantly. "All right, but you get him out of there."

James and Abigail nodded at each other, and he sent her off as the security guard came back out to get her.

"James, watch the water and be ready to hoist him out the moment we find him." Autumn's heart felt like it was beating out of her chest now.

Lainy and Anabeth rushed up beside them both, panting deeply.

"We're here. What happened?" Lainy exchanged looks with Autumn and recognized that things were serious.

"A man fell into the water, and I need you both to help us get him out. Rescue services are on the way, but it's up to us right now." Autumn glanced at Anabeth and noticed her wearing the long hemp scarf she'd purchased from Parchment and Pine several days ago.

Autumn then met eyes with Lainy as James and Anabeth scanned the waters for any sign of Dillon. "Lainy, we have to melt the ice so we can find him."

"Right. Okay." Lainy looked down at the hole in the ice and then back up at Autumn.

Autumn whispered something under her breath and bent down onto the ice, along with Lainy. They put their palms directly onto the surface and locked eyes.

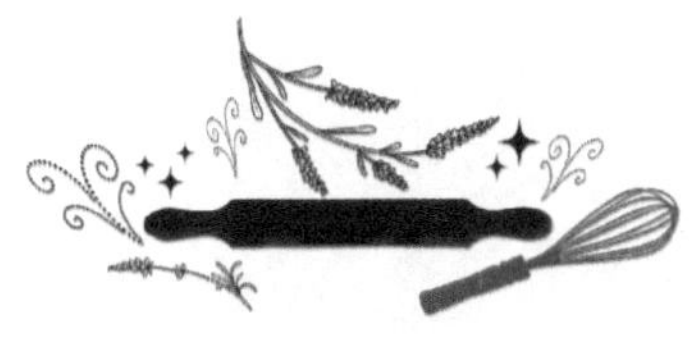

Eve's Gingerbread Muffins For Well-Being

For the muffins:

2 1/2 cups all purpose flour

1 1/2 tsp baking soda

1/2 tsp baking powder

1/4 teaspoon salt

2 tsp ground cinnamon

1 tsp ground ginger

1/2 tsp ground cloves

1/2 cup light or dark brown sugar

2 eggs

1/2 cup butter, melted

1/2 cup (180ml) light or dark molasses

1/2 cup (120ml) milk

1 tsp vanilla extract

For the glaze:

1 cup confectioners' sugar

1 tsp vanilla extract

1 Tbsp milk

Preheat oven to 425°F. Line a muffin pan with papers and set aside. In a large bowl, whisk together all of the dry ingredients while saying,

For warmth, health, and protection through our days.

In a separate bowl, whisk together molasses, milk, melted butter, eggs, and vanilla extract. Add wet ingredients to dry ingredients with a wooden spoon. As you stir, draw the shape of a star in the batter three times while saying aloud,

Earth, air, fire, and water, give these muffins protective power.

Divide batter among prepared muffin pan. Bake at 425 degrees Fahrenheit for 5 minutes. Then, reduce the oven temperature to 350 degrees Fahrenheit and continue baking for about 15 minutes more until the tops are cracked. Test with a toothpick to ensure the center has set. Allow to cool for 5-10 minutes in pan before glazing.

As the muffins cool, mix all of the glaze ingredients together in a medium bowl. Add more milk to thin out as needed. Drizzle on top of warm muffins and enjoy.

CHAPTER 23

The ice beneath Autumn's hands stung her skin, and she knew they only had a few more minutes to get Dillon out of the water. She began chanting, and Lainy joined in.

"Fire within us, melt the ice hiding the waters below."

They repeated the chant several more times, not taking their eyes off each other. Both of them lay flat on their stomachs on the icy surface. The glowing green of Autumn's necklace radiated from her chest while the most intense heat she'd ever felt coursed through her hands.

Then, they both felt a wetness beneath their hands rather than the solidity of the ice. Autumn looked under her palms to find a pool of water growing larger by the second.

"It's working! Scoot back on the ice and keep going." Lainy pushed herself a few inches further from the hole in the ice.

As the girls moved, James and Anabeth followed their lead. The ice in front of them broke off and melted directly into the gaping hole.

"Anabeth, give me your scarf!" James threw his hands out to take the scarf from her. He wrapped one end of it tightly around the top of his arm. "Help me tie a knot."

Anabeth did her best to tie the scarf into a triple knot and test its strength. "That should work. Fingers crossed."

James and Anabeth bent down at the edge of the water and scanned it again for his uncle while Autumn caught the scent of vanilla rising in the air again.

"I see something!" James fed the loose end of the scarf down into the icy waters and allowed it to float around. "He's there!" James pointed across the hole to the other side of Anabeth. He slid his body across the ice and plunged his hand into the freezing water.

Autumn's heart beat faster as she watched him lower into the hole a little. "Lainy, the water." Autumn moved herself forward and put her own hand into the hole. "Fire within me, heat the water to save this life."

Lainy moved up against Autumn and placed her hands down into the water as well. They repeated the chant together. "Heat the water to save this life."

Both of their hands shimmered under the surface. Autumn watched as the sparkling dark vine-like tentacles melted toward the water's bottom, and their hands shined brightly with golden sparks at the top.

"I've got him!" James pulled his arm from the water with Dillon's hand wrapped tightly around it.

Autumn let out a breath of relief, and the sun poked free of the clouds overhead. In an instant, the reflection of something caught Autumn's eye in the tree line across the pond. She squinted to see as James and Anabeth pulled at his uncle. Autumn glimpsed what looked like a shadowy figure in a navy ice fishing jacket. The figure scurried away and left the tree line bare again.

As James made one more heave to pull Dillon clear of the water, rescue workers swarmed up behind them and grabbed them both from the water's edge. Anabeth slid back on her ice skates and took in the scene as the medics did their job to check vitals.

Autumn and Lainy moved back to give them space. They immediately hauled Dillon away on a stretcher. As James watched him being wheeled away, he saw Abigail meet up with the medics and go with them to the ambulance. He flopped down on the ice and rested his arms over his knees as he panted.

"He's okay." James closed his eyes and repeated the phrase to himself again.

Another medic came over and wrapped James in a blanket just as Chief Walsh and a few officers appeared. Autumn turned on her skates to face Chief Walsh and gave him a grave look.

"We'll talk in a moment." He nodded in Autumn's direction. "Uh, Ms. Greenwood, is it?" The chief turned toward Anabeth and put his arm around her. "Why don't you go over and sit next to Autumn for a minute while I talk with James, okay?"

Anabeth gave Chief Walsh a relieved nod and slid over to Autumn and Lainy. The three of them skated back from the melted ice.

"Anabeth, we couldn't have saved him without you." Autumn hugged her with a soothing smile. "It was lucky you had that hemp scarf from the shop with you."

She looked up into Autumn's eyes in realization. "You're right. It was lucky. How did you know I would need it?"

Autumn glanced at Lainy and then back at Anabeth with a shrug. "It just seemed to work out. You having it today, and me knowing that hemp is one of the strongest fabrics. As soon as I remembered you wearing it, I knew it would be our best bet to hold Dillon."

Anabeth shook her head in amazement. "I don't even understand all that happened here. I mean, you both melted that ice, and I saw light coming from you into the water. How is that possible?"

"Anabeth . . ." Lainy tried to explain, but Autumn put her hand on Lainy's shoulder to suggest she could handle it.

Autumn stood as firmly as she could on her skates and looked Anabeth directly in the eyes. "We got incredibly lucky today when the ice kept cracking and exposed the water for us to find Dillon." Autumn focused her mind on sending the message to Anabeth as she stared into her eyes. "The ice cracking on its own allowed us to see more of the water. That's what happened." She searched Anabeth's eyes to ensure her memory altered enough to release all questions.

Anabeth nodded and repeated Autumn's version of the story. "I can't believe how lucky we were that the ice cracked for us to see into the waters. That man got so lucky."

The girls gave Anabeth a smile, and Chief Walsh glanced over to see that Autumn had taken care of the situation. Lainy tugged on Autumn's sleeve and pulled her out of earshot of Anabeth.

"How did you do that? Will she remember what really happened?" Lainy's mouth hung open in confusion.

Autumn laughed a little under her breath. "Air energy is my primary element. I realized recently that I can reframe memories. It doesn't take them away or anything, but it reinterprets them for people. I think they need to be subconsciously open to reinterpretation for it to work, but it hasn't been a problem."

Lainy's head tipped back in surprise. "I better stay on your good side."

Autumn rolled her eyes at her. "Seriously, though, I wouldn't have been able to do any of that without you. Your fire energy is incredibly strong."

Lainy could feel the pride welling up inside her. She'd felt so distant from everyone her whole life, including her own sister. Now, though, she had a purpose in Hollow's Glenn and a family that understood her. "I'm really glad to be here and to know that somehow I'm needed."

They stared at the police officers getting a statement from James and Anabeth and shook their heads. Autumn broke the silence with what she hoped Lainy needed to hear.

"We do need you. Not just because of your fire, but because you're you. And I'm happy you took that job at city hall. Although . . ." Autumn stopped and glanced over at Chief Walsh.

Lainy wrinkled her forehead at Autumn. "What is it?"

"This was supposed to be a city hall event, and it definitely wasn't an accident that Dillon fell in the water. I saw someone over there in the tree line watching us."

"So . . . you're saying someone wants to hurt somebody from city hall? Dillon doesn't work at city hall, though."

Autumn moved back and forth on her skates as she thought. "No, but his wife does. And there have been a lot of connections with Tom Leslie around land preservation and complaints filed at city hall. Dillon may not have been the intended victim here, but maybe there is some kind of connection with city hall somehow. I don't know. I'm just . . . thinking out loud."

Chief Walsh and Ben walked over to the girls as James and Anabeth headed out with the medics. James caught Autumn's eye for a moment, and he signaled he wouldn't go far.

"Autumn . . . and Lainy, right?" The chief dipped his head down to check with her.

"Yes, it's Lainy." She smiled awkwardly at him. The first time she'd met him at the police station had been during the hardest situation of her life.

The chief nodded at her and brought his attention back to Autumn. "I have a feeling you're the reason we have a man who's still breathing instead of drowned."

"It was a group effort, and I'm so thankful we got him out alive. But Chief, this was no accident." Autumn stared at him with seriousness in her face.

He rested his hands on his belt, glanced at Ben by his side, and then focused on what she was saying. "Go on. We're listening."

"I saw someone in the trees watching us." She lowered her voice to a whisper. "And I could tell the water had changed. It's being manipulated by someone, but this was . . . very deliberate and premeditated."

"Okay, I want you to tell Ben as much as you know. Whatever you saw, we'll investigate. Confidentially, if we have to. But just to be clear, I can't make any arrests without concrete evidence."

Autumn nodded and looked over at Ben. "I'll tell you all I can, but some of it we obviously can't disclose. So, I guess you'll have to weed out what you can't substantiate."

"We'll do our best, Autumn. Chief, I'll take them over to the ambulances and get their statements there." Ben lifted his arms behind the girls to usher them toward the parking lot.

"Ben, it needs to be your eyes only on that statement." The chief gave his son a look and then called a few other officers over to cordon off the area.

Autumn and Lainy skated back to the ice hut to grab their shoes and talk with Ben, when the wind picked up around them. Autumn's hair swirled to the sides, and she slowed down to a stop on the ice.

The voices on the wind whispered, "With water flows the poison."

"I know that already, don't I?" Autumn questioned the air around her as Ben and Lainy eyed her.

"Know what?" Ben wasn't sure what Autumn was talking about or why she had stopped so suddenly.

"I'm not sure exactly, but maybe my cousin will have some ideas." Autumn started skating toward the hut again with a quickened pace.

"Simone? Wait, Autumn! I'm coming with you," Ben shouted as he slid across the rest of the ice to keep up.

CHAPTER 24

Simone slammed the door to her black Jeep SUV. She jogged up the driveway to her mother's front porch just as Autumn, Lainy, and Ben pulled up. Ben Walsh parked his squad car out on the curb, and the second Simone saw him coming out, her stomach dropped.

"Ben, what's going on? Autumn called me in a rush and told me to meet her here right away," Simone yelled across the front lawn.

Ben glanced over at Autumn with tight lips and then headed straight for Simone at the porch. "Simone, everyone's okay. Let's just go inside so Autumn can talk."

He climbed the front steps and grabbed her hand. "I'm glad you're here and safe."

"You're freaking me out." She looked across the lawn. "Autumn, where have you been? I thought you'd be home hours ago." Simone propped open the front door to wait for her cousin when she realized Lainy was there, too. "Lainy, what are you doing here? Something is definitely going on."

They all hurried inside, where Jo and Penny stood in the front hall, wondering about the commotion.

"Officer Walsh, what's happened? I had a strange feeling I'd be seeing you tonight." Jo started in on him quickly.

Ben put his palms out and tilted his head at her. "Everything is fine, Ms. MacKinnon. Would you be so kind as to lead us into your living room where we can chat?"

Jo nodded and led them into the front sitting room where the fireplace was already alight. They each took a seat around the room, but Ben stood next to where Simone sat.

"Well, let's hear it. What's this all about?" Simone tucked her legs under her on the couch and leaned forward, waiting for someone to speak.

"Dillon Ross almost drowned this evening." Autumn shot her eyes over to Aunt Jo to gauge her expression.

Jo covered her mouth with her hands and gasped. She turned to her sister and grabbed her hand beside her. "Oh, Penny! I sensed something wasn't right. I must call Sorcha!"

"Ma'am, please wait. Mr. Ross is with his wife now at the hospital, and they'll be able to call anyone who needs to know. It's best if Autumn recounts the events of the evening, and I'm going to take her statement here, along with Lainy's, as they were both present at the scene."

"You mean, you saw him almost drown? Where? The river again?" Simone bit her fingernails while listening intently.

"No, we were all at the reservoir. They opened up the ice for skating today, and city hall hosted a social event for the kickoff. So, there were loads of people there," Lainy chimed in as she crossed her legs and rubbed her arms to get warm.

"Yeah, I guess Dillon's wife works at city hall. He must have taken the day off to be with her at the event, so they were skating together." Autumn eased out of her wool coat and slid down to the floor beside the fireplace.

"I didn't know you planned to go skating today. I thought you were out at the Leslies' farm." Simone blurted the words out before she realized Ben hovered over her. She gave him a look and rolled her eyes as if it were no big deal.

"Well, when James and I delivered Gran's tea to Mrs. Cunningham, she suggested we go over to the ice pond. It was so close, and I owed James a proper date . . . So much for that." Autumn warmed her hands by the fire when she heard a meow and little paws coming into the room.

"Aw, Tav! Am I glad to see you!" He went straight to Autumn's arms and curled up in them.

"As soon as you called, I figured I better bring Tavish along with me. He always makes everything better." Simone gave Ben a sideways glance and smiled to herself.

"Okay, so out with it, girls. What happened to Dillon Ross?" Jo couldn't take the suspense for the rest of the story.

Ben pulled out a notepad and pen and signaled to Autumn to describe what happened.

Autumn sighed, preparing herself to relive it. "James and I heard Dillon's wife screaming across the pond, and we skated over there as fast as we could to find the ice cracked. There was a hole where Dillon fell in, and I could only imagine how cold and scared he must have been underneath the ice."

"That's when Autumn sent a security guard to find me and Anabeth." Lainy kicked off her heels and her belted coat as she spoke.

"Anabeth? As in the reporter Anabeth Greenwood who came into the shop to grill me the other day?" Simone bent a knee up and wrapped her arms around it as she huffed.

"Yeah, she was there at the pond. And when I first saw her, I knew she was out to get a story on the latest happenings in town. But then, after Dillon fell in, I immediately knew she was there to help. Not that she knew it, but that hemp scarf you sold her the other day came in handy. She was wearing it tonight, and it made all the difference."

"So you're saying she helped you rescue Mr. Ross? And did she wanna write an entire story about it afterward?" Simone's cynical side came through.

"She actually remained pretty calm and helpful, especially while we were melting the ice," Lainy interjected, turning toward Autumn and then herself, realizing Ben still stood there. Lainy's mouth dropped open, and she raised her hand to her chin to think of how to backpetal from her comments.

"It's all right, dear. Ben knows about our gifts. We can speak freely in front of him and his father," Jo reassured her on the spot.

"Autumn, you used your gifts in front of all those people?" Penny gave her daughter a worried look.

"Yes and no. We were so far away from the crowd on the other side of the lake that no one else would have seen what we were doing. Anabeth did, however, see it all firsthand. I think I adjusted her memory of it well enough that she now thinks the ice cracked on its own."

"But what really happened? You melted it?" The story was getting good now that Simone knew everyone was fine. She wanted to hear every detail.

Autumn turned to Lainy next to her and smiled. "We melted it. Together. There's no way I would have gotten through that ice on my own. It was a good thing Lainy was there to help because we couldn't see Dillon in the water at all until we made a bigger hole in the ice."

"The water was so dark, and the hole he fell into wasn't very big. We had to expand it to even find him below the surface. So, while James and Anabeth searched and made a rope with Anabeth's scarf, Autumn and I sent fire energy into the ice." Lainy stretched out her legs and wiggled her toes by the fire. She still couldn't quite get warm enough from being close to the ice for so long.

"Next to the water, I saw the black vines spreading under the surface. It took all we had combined to make them melt down into the lake so we could pull Dillon out. Well, allow James to pull him out." Autumn snuggled Tavish into her neck for comfort as she thought about it. "And that's when I saw the figure in the trees."

Ben looked up from his notebook to listen intently. "Can you describe the figure?"

Autumn closed her eyes, trying to recall what she'd seen. "A tall figure hiding in the shadows of the trees. I only noticed because of some sort of reflection when the sun creeped through the clouds. It looked like the person wore a navy-blue ice fishing jacket. You know, like those waterproof jackets you see the outdoorsy types wearing sometimes around here?"

Ben nodded and jotted a few things down. "But you didn't see the person's face or any features?"

Shaking her head, Autumn drew Tavish into her. "No, unfortunately. Just the coat, and then they were gone."

Ben and Simone exchanged a serious look before returning their attention to Autumn and Lainy. "Okay, if you remember anything else, then contact me or my father at the station. I'm gonna head back and check up on everything."

"Well, how is James? Was he hurt at all when pulling his uncle out?" Being the constant healer, Penny wanted to ensure everyone was all right now.

"He's fine, Mom," Autumn interjected with a calming tone. "They checked all his vitals in the ambulance before we left the scene. I made sure he was okay before heading out, and he promised to check back in with me when he went to the hospital to see his aunt and uncle. He's probably there now. I planned to head over there as soon as we let you know what was happening."

"If you're going to the hospital, then I'm coming with you." Simone stood up and put her hands on her hips.

"The weather was supposed to have turned by now. They're saying several inches of snow will come tonight and into tomorrow, so I don't want you girls out in that. It worries me." Jo played with the rings on her fingers as she stood up and made her way to the front window. "It's already started. The flakes are accumulating on the porch."

"Try to stay close to home tonight. If you're gonna go, then make it quick and be back before we get any substantial weather. And promise me you'll be safe and not cause any more work for me tonight." Ben eyed Simone, knowing how stubborn she was.

Simone raised her hand in the air. "Promise, we'll be careful. I'll just go with Autumn to check on James's family, and we'll head back. I swear." Simone turned toward Autumn, and she agreed.

"And Lainy, you're welcome to stay here tonight if you don't want to be alone at home," Penny suggested, hoping she could entice her to stay close by.

Lainy shook her head and rose off her chair. "Oh no, I'll be fine, but thank you. My place is pretty cozy, and if we end up being snowed in, it'll give me a chance to catch up on some candle making."

"Well, then, I'll leave you all to it for the night. Please remember to call if anything at all comes up." Ben started toward the front door as Simone and her mother followed him out.

As Simone opened the door for him, he turned back to look at her one more time. "Be careful tonight. I don't like that someone may be out there trying to hurt people on top of this storm coming in. Too many layers of uncertainty for me."

Simone smiled at him and leaned in to whisper, "Uncertainty is my wheelhouse. We'll be fine." She kissed his lips as she gently grazed her hand across his cheek. "Goodnight, Officer Walsh."

"Goodnight, everyone." He waved his hand and walked out to his squad car.

Autumn, Lainy, and Penny all gathered in the front hall along with them. The girls pulled their coats and boots out and got ready to face the cold again.

Jo peered out the side window at the front door as the snow fell in larger chunks. "Girls, call us the minute you get where you're going, all right? I sense this night hasn't finished causing trouble yet."

They hugged one another and nodded. "We'll let you know, Aunt Jo. Simone and I will head home after the hospital, so don't wait for us to come back."

"All right, dears, be safe. I'll put a quick protection bubble around you as you walk to your cars." Penny waved as they walked out the door.

Lainy stopped out on the front walkway as Simone and Autumn stood at the SUV in the driveway. The clouds above them rumbled, and they watched blue static flicker in one of them as snow dumped down around them.

Autumn peered over to Simone with a questioning look. "Is that . . .?"

"Thundersnow. That doesn't happen here in the mountain region, even with our lakes." Simone walked around to the back of the SUV to watch the sky with Lainy and Autumn. "Someone must be messing with the weather."

"That's pretty serious magic you're talking about. Creating thundersnow?" Lainy raised her eyebrows at Simone as she wrapped her coat tighter around her.

"If someone's messing with the weather, you're talking about manipulation of the air now. Not just the water?" Autumn thought for a moment about what Simone was saying.

"No, not the air. Well, maybe, but I can feel the imbalance in the snow." Simone waited for a few flakes to fall into her palm and give her an intuitive download. "My guess . . . warming the water temperatures disrupts the cold air above and activates the storm. This snow feels fragile and tainted, so that's my best off-the-cuff idea. Whether or not it's right, this thundersnow isn't natural."

Autumn let the snow gather on the sleeve of her coat and squinted her eyes at the flakes. They appeared to be more like viny tendrils than structured branches, and as she lifted them closer to her face, she caught a hint of rotten eggs in the air.

CHAPTER 25

Autumn pushed the elevator button again as she and Simone waited impatiently for it to appear. She already knew James was all right. Yet, the thought of how close his uncle had come to drowning made her eager to confirm he didn't have any permanent damage.

The elevator dinged, and the doors opened to reveal James's aunt Abigail and his mother, Sorcha, on the other side.

"Autumn!" Sorcha quickly came out of the elevator to wrap her arms around her. "Oh, Simone, it's good to see you, too, dear." She turned toward her sister-in-law. "This is Abigail, Dillon's wife."

Autumn nodded. "Yes, we met briefly at the reservoir. How is your husband?"

Abigail sighed with relief and hugged Autumn tightly. "He's stable now, and thanks to you and James, he's alive. They're monitoring his blood oxygen levels and will most likely do some scans over the next several hours. But I'm so thankful he's still here with us."

"I know it must have been an incredibly scary experience for you both. Are you holding up okay?" Autumn gave the woman a soft, empathetic expression.

"As best I can be under the circumstances. Sorcha and James have been a godsend here with me, though." Abigail grasped Sorcha's hand and smiled.

"Girls, why don't you go up and see James? They gave him the all clear, and he's in Dillon's room now, 204. Just knock gently since Dillon may be sleeping." Sorcha hugged Autumn and Simone and headed toward the cafeteria with Abigail.

The elevator dinged again, and the girls hopped on it to head upstairs. When they reached the door to Room 204, Autumn heard strange mumblings coming from inside. She peered through the strip of glass over the door handle to see Dillon asleep in the hospital bed and James asleep in the chair beside him. James jerked his head from side to side while keeping his eyes closed. Autumn pushed through the door and eyed him.

"Through the flames," James murmured as he slept. "The flames are the way!"

Autumn shook him slightly to wake him from whatever dream disturbed him. She glanced at Simone, wondering how to wake him as his eyes shifted back and forth under the lids.

"Let's both try it." Simone stepped to the other side of James, and they shook his body back and forth to jolt him awake.

James nearly fell out of his chair as he opened his eyes, stunned at where he was. "Autumn? What's going on?"

She brushed her hand across his forehead and looked into his eyes. "Are you okay? You were talking in your sleep, and you seemed pretty agitated. Simone and I had to wake you up."

"Oh, uh . . ." He ran his hand over his face to wipe off the stupor. Catching his breath for a moment, he looked into Autumn's green eyes. "That dream. It was so vivid and surreal."

Simone pulled a couple more chairs over from the side wall, and they sat beside James as his uncle continued to sleep.

"Do you wanna tell us about it?" Autumn worried when she saw the stress in James's face.

"This one was different. I didn't feel the connection like I did with the drowning dream." James looked over at his uncle on the bed. "Now I know why I felt that so deeply. Dillon's always been close to me."

"I know. This must have been so hard for you, having to rescue him like that. But we saw Abigail and your mom downstairs. They said he's stable, and they're monitoring him." Autumn put her hand over his.

James rubbed the back of his neck with his other hand. "I just wish I would have known earlier that it was him in my dream. I could have prevented it. And now, with this new one, I can't really tell what's what."

"What do you mean? Do you remember most of it?" Simone leaned over and put her forearms on her thighs as she waited for his response.

"I saw a ring of fire rising on the surface of some water. Someone pushed their way through it, but under the surface, another figure swam around. I could swear it moved like . . . a mermaid gliding through the water. And I could feel the tension and anxiousness of the dream, but there was a calmness to the water and the flames. Almost like being calm under pressure, if that makes sense." James pressed his fingers onto his eyes and then blinked them open a few times.

"A mermaid and a ring of fire. Your dream sounds like an underwater circus." Simone raised her eyebrows and sat back into her chair, crossing her arms over her chest.

James threw his hands up. "Yeah, well, they just come to me. I never really know what they mean until it's too late, and I don't know how to prevent that. I just wish there was a way for me to decipher these things sooner so no one got hurt."

Autumn rubbed his back. "It's okay. We'll figure it out together. They're definitely messages, and you need to learn how to speak the dream language better. Like now you know that when you feel connected and actually sense what's happening in the dream, then you could be related to the person."

James watched his uncle as he slept. "Yeah, I absolutely felt what he was going through in that dream. I felt the fear of drowning in that icy water." He swallowed hard and shook his head. "Thank God we were there." James sat up straighter and removed his phone from his pocket. "That reminds me. I got a message from my dad before all this happened." He pulled up the message and handed the phone to Autumn.

Autumn read the beginning of the message aloud. "Test results..."

"They're from the samples we ran at the river. My dad had the water and the soil tested at an environmental engineering lab nearby. Turns out, they found high levels of pesticides and some arsenic in the water. Both of which were banned in manufacturing here some time ago."

"Arsenic, are you serious? The river feeds into the water treatment facility for the town. We could have those pollutants in our drinking water, making the residents incredibly sick."

"Which is why my father sent it directly to city hall with an immediate action notice. They'll most likely redirect the drinking water from the Ivansedge water tower for the time being until we can get this under control. But that's not the only thing found in the report." James took the phone from Autumn and scrolled down the page to the bottom. He pointed to a grayed-out line of text.

Autumn read over it to herself first but wasn't sure what she was looking at. "Hydrogen sulfide. What does that mean?"

"It means the bacteria in the water is increasing exponentially, and it's creating a significant amount of sulfur. I bet people will start smelling it soon, but we won't give them a chance to taste it if we can redirect water from the Ivansedge tower."

"Is sulfur harmful? I thought it just smelled bad." Simone shrugged and gave James a questioning look.

"Well, that depends on a lot of things. I mean, sulfur is highly corrosive. So, it'll start eating away at pipes and causing a lot of scale and deterioration, not to mention it's harmful to people, especially in these amounts. But the way the sulfur appeared on the report was the strange part. They found it with an herbal carrier in the water sample. A flower that seemed to be attached to it." James ran his finger over the line below on the report. "Winter jasmine."

Autumn gasped and put her hand over her mouth. "Winter jasmine. That's what Tom Leslie foraged near the river. It's the reason he would go out there, including the night he died most likely."

"If those are the flowers we saw in the Leslies' shop, then those don't grow right up to the river." Simone leaned forward again and shook her head. "I've gone running along there enough times to know that they're like ground cover that grows away from the river's edge, even though they're in that same area. But they wouldn't just end up in the river naturally. Someone intentionally had to put them in there."

"Someone who's also using enough black magic to produce significantly higher amounts of sulfur than usual." Autumn moved her eyes between Simone and James as she thought. She realized the water and the wildflowers intertwined somehow in all the recent events.

James sighed. "I'm afraid this same someone won't stop until they go a lot further. Maybe even to where rings of fire burst through the water like in my dream." James lifted an eyebrow as he spoke.

Autumn knew he was right. They had to find the connection between Dillon's mishap and Tom Leslie's death before someone else got hurt and the entire town felt the consequences of the contamination.

CHAPTER 26

Simone scooped one last shovelful of snow away from the driveway in front of the girls' home. She wiped the hair away from her face with her thick fleece gloves.

"Man, the storm last night really came out of nowhere and dumped on us." Simone panted as she walked over to Autumn, throwing another shovelful onto the lawn.

"Yeah, this is pretty deep. I didn't expect to get this many inches, not to mention the thunder that came along with it last night. I hope everything's okay at the shop. We need to get going and check everything out. Mrs. Lachlan is supposed to come in today to go over the supplies for her son's welcome home party. I'm hoping that'll give me an opportunity to dig further into how much her husband disliked Tom Leslie." Autumn tapped the snow shovel on the ground to remove any last snow before heading up to the porch.

"Well, I guess we better grab Tavish and get going, then. I wanna make sure that our computer is still intact at the shop. I backed everything up, but getting a new computer is not in the budget right now. So fingers crossed the storm didn't cause any damage." Simone followed Autumn into the house to grab their things and scoop Tavish up into his cozy flannel-lined carrier.

"All set. Let's go." Autumn locked the door behind them and headed to Simone's SUV.

Simone started up the heat, and as soon as Autumn and Tavish hopped in, she pulled out. The girls made their way down the wooded road, when Simone slowed to watch Mrs. Pendleton out shoveling her driveway. She looked up at them and flagged them down.

Simone rolled down the window just as their neighbor tramped through the snow to get to the road.

"Oh, girls, can you believe this mess? We must have gotten at least a foot of snow last night." Mrs. Pendleton pulled the scarf down from around her face to speak. "Speaking of, did you hear what happened to the mayor?"

Simone and Autumn looked at one another with a pang of nervousness and shook their heads.

"No, we didn't. What happened?" Autumn leaned further over to get a better view of Mrs. Pendleton out Simone's window.

"He ran off the road last night. Apparently, he drove near the marina where the weather was the worst, and the roads had already iced over, not to mention the poor visibility." She put her gloved hands on her hips and took in a cold breath as she continued. "Long story short, he veered off the road straight into a telephone pole. Almost killed him, but he's stable in the hospital now."

"Almost killed him?" Simone turned toward Autumn again. "We're really racking up the crazy accidents around here."

"Thankfully, he's fine, though. The hospital fixed him right up, and he'll be back on the job in no time. Now, I've gotta finish the drive, but you girls be careful going out today."

"We will, Mrs. Pendleton. Thanks for letting us know." Autumn waved at her as she walked away.

Simone shook her head as she put the window back up and drove away. "I'm betting that was no accident. And this crazy thunder snow wasn't either."

"You're right. This is all connected somehow, but we're definitely missing something. She mentioned the mayor was near the marina, so this all occurred around the water. First the river, then the ice on the lake, and now this right near the lake marina. Plus, the voices told me that with the water flows the poison. I just can't understand what that has to do with each of these people. Mr. Leslie, James's uncle, and now the mayor. I don't get it."

Tavish poked his nose out of his carrier in the backseat to give a meow, and Autumn turned back to scratch his chin. "Aw, Tav. I know you wanna help. Let's go warm up at the

Pine, and we can think things over with some hot chocolate and a cozy fire."

Simone turned down the back alley of the shop and slowed down. "Who is that with Karen Leslie?"

Autumn squinted to see a girl with dark hair half pinned up in a bun and the rest draping over the shoulders of her wool coat. She helped Mrs. Leslie carry a covered box from the flower shop van to the back door. "I think that's her daughter, Quinn. I haven't seen her in ages, but Vera Cunningham mentioned she might be back in town."

Simone parked her SUV behind the Pine, and the girls, along with Tavish, bundled up to head straight inside the shop. The wind and snow died down outside, but the air remained frigid. Autumn plopped Tavish down on the ground in the back office, and he hopped right out and headed for the hearth room.

"Why don't you check to see if there's any damage, and I'll get some hot water going and open the shop." Autumn unwrapped herself from the many layers she wore and got going with her checklist.

Simone made her way to the front and checked on the computer first. "No damage to the computer, thank God. Looks like everything is still intact."

Autumn made her way up to Simone with two giant mugs of hot chocolate in hand and placed them down on the counter. "Good, I was nervous we might lose all our designs."

She headed into the hearth room to start the fire just as the piano music started over the speakers.

Simone looked up at the ceiling. "Ooh, good choice. I like piano notes on a chilly day. It feels soothing somehow." Simone raised a finger and leaned over the computer to glance at Autumn. "But as far as our designs go, you don't need to worry about the lantern collection. We already have enough printed to cover us for the festival and all the way through the new year. So even if something happened, we'd have plenty of time to regroup."

Autumn lit the starter log for the fire and called back to Simone. "I know, you're right. I just don't like changes to our plans. Although, these days, I'm getting more accustomed to things going wrong and causing trouble. Maybe I am leaning more into some of this water energy and going with the flow."

Tavish trotted over and spun in a circle beside the warming fire before easing into a spot on top of a navy-and-evergreen plaid blanket. Autumn smiled at the cat and headed to the front of the shop to flip the sign to open.

"I have noticed that, you know?" Simone smirked to herself. "The water got stronger in you, and you've loosened up a bit. Before, you would have stressed about any little detail going awry, but now that everything has been turned upside down lately . . ." Simone shook her head and looked up at her cousin. "You're just . . . handling change differently. And I'm proud of how you've taken all this. First Gran's death and becoming the four-points witch, and now all this new responsibility. It's hard responding to change, but you're doing it in your own way." Simone tilted her head toward her shoulder. "That's a good thing."

Autumn smiled at her and sighed. "I don't know, is it? It feels like I'm drowning in all this, just trying to keep my head above water. I know that's not the best analogy since someone almost actually drowned, but that is what it seems like these days."

Autumn adjusted the lanterns on display in the front window and came back to the counter with Simone. She pulled out a large binder from underneath the countertop and started flipping through the pages of invitations.

Simone gave her a nudge. "Hey, it's gonna take time to settle into this new way of life. Don't beat yourself up for things not being completely perfect right away. Just be thankful you've got me to keep you in check." Simone laughed as she looked over Autumn's shoulder at the invitation book. "Do you know what Mrs. Lachlan is gonna want?"

Autumn nodded as she flipped back and forth between two pages. "I think so. Although, I have this weird idea that the party they're throwing isn't actually wanted. Like maybe it's for appearances, and the person of honor isn't really interested. That's why I'm going back and forth between this elegant, formal invitation style and this darker, more modern one." Autumn shrugged and looked at Simone. "I'll just bring them both out, and I'll be able to read Mrs. Lachlan better when she gets here."

Simone raised her chin toward the door. "Speaking of . . ."

The front chime rang, and two figures scurried inside to escape the cold. The woman pulled her face out from underneath her wrap and revealed an older woman with a well taken care of appearance. Her natural makeup looked beautifully simple, and she delicately removed each of her layers with a simple elegance to her movements.

"Hello, Mrs. Lachlan. I'll take your coats." Autumn made her way up to the front and grabbed Mrs. Lachlan's belongings to place them on the wall hooks. Autumn turned toward the younger, lanky man accompanying her. He was dressed in a high-quality black coat and sweater with dark-blue jeans, and he ran his eyes around the shop as if unimpressed. Autumn put her hand out toward him with a curious smile. "I'm Autumn."

He looked at her with hesitancy to shake her hand, but then succumbed to the polite request. "Yes, I've heard."

"Autumn, this is my son, Cory. He's the one we'll be hosting the party for, so I thought I'd better bring him along." Mrs. Lachlan cleared her throat and gave her son a glare.

"My mother insisted we have a homecoming party, although I'm not sure how long exactly I'll be here." Autumn put her hand out to take his coat from him, but he lifted his palm to decline as he removed the coat himself.

"Well, we'll get everything sorted out for the party, so you and your mother won't have to worry about any of the details." Autumn led them back to the hearth room, and Simone brought out the big binders full of invitations. Mrs. Lachlan sat in one of the wingback chairs, and Autumn scooted a stool over beside her.

"Oh, this is wonderful. I thought we'd do an elegant cocktail party. Cocktails, wine, and cheese. A string quartet playing in the background. I want this party to show that my son is taking his rightful place with the family once again." As his mother spoke, Autumn noticed the clear disdain on her son's face.

Mrs. Lachlan ran her hand over the elegant invitation Autumn had picked out before they'd arrived. She smiled to herself and nodded before continuing to the next few pages. When she came to the page with the darker, more distinguished invitation, Cory put his hand over the invitation.

"That one. It has a commanding mystery to it that works well with this charade, don't you think?" Cory raised his eyebrows at his mother and then walked over to the fireplace. He eyed Tavish on the floor and put his forearm on the mantle. Tavish sat up abruptly and gave a slight hiss as he moved away from Cory.

"Oh no, we couldn't possibly go that dark. Could we?" Mrs. Lachlan looked over at Autumn with an expression that seemed to request assistance.

Autumn tilted her head and eyed the invitation. It was a deep charcoal color with white script font and modern, gothic flowers in an architectural arch pattern around the edge. "This one might work well for an evening cocktail party. It has a dominant but refined energy about it, and this style pairs nicely with the idea of a string quartet and hors d'oeuvres. Of course, it would be more dark luxury than elegance." Autumn waited for a moment, giving Mrs. Lachlan a chance to ponder the idea.

Cory sighed and came back to the table with the invitations. "Mother, just choose the dark one so we can be on our way."

Mrs. Lachlan straightened her back and lifted her chin. "You'll have to excuse my son. Sometimes he forgets his place."

Autumn pursed her lips together and leaned back on the stool to let them hash out the decision between them.

"Very well, we'll go with the dark invitations since Cory is the guest of honor. Autumn, I'll take your best black paper lanterns to hang from the ceiling, labels for the food tables, and small tags to go around each miniature bottle of wine that guests take home with them. There should be about fifty guests, and I'll have our house manager pick up the order from you, if that's all right."

Autumn nodded. "Absolutely, I'll get that order placed right away. Just follow me up to the counter, and we can wrap this up." Autumn stood up to head toward the counter while thinking of a way to bring up Mr. Lachlan and his dealings with Tom Leslie. She hadn't expected them to hurry through their selections so quickly, and she needed some time to get more information out of them.

Autumn opened the binder at the counter so Simone could input the order into the computer. "It'll just be a moment while we get the details." Autumn took a breath, and Mrs. Lachlan fumbled to find her wallet. "Mrs. Lachlan, how have things been at the marina? So much has happened. Has your husband been able to maintain business through all this?"

Mrs. Lachlan waved her hand through the air. "It's a complete mess, as you well know. The waters have been quite . . . trying as of late, and it's certainly testing Bryce's patience. And on top of the peculiar waters, we now have to contend with the incident at the skating area. It's been a stain on the marina. But that's just one more reason we need to have this party and show everyone our next generation will have no problem maintaining a thriving marina." She patted her son's arm and smiled proudly.

"Oh, so Cory will help with the marina now that he's home?" Autumn raised her eyes toward him with a smile, but he returned it only with a disgusted look.

His mother answered for him as he walked toward the front door. "Yes, that is the intention. We have to uphold the line, after all. You know the responsibility we hold." Mrs. Lachlan nodded gravely at both Autumn and Simone.

"Right." Simone nodded back to her from behind the computer. "Founding families."

Mrs. Lachlan pursed her lips as she handed Autumn the payment for the order. "That's right. It's our duty to maintain not only the marina but also our line here. And as we grow the marina, our line will thrive to support the mountain region."

"I see." Autumn nodded as she felt the locket on her skin heat up. "So, you intend to expand the marina? I thought

Mr. Lachlan mentioned something about a conservation easement. I didn't realize you could expand."

"Oh, that's just a minor hurdle. It shouldn't be an issue now." Mrs. Lachlan shook her head and looked back at her son. "Now that Cory has come back, he can help Bryce. We'll be able to develop the land and expand with a restaurant and hopefully an even larger recreation center. That's the beauty of having your children take over the family business. Long-term viability."

Autumn felt the heat intensifying on her chest, and she grabbed for her water bottle tucked underneath the counter. She took a sip to cool herself down as Simone went to the back office to retrieve the printed order receipt and bring it back to Mrs. Lachlan.

"Right, well, here's your invoice. Just keep this for your records."

"I'll have everything ready for when your house manager picks up the order. Just have her call before stopping by." Autumn smiled and came around the counter to walk Mrs. Lachlan out.

"Thank you both. It'll be a lovely affair thanks to your gorgeous designs. Really, the shop is such a staple in our town, and I'm so glad to have you here for these events." Mrs. Lachlan took Autumn's hand in hers. "Tell your aunt and your mother that we said hello."

"We will. Thank you, Mrs. Lachlan." Autumn looked over at Cory as he opened the door for his mother. "Welcome home, Cory."

Cory kept a stone face and responded, "Home is a relative term." He walked out the door with his mother and opened the door to the black BMW at the curb for her.

Autumn peered out the front window at the two of them, and Simone and Tavish joined her at the window. She heard the air stirring as she watched them, and the voices began whispering.

"Unmask the pain. Reveal the darkness below."

Autumn held the heavy front curtains back and waved at Cory as he got into the car and sped away. She sighed and gave her cousin a serious look. "There's something going on there."

Simone raised her eyebrows and walked back to one of the wooden hutches that stood on the side wall. "Yeah, tell me about it! That guy had a seriously dark aura. All deep maroon and almost a muddy black. I've never seen anything like it." She pulled a sage bundle from inside the hutch and went back to the hearth room to light it in the fireplace. "I'm gonna smudge this whole place and try to get rid of the energy they brought in here."

"Strange, I've never felt that energy around Mrs. Lachlan before. It was mostly her son. Although, my necklace glowed while they were here. She was talking about expanding the marina, and the conservation easement not being a problem. There's gotta be something to that because Tom Leslie was involved, too." Tavish walked around beside Autumn's feet as she moved through the shop toward the back near Simone. "Plus . . ."

Simone wafted the sage stick through the air and gave her cousin the eye. "Plus what? Something came to you?"

"The voices. Something about unmasking the pain to reveal darkness. I'm getting the feeling there's more to the Lachlans than they're leading people to believe."

"They're giving me the creeps, that's for sure. And that's pretty hard to do considering I'm pretty comfortable with things that go bump in the night. The moon is in my blood."

Autumn laughed and picked up Tavish to snuggle him in tight. "Yeah, that's saying something if they can freak you out, Ms. Dark and Mysterious. But the one thing that concerns me, though, is they're a founding family. A water-connected family. And that means Bryce Lachlan now had a motive to kill Tom Leslie. That would get rid of the easement and expand his business for his son to take over. He also has magical abilities, which puts him in a perfect place to contaminate the waters. Plus, he's privy to all the founders' information. He was at the dinner and the river demonstration when we removed some of the black magic. He knows what we know and what we can do."

"This is getting worse by the second. We better figure out how to handle another founding family in case it comes down to that."

"I agree, although I'm not completely convinced that's where we should place all our efforts. I still have a nagging idea that Emily Campbell may be involved somehow, and I know now she also has the capacity for magic. And that hasn't even ruled out Grant Ferguson, who had the land dispute with the Leslies. I still don't know whether he has any potential magical connections or if that's a dead end."

"Sounds like you better tie up that loose end first." Simone lifted her chin toward the wall they shared with the flower shop next door. "Besides, we haven't determined exactly who was with Karen Leslie this morning. You better head over there and do some sleuthing. Karen's probably expecting you to stop by again, anyway."

Autumn nodded in agreement. "Watch the shop for a few minutes while I pop over there?"

Simone slid onto the counter stool behind the computer again. "You know it."

Autumn laughed at her cousin as she grabbed her coat from the back and moved toward the front door. "We're close. I know we are."

Simone peeked out from behind the computer. "I can feel it, too. But I also feel like the waves are about to throw us overboard somehow, so just keep your guard up, okay?"

Autumn nodded and bundled up her coat around her neck. She pushed the shop door open. She couldn't help noting the crisp air had turned to a pastel shade of yellow, the color of knowledge. They were, in fact, getting closer to the truth, but the question remained, how much would that truth cost them and the town to find out?

CHAPTER 27

Autumn pushed the door open to the flower shop and shivered. Just being outside for a moment gave her chills from the frigid air. She unraveled her scarf slightly and walked through a few customers to the counter.

The dark-haired woman she had seen earlier behind the shop looked up from the counter and squinted at her. "Hello, can I help you?"

"Hi, yes. Quinn, right? I'm not sure if you remember me, but I'm Autumn. We went to the same school growing up, but now I run the shop next door, Parchment and Pine."

Autumn turned to see Karen making her way out from the storage room in the back. "Oh, Autumn, dear! I'm so glad you're here! Do you remember my daughter, Quinn?"

She nodded and smiled at Mrs. Leslie. "Yes, I mentioned we went to school together."

"MacKinnon, right? You were a couple years behind me in school." Quinn wrinkled her forehead as she thought about it.

"That's right. I remember you being on the student council and the debate team. How have you been?" Autumn moved to one side of the counter so Quinn could ring up another customer's order.

"I've been doing pretty well. I live in the city and am pretty close to making partner at my law firm. So things had been good until my dad passed." Quinn helped her mother bundle a bouquet for a customer and thanked them as they left. "Anyway, I'm here to help my mom with the funeral arrangements and sorting things out before I head back to the city."

"Yes, Quinn will be here for another week. I mentioned you helped me with a few things for the shop, but I know you have your own things to tend to. We're still working out what to do when it's just me again. It's been so busy here lately with all the extra publicity, even though it was regarding Tom's passing. I want to see it as a blessing from a terrible circumstance, but I don't know if I can handle all this myself." Mrs. Leslie wrung her hands together and gave them both a worried look.

"Actually, Karen, I meant to ask you about something else. I saw there's a dispute about your property lines. I don't mean to pry, but . . . well, if you take over more land, won't that just contribute to overwhelming you right now?"

Quinn laughed under her breath a bit. "Good old Hollow's Glenn. News always traveled fast here." Quinn wrapped her arm around her mother's shoulders and gave her a tight-lipped smile. "I've already gone over all that with my mother. That was my father's dispute that started over a year ago. He wanted to expand and create new flower plots, but there's no reason for my mother to continue pursuing that now. She's got enough money to support herself, and going through a property dispute just to have more of a burden isn't a step in the right direction."

"That's right. She's settling it all with Grant's lawyer so we can be done with that mess. I mean, I love Tom for trying to pursue more opportunities for us, but there's no reason to rock the boat with good neighbors. You know, he mentioned to me he saw you the other day out that way. Did you come out to see me, dear?"

"Oh, I needed to bring a batch of Gran's teas out to Mrs. Cunningham, and I thought I'd stop by. It was a quick stop, but he mentioned the dispute. So I wanted to check and make sure everything was okay."

Mrs. Leslie came around the counter to give Autumn a hug. "You're very sweet to check on me, but things are all right now that Quinn is here. And Grant and his wife actually came by with a basket of fruit and stayed to have tea now that this dispute is being settled. That was the first time I really spoke to them since this whole thing started, and I'm so relieved that we're putting it behind us."

"Oh, so Mr. Ferguson was cordial about it all?" Autumn casually tried to prod for more information.

"He was, right, Mom? It surprised me because I remember him as somewhat gruff. But I could see he and his wife really wanted to come give their condolences to my mother and put all that aside. There was even a sadness about the fact that they hadn't spoken to my father in over a year, and now he's gone. I could tell they missed him. Mr. Ferguson even mentioned how much he missed spending time with Dad at their Thursday night whiskey tastings. I guess my dad stopped going a couple months back."

Mrs. Leslie's eyes welled up with tears as her daughter spoke. She pulled a tissue from the box at the register and dabbed her eyes. "I'm just grateful they're coming back around now because they were good friends throughout the years. I wish my Tom were still here with us all."

"Mom, it's gonna be okay. We'll figure out how to get you some help for the shop if you really want to stay here, and I'll do my best to come visit more frequently."

"Autumn has been a wonderful help since she and her cousin, Simone, opened the shop next door. I hate to lean on you girls for much, but I'm so appreciative." Mrs. Leslie heard the bell ring at the front and waved to the customers. "I have to keep up with the customers, but you two finish your conversation. Autumn, thanks for stopping by." Mrs. Leslie gave Autumn another hug and made her way to the new customers.

"Seriously, thank you for helping my mom before I got here. I could tell she was really distraught and in need of support."

"Oh, of course. Like she said, Simone and I run the shop right next door if she needs anything. I am curious, though, what she intends to do about this shop. I'm worried about rumors regarding developers interested in buying the properties along Main Street. Do you think it's a possibility she might sell?"

"Honestly, no, I don't. Don't get me wrong, I would love it if she sold the shop, because then she could move closer to me. I could take care of her better in the city. My mom won't even think of it, though. She loves this town and everyone in it, and I'd have to pry her away kicking and screaming, especially now that there are customers in the low season." Quinn typed a few things into a spreadsheet on the computer and then turned back toward Autumn. "But I'll get her some help here before I leave and make sure she's not doing everything herself."

Autumn couldn't help but wonder if perhaps the abundance spell she'd done the other day triggered all this foot traffic. Even though some black energy still lingered around the waters, something positive existed here on Main Street. Something that could shift the energy in the town's favor and reset the balance in the region.

She looked at Quinn with a sense of hope and replied to her plan. "That makes sense. Your mom is lucky to have you looking out for her."

Autumn watched as another batch of people scrambled into the shop from the cold. "Well, I won't keep you. Looks like you're going to be pretty busy with orders for holiday parties and events. Please, just let your mom know that we'll help with anything else she needs."

"I will, thank you." Quinn smiled at Autumn and walked over to help a few new customers pick out their flower orders as Autumn left.

She was glad she'd made it over to see Karen and learn about the property dispute being settled. If the Fergusons had been longtime friends of the Leslies, then maybe Grant Ferguson didn't deserve to be on the suspect list after all. It seemed highly unlikely the dispute could push him that far to kill a friend he missed spending time with. Plus, the whiskey-tasting group Quinn had mentioned sounded like a reasonable alibi for Mr. Ferguson. Autumn would bet he was there the night Tom Leslie died, and that took him off the table entirely.

Autumn remembered the mayor also had an affinity for whiskey. She owed the mayor a visit once he got out of the hospital, anyway. So he seemed like the next right step in putting the pieces together, whether to confirm Grant's alibi or to tie them all further together.

Simone dried a few last dishes and waited for Autumn to settle onto a kitchen stool with her after dinner tea. The last few nights during Simone's evening runs on the river trail, Simone experienced something new. She wanted to talk it over with Autumn, but there had been so much going on that there hadn't been time until now.

"Hey, Autumn, I know it's been a long day, but there's something that's been happening on my runs. I don't know what it's all about, but my gifts may be manifesting differently."

Simone wound the dish towel she used through the handle of the oven and sat down on another kitchen stool. She brought her legs underneath her and twisted her mouth to the side, hesitant of what to say.

"Okay, tell me what it is." Autumn put her tea mug down and gave her attention to her cousin.

"Well, there's this high-pitched singing that I've started hearing when I'm near the water. Almost like something's calling me and trying to communicate. It's peaceful singing, like a woman's voice, but it's only for a moment. Then, it stops. Has that ever happened to you with the voices you hear?" Simone bit her lip and stared at Autumn curiously.

"No, I don't think so. It's always voices for me, and they speak in messages through the air. It's never music. When did this start?" Autumn pulled her sweater sleeves down over her hands to warm them as she listened.

"A few days ago on my runs. I kind of dismissed it at first and figured it was music in town somewhere, but it kept happening. And then, it also happened here at home last night and tonight. I heard the music, and I felt this pull toward Gran's wardrobe." Simone motioned to the wardrobe that stood behind the front entryway. All the family's magical heirlooms lived in that cabinet and only revealed themselves with a worthy intention.

"Gran's wardrobe? Was the music coming from inside it?" Autumn stood up and walked over to it in the living room, and Simone followed.

"I don't think so. I heard the singing all around me, calling from somewhere in the distance. But the wardrobe . . . I don't know. It's like I have this intuitive feeling there's something inside that I'm meant to retrieve."

The girls stood in front of the tall, wooden wardrobe as Tavish sauntered up next to them, stretching his legs. He purred as he rubbed his head along the edge of the wardrobe, and the girls noticed a slight emerald-green light slowly erupting from the slit between the two doors. They looked at one another with surprise, and Autumn put a hand on the doors. It felt warm to the touch, and her necklace glowed on her chest to match the light of the wardrobe.

"Okay, then. Looks like we're meant to get whatever's waiting inside." Autumn walked over to the coffee table and pulled open the drawer to grab a lighter. She lit the white pillar candle that sat on the table and reached her hand out for Simone to hold. Tavish jumped up onto the coffee table between them.

"What's our intention? To retrieve what we're meant to find?" Simone questioned.

"Sounds good to me. The wardrobe already wants to show us something, so let's try it out." Autumn closed her eyes, and Simone did the same.

She cleared her throat and focused on the intention of unlocking the wardrobe. "Ancestors and four corners, we call on you to bring forth what lies within the wardrobe. Allow us to retrieve what we're meant to wield. Unlock the wardrobe, reveal the heirloom."

Simone joined in as they repeated the phrase together. "Unlock the wardrobe, reveal the heirloom. Unlock the wardrobe, reveal the heirloom."

Autumn sensed the locket around her neck holding the key. She dropped Simone's hands and pulled the necklace open to reveal the tiny antique key inside. She held it up for Simone to see just as Tavish gave a big yawn and jumped down from the coffee table, as if his work there was done.

The girls walked over to the wardrobe, and Autumn slid the key inside the lock. She twisted the knob to open the doors as more emerald light poured out in front of them. The wooden heirloom box sat at the bottom of the wardrobe as it had done before when they'd needed it.

"Go ahead." Autumn raised her chin toward the box. "You're the one meant for whatever's inside tonight."

Simone swallowed hard and knelt to pick up the box. She brought it out to the coffee table and placed it beside the white pillar candle. The edges of the box glowed in her hands as she sat it down. The lid creaked slightly as she lifted it back onto its hinges. Inside lay an assortment of heirlooms, including the MacKinnon Book of Spells that they had just used to clear the waters. All the pieces sat on top of the MacKinnon plaid flannel and kept their places without being jostled at all.

To one side, a small orange-coral-colored box beamed with the emerald light. Simone lifted the box out and removed the top to reveal a dried starfish inside.

"A starfish? That's strange." Simone held the starfish between her fingers and moved it back and forth to look at both sides. "We don't have salt water in the mountain region."

Autumn pulled the lid out of Simone's other hand and looked inside it. "There's a note here. Carried by our ancestors from the North Sea."

"A piece of the old land, sea, and sky brought to the new. Huh . . . I wonder if this is the thing calling to me." Simone gave Autumn a questioning look.

"It could be some kind of ancestral message being carried through the water energy in the starfish. I mean, energy never goes away, right? It only transforms. So maybe this serves as a communication link to the water."

"My mom may know more, but for now I guess I'm supposed to keep it with me or something." Simone shrugged, unsure of what to do next.

"Yeah, just keep the box with you and see if the singing continues. You're obviously meant to have it for a reason, so trust your intuition and stay prepared. That's all we can do for now." Autumn handed the box lid back to Simone to put the starfish away as she cleaned up the larger wooden box and locked the wardrobe.

Autumn reached for Simone's hands again and closed her eyes. "Ancestors and energies of the four directions, thank you for supporting us in maintaining the balance. We shall honor the land, sea, and sky by respecting this heirloom and using it for the region's highest good. And so it is."

As she said the closing words, Autumn felt a strange slipperiness to Simone's hands in hers. The girls both opened their eyes at the same time. Glancing down at their hands, they blinked and stepped back in amazement. Simone lifted her arms in the air to display shimmering silver scales lightly running across the length of her skin. An instant after the girls watched the scales reflect from Simone's body, the white candle flickered out, and the shimmering scales vanished.

CHAPTER 28

Customers packed into the Pine the next day, gathering their paper lanterns for the winter solstice festival. The lanterns would soar through the trees up to the stars until they completely dotted the dark with light. They represented the sun gradually taking over the dark days to start a new cycle of life again.

The girls' shop supplied most of the festival lanterns, which meant an incredibly busy upcoming week before the event. Customers hustled into the shop all day long to select their lanterns before they were gone. Autumn busied herself with boxing up several orders and ringing up customers at the counter with Tavish underfoot. Simone walked others around the shop, explaining the differences between each lantern type so they could make their choices.

Autumn pressed four paper lanterns down flat into a kraft paper box and laid four tea candles beside them on a bed of shredded paper. She placed the lid on the box and wrapped it with a silk evergreen-colored ribbon. Turning around to hand it to the customers, she looked up to see Simone wandering back to the register.

"Thank you so much! Enjoy the festival!" Autumn smiled at the last of the customers as they walked out.

Simone flopped onto the stool behind the computer and sighed. "I love all the business, but man, we've never been this busy!"

"I know. I talked to Karen about this the other day. She thought all the business was because of the article in the paper about her husband's death. Karen assumed people came in to be nosy and then ended up placing orders, but I'm wondering if it's that abundance spell I did the other day."

Simone straightened up from her seat and raised her eyebrows. "Oh, yeah! I completely forgot about that! It has to be that, Autumn. Main Street hasn't been this busy in a very long time, but now the winds have changed. See, I always knew I should keep you around."

Autumn laughed and shook her head. "You don't have a choice but to keep me around."

"Hey, there's always a choice. It's just that sometimes the universe nudges us closer to the most aligned choice for us. So I guess it's in my best interest to be around you so much." Simone smiled as the bell at the front door rang with someone new entering the shop.

"Oh! Mr. Mayor!" Autumn hurried around the counter toward the front of the shop as the mayor walked in on crutches with Chief Walsh and Ben close behind him.

Simone hopped off her stool and flattened her hair with her palm. She headed to the front and locked eyes with Ben as he came inside. Simone gave him a small wave and stood beside Autumn.

"Hello, Chief, Ben." Autumn nodded at the men. "Mr. Mayor, I didn't expect you to be out of the hospital so soon! How are you?" She raised her arm to signal that they all follow her into the hearth room to sit.

"Well, I'm all right now that I've had some fine people fix me up a bit." The mayor sighed as he sank into one of the wingback chairs next to the fire. "It seems my troubles may be more connected to everything else that's been happening, though, and that's what's got us all worried."

The bell at the front rang again, and Autumn and Simone turned to see their mothers walking in. Simone motioned her thumb toward the door and headed over to greet Jo and Penny.

Chief Walsh rested his hands on his belt and gave Autumn a serious look. "We asked your mothers to join us here to discuss a few things."

Autumn nodded and noticed her aunt, Jo, flipping the front door sign from open to closed before heading back to the hearth room. They all congregated inside the little archway space and waited for someone to explain.

"From what we suspect, none of the recent occurrences happened accidentally." The mayor leaned forward toward the table and clasped his hands together on top of it.

Autumn squinted and crossed her arms over her chest. "I thought your car ran off the icy road the other night."

Mayor Halpin nodded in agreement. "It did . . . However, that road was only a bit wet when I got into the car and pulled away. The snow came down some, but the temperatures hadn't dropped yet. Somehow, the road iced over in a matter of seconds and buckets of snow dropped on me all at once. Now, the rest of the region got the snowstorm as well, but that small section of town I was in was the unusual part."

Chief Walsh continued explaining the situation. "That's right. Weather sources tell us the storm in that area right around the marina produced a significantly higher amount of precipitation. And it happened over the course of just ten minutes or less. Now, if that isn't an anomaly, then I don't know what is."

"And with this on top of Dillon Ross's ice incident and the strange shimmers in the river, well . . . we're inclined to believe someone with elemental abilities is targeting people in town."

"Oh my word! How on earth has this happened? We should have been protected against something like this, but everything is out of balance!" Aunt Jo covered her mouth with her hand and gave Chief Walsh a worried look.

"Let's just take things one step at a time, Jo, and walk through the possibilities." The chief put his hands out in front of him to get her to calm down.

"There's definitely a connection between all of this. I know there is," Autumn chimed in. "Plus, magic keeps coming up in the background of each incident. Mayor, you and Dillon are both founding members with magical abilities yourselves. Tom Leslie didn't have any gifts, but that doesn't mean he wasn't involved with people who had gifts of their own."

"Exactly, that's why the chief and I are going to err on the cautious side and suggest that there's a possibility of the founding families being in danger. We don't know how this is all connected, but we know black magic is involved somehow." The mayor tightened his lips.

Ben stepped forward to agree. "Autumn, you alluded to it yourself the night Mr. Ross fell into the ice. When I took your statement, you noted someone hiding in the shadows of the trees, looking on at your rescue attempt as if they were being thwarted. That may have been the someone who's been altering the elements to do their dirty work for them."

"We have to be vigilant about keeping watch over one another right now, especially the founding families. So, we need to notify everyone to stay together and pay attention." The chief looked around the room to get everyone's agreement.

"What if . . ." Autumn hesitated and moved her eyes from Aunt Jo over to the mayor and then the chief. She swallowed hard before continuing. "What about the possibility that a founding member is behind these attacks?" Autumn knew the idea would meet some dismissal, but she had to put it out there.

"A founding member doing all of this? Good grief, we'd be in for a storm of enormous proportions." Aunt Jo fiddled with the rings on her fingers and wrapped her sweater more tightly around her body.

"You suspect someone, don't you?" Mayor Halpin eyed Autumn curiously. "I'm inclined to believe we can trust every person in this room. Autumn, I know you have a strong wisdom about these things just like your grandmother did, so I'll let you decide what you'd like to share. But if we're going to figure this out and support you as the new four-points witch, then you've gotta trust us as well."

Autumn turned toward her mother, Penny, and stood for a moment in silence. She felt a strong wind sweep down the fireplace chimney and into the room, giving off the powdery yet earthy scent of iris flowers. Autumn's eyes brightened as she recognized the scent from a spring day in her gran's garden.

"Iris," she whispered under her breath.

Penny smiled as she heard her daughter whisper the word. Nodding with relief, Penny realized what Autumn sensed in the air. "Mmm . . . one of Gran's favorites. Hope can pull even the most downtrodden out of the shadows."

Autumn returned her mother's smile with recognition of the phrase her gran had used when tending to the irises. She took a deep breath and addressed everyone in the room. "I trust you all, and I have hope that together we will solve this. But I suspect Mr. Lachlan in all of this. Maybe not entirely, as I also have suspicions around the lumber mill owner, Ms. Campbell, and the Leslies' neighbor, Grant Ferguson. But Mr. Lachlan concerns me the most."

The mayor sighed and rubbed his palm over his eyes. "The Lachlans . . . they're a proud family, and a founding family. I've known Bryce Lachlan for many years. We grew up together, in fact. I know he has an edge, and he can be quite ambitious. But I can't see him going as far as killing someone."

"He is a water element, Stephen." Jo looked directly at Mayor Halpin with concern in her voice. "As I well know, water has the potential for deep shadows under the surface. We cannot fully understand the depths of a water element's spirit. You can only try to work with it in harmony. But if you underestimate it, there could be great consequences."

"Emily Campbell, the lumber mill owner, is also a water-line descendent. I found out at the library that she's tied to the Ross bloodline. There could be something there as well." Autumn paced slightly between everyone in the hearth room as she spoke.

"We've been looking into Ms. Campbell already. Those water samples led us to the mill. Right, Ben?" The chief glanced over his shoulder at his son to confirm.

"That's right. Our information currently points to Ms. Campbell as the likely suspect, but I don't wanna make assumptions until we have something firm. And as for the neighbor Mr. Ferguson, whom Autumn brought up, he was also on our watch list until recently, at least for the Leslie case, anyway. Turns out he has an alibi for that night. Mr. Mayor, you confirmed it as well." Ben nodded at him to suggest he interject.

"Yes, Grant goes to our weekly Scottish whisky tastings over at the Ridgeline Inn. It's something I used to frequent regularly, but I just started going again about a month ago. Grant is a regular, and Tom was, too, until recently. I'm not sure why he stopped going."

"So Grant attended the whiskey club the night Tom was killed. I heard about it from Karen's daughter, and she also mentioned her father had stopped going. My suspicion is that he reserved those Thursday nights for wildflower foraging at the river. That's when he met his contact from the lumber mill and received a payoff for keeping quiet about the water runoff." Autumn spoke as though she was thinking out loud, but she directed her thoughts to Chief Walsh.

"A regular meetup for bribes? If that's the case, then maybe whoever kept Tom quiet didn't want to do it anymore. Making regular payments gets old after a while. Ben, follow up on that and have Ms. Campbell come in for another round of questioning." The chief nodded to his son as he started toward the archway of the room. "Looks like the water energy is our best clue to go on right now. Jo, if you and Autumn wouldn't mind notifying the founders to be on their guard, I sure would appreciate it." He smiled at Jo and placed his hand on her forearm for a moment before moving out of the room with Ben.

"What about Bryce Lachlan? Should we tell him we're being cautious?" The mayor rose to his feet and placed his crutches under his arms to walk out with the officers.

"Why don't we give him a variation of the story for now? Tell him we're concerned for the safety of those in business or leadership positions around town, and we want to make sure everyone keeps together. Nothing about the founding families or their magic. Just keep it more general, alright?" The chief waited for Mayor Halpin as he hobbled along on his crutches toward the front door.

"Yes, we'll do that. Jo, Autumn, you've got that, right?" The mayor looked back at them to confirm.

"Yes, Mr. Mayor. I can notify people at the preservation meeting tonight. You'll be there, won't you?" Autumn headed to the front to open the door for everyone.

"Of course, I wouldn't miss it. We've all got to get those paper lanterns from you this evening and prepare for the festival. I want the event to go off without a hitch! So it's important everyone be on their toes and watchful of anything out of the ordinary." The mayor walked out the door onto the sidewalk with Chief Walsh and Ben.

"I'll see you over there. Chief, thanks for stopping by." Autumn smiled and held the door open, and Simone slipped out onto the sidewalk beside Ben.

"Hey, I know the festival is a week away still, but I was wondering if you might wanna hang out with me to light the lanterns." Simone crossed her arms around her chest to keep warm as she waited for his answer.

Ben took a step closer to her and smiled. "Yeah, I think I can manage that. Where should I meet you?"

"By my grandmother's bench at the downtown fountain. I'll bring the lanterns. You bring a lighter and a blanket." Simone smiled at him before turning to head back inside the shop.

The three men waved and made their way down Main Street as Autumn closed the shop door. She moved toward the front window alongside Penny and Jo.

"What do you both make of all this?" Autumn picked up Tavish, who had appeared at her feet.

Penny sighed and looked between them. "Black magic isn't something you can just experiment with once or twice. Once it has you, it won't let go. And something like that carries grave consequences."

"Your mother's right. Someone's playing with very dangerous magic. If it's a founding family, which I'm fearful it may be, then our founding council will have no choice but to take drastic measures. I've never seen it done in our lifetime, but we may need to consider the implications. And Autumn, as the four-points witch, you would have to enact the final decision." Jo pursed her lips and patted her sister on the back as she walked toward Simone at the back counter.

Autumn knew her responsibilities as the four-points witch kept growing, but she didn't realize how much she'd have to preside over concerning the founding families. She still felt like the little girl who talked to the wind and lived a simple life playing in the woods. Somehow she'd ended up the one everyone turned to when a storm brewed. And now, she wasn't sure she liked the burdens that came along with it.

Simone eyed her cousin as her aura changed to a worried shade of light yellow. "It'll all work out, cuz. Don't stress. Just go to the preservation meeting and come back for some tea."

"Yes, go, sweetheart!" Penny chimed in. "No sense in us continuing with this dark vibe. In fact, I should probably test out a new tea blend for that. Something to hedge against negativity. I'm thinking . . . juniper berry!" Penny raised a finger and walked toward the back of the shop. "We'll be fine here until you return. I'll put the teakettle on, and we'll help Simone close up the shop."

Autumn smiled reluctantly and grabbed her coat and backpack from the back room. She bagged up a few ribboned boxes of paper lanterns and headed toward the front door. "Okay, I'm off. Keep the tea warm until I get back."

She walked out the front door with bags in hand and headed down Main Street for the Forest Brew. The wind whistled around her, and Autumn let it carry her worries away for the time being. She took a deep breath and blew it out with a sigh, watching as her exhale turned into tiny ice crystals that dropped to the ground right in front of her. Perhaps this would be how she could maintain her own balance while the world pulled in so many directions around her. One breath at a time.

CHAPTER 29

At the end of the preservation meeting, Autumn handed out the kraft paper boxes of paper lanterns as everyone got up from the table. She raised her eyes, lifting another box out of her bag, and caught eyes with Marion Bennett in front of her.

"Autumn." Marion continued putting on her leather gloves as she spoke. "I just wanted to note that you're doing a good job here for the preservation committee. I was hesitant that you may not be open to new ideas for the town, but I can see your interest in breathing new life into the town's charming character. And this lantern festival shows me you have a smart business sense on top of it. I'm just sorry I didn't recognize it sooner."

Marion had butted heads with Gran in the past, and Autumn had had a rocky start with her when taking over the MacKinnon position on the preservation committee. Now, though, Autumn realized Marion was warming to her and she to Marion, and the woman exhibited a loyal personality. Although stubborn in her vision, once you were on her good side, she advocated for you as well as her own ideas.

Autumn smiled back at her and lifted one of the kraft paper boxes. "Thank you, Marion. I appreciate that very much. This lantern festival adds to our town's sense of community, and I knew we had to bump it up a notch this year. We need more people actively engaging in town events and getting into our shops and restaurants." Autumn moved the lantern box closer to Marion for her to take it.

"Precisely." Marion grabbed the box from her with curiosity. "Our businesses need this boost now more than ever, and I'm happy to see everyone on board with it." She placed one hand on top of the box and tapped it gently. "I didn't order any lanterns."

Autumn tilted her head to one side. "No, but I figured bringing an extra box would be a good idea. This one's for you."

A tiny smile crept across Marion's face. "I assume I'll see you at the festival, then, and I will tell everyone where the best lanterns in town came from."

Autumn nodded at Marion and walked her to the door of the meeting room just as someone put their hand on Autumn's shoulder. She turned around to see Dillon Ross and James standing beside him.

"Oh, Dillon, it was so good to see you here tonight. How are you feeling?" Autumn stepped to the side so others could make their way out the door.

"I'm all right, considering. The only reason I'm here at all is because of you and James. I don't know how I'll ever repay you both." He wrapped his arms around Autumn and James in appreciation.

"Nonsense, Uncle Dillon. You don't owe us anything except maybe dinner one night with you and Aunt Abigail." James smiled at his uncle and then back at Autumn.

"Yeah, we're so glad that you're okay. You definitely gave us a scare." Autumn saw the hesitation in Dillon's face as he looked back on what had happened.

He sighed and shook his head. "It's all over and done with now. Although, I do still feel a strange cloud hovering over me, almost like a haziness. My health is slowly on the mend, though. I just need to work on my motor skills with the therapist for a while, but I've been quite lucky. Really, as long as I can see Abigail's face every day, then all is well. I don't know if I'll ever go near the water again, though, which saddens me." He raised his head as a thought came to his mind. "That reminds me, James. The tests your father's company ran on the water samples. There were some anomalies in the water. Have you addressed them with the others, especially Josephine MacKinnon?"

Autumn and James both nodded. "My aunt Jo and Chief Walsh both know about the findings, Dillon. James talked to me about the sulfur in the water, too, and we're figuring it out."

He nodded in relief. "Good, good. It's been in my dreams as of late. Usually, James, it's your mother who I'd talk with about these things, or Josephine, but you two seem to be in the thick of this. And something tells me it's someone else who must cleanse the waters. Someone just coming to know and more deeply understand what they're capable of."

"Your dream didn't show you who that might be, Uncle Dillon?" James lowered his voice a bit so the last few people in the meeting room wouldn't hear.

Dillon shook his head. "I'm sorry, but I don't know for sure. I only feel someone else connected to the water in a positive way. It's someone familiar, though, and I'm hopeful when I have the dream."

"Well, that's the first bit of good news we've heard in a while." James raised his eyebrows and turned toward Autumn.

"Yeah, we could all use that sense of hope right now. Thanks for sharing that with us, and please don't be shy if anything else comes up." Autumn gave Dillon a warm hug as he headed for the door.

She gathered her things as James stood by her side, appreciating her. She looked up at him as he met her eyes with his. "What is it?" She laughed at him.

James shrugged. "Nothing. I was just . . . admiring how you have a way with people."

"What do you mean?" She walked out of the meeting room and toward the pastry counter as the Newburys cleaned up the Forest Brew for the evening.

"I mean, you're incredibly perceptive, and you have a way of making people feel at ease in your presence. Even the stiffest people open up to your compassion and understanding. It's captivating just watching you interact with someone. Not to mention, you've got me under some kind of spell because I can't stop thinking about you." James grabbed Autumn's hand and brought it to his lips.

She blushed slightly and moved closer to give him a proper kiss. "I'm glad you walked into my shop that day. Even if it wasn't the best of circumstances, it brought you into my life."

He put her hand on his chest and nodded in agreement. "Me, too."

Autumn peered over James's shoulder to see Eve eyeing the two of them with a smirk. "Uh, James, I need to speak with the Newburys. How about I meet you for lunch one day this week?"

"Sounds good. I'll even let you choose where we go." He leaned over and gently kissed her lips one more time. "Be careful getting home tonight."

She smiled and waved as he headed toward the door and she toward the counter where Eve stood. Eve cleared her throat as she wiped the counter down with a rag.

"He must be that cute contractor I keep seeing around town. Isn't he the one with water energy in him?" Eve popped her eyes up to Autumn as if she didn't mean to overstep at all. "I don't mean to pry, so you don't have to tell me if you don't want to."

Autumn laughed at Eve's youthful quirkiness. "It's okay, Eve. James works for his dad's construction company. They're doing the restoration work downtown, and yes, he's part of the water bloodline. The Ross family."

"Oooh, okay. So I was right." Eve put down the rag and saw that Autumn wanted to ask something of her. "You look like you need something. What is it?"

"Actually, I was thinking about the sweetener jars we made the other day. How did they work in the coffee shop?"

Eve pressed down her forearms on the counter and leaned over. "They were amazing! The regular customers who'd been quite grumpy lately seemed to sweeten right up. I couldn't believe how well the jars did the trick, so I put a few more out over the last couple days. It feels like the energy completely shifted in here at lunchtime."

"Wow, that's amazing! I was kind of hoping you might make a jar or two for us at the Pine. Someone came in the other day for a party order, and they had a really negative vibe. I don't want that to continue in the shop, and I remembered we made those jars to make people sweeter. Can you make more?"

"Of course! But I actually got so excited about them I already made a few new ones just to have around. They should work for the Pine. Let me grab one out of the back for you."

Eve put her pointer finger up to signal Autumn to wait a moment just as Mrs. Newbury came over.

"Autumn, how is everything going? Graham said the meeting tonight was uneventful, but I'm more concerned with what's happening down at the water." Mrs. Newbury came around to the outside of the counter and took a stool beside Autumn. The customers had all left for the night, and Autumn was the only one to remain now.

"That's what I wanted to talk about with you and Mr. Newbury." Autumn moved her gaze between Catherine Newbury and Eve just coming out of the back to hand her a sweetener jar for the Pine.

"I'm sure you heard about the mayor's car accident?" Autumn waited for them both to confirm. Autumn exhaled deeply before continuing. "Well, we believe it wasn't an accident. There may be someone targeting prominent people in town. In fact, it may even be the founding families in particular."

Mrs. Newbury gasped, leaning back on her stool and putting one hand over her mouth. She stiffened herself upright again and waved her husband over. "Graham! Come over here and listen to what Autumn has to say."

Mr. Newbury gathered up several empty glasses from the meeting room table and made his way up to the counter. "What's going on?" He looked at the three of them questioningly.

"I was just telling them I spoke to the mayor and Chief Walsh. We think someone is targeting the founding families. It's important we keep together and watch our surroundings so there isn't another mishap."

Eve helped her father place the glasses down behind the counter as they all considered the implications of what Autumn had said.

"So Tom Leslie's death is connected to these recent accidents? Dillon's as well as the mayor's?" Graham looked at Autumn as she confirmed.

"We think so, yes. And it's most likely all tied to the black magic in the river. We haven't pinpointed how, though." Autumn glanced at Eve with a grave look. "We're going to need to draw from all four energies if we're to fight this and stay safe."

Eve stood a little straighter and gave Autumn a confident head nod. "We will. One way or another, we'll restore the balance."

Autumn drew in a breath and turned toward Mr. and Mrs. Newbury. "There's one other thing." She hesitated, knowing that the Newburys were close to the other founding families. "We suspect who's behind this, but it may end up being someone closer than we'd all like."

Mr. and Mrs. Newbury gave each other a surprised expression.

"In what way do you mean?" Mrs. Newbury rested her elbows on the counter and covered her mouth again as she waited for an answer.

"I can't discuss anything for certain, but please don't disclose what I've told you to anyone outside of your family and mine. You know the MacKinnon family stands by the mountain region no matter what, but I'm afraid the allegiance of some others may be flawed. Of course, it's still in question, but for your safety, please keep this to yourselves."

Mrs. Newbury leaned over and wrapped her arm around Autumn. "How did all of this happen? I worry about you girls. I don't like you being caught up in this mess, so you both promise us you'll stay safe as well."

Eve and Autumn nodded at each other. "We will, Mom. Don't worry. Our coven is getting stronger by the day, and our gifts are all advancing."

Mr. Newbury sighed. "You've both grown so quickly. It's hard to believe you're now the ones protecting these lands. I'm proud of you both, and I know you're powerful. But I'm still a concerned father. So, I'm going to drive everyone home tonight to ensure we all get there safely."

"Oh, Mr. Newbury, you don't have to do that. My family waited for me at the shop, so I'll be fine." Autumn waved her hand in the air to dismiss the idea.

"Nonsense. If you need to head back to the shop, then we'll drop you off. Better to stick together, like you said a moment ago. I just need to close the kitchen and lock the doors." Mr. Newbury grabbed the empty glasses off the counter and headed back to the kitchen.

"I'll feel so much better once this is all behind us! What a mess this has all been!" Mrs. Newbury grabbed her daughter's hand over the counter.

"It's okay, Mom. We just need to stay grounded and focus on what's right in front of us." Eve smiled at her mother.

Autumn stared at Eve for a moment, getting a download in her mind. "Speaking of which, Eve, are you available to come for breakfast tomorrow morning at my house?"

"Sure. Did you want to do some magic practice?" Eve squinted her eyes and considered Autumn's request.

"No, but something tells me your earth energy will come in handy. How's nine thirty sound?" Autumn got up from her stool as Mr. Newbury came out of the back with their coats.

"Sounds good. I'll be there, ready for anything." Eve smiled and gave Autumn a cheesy salute.

They all headed out the back to the Newburys' minivan, and Autumn couldn't help but notice the eerie quiet that lingered in the air that night. Something told her the stillness here meant trouble stirring elsewhere that same night.

CHAPTER 30

Autumn pushed her head through her favorite oatmeal-colored cowl-neck sweater and threw on the evergreen cape her gran had given her on top. Tavish meowed at her intensely from below.

"Tav, I'm only going to be a few minutes, and then I'll be back. I just need to ground myself in the woods and speak to the elements. It's too cold out there in the snow for your little paws, so stay here with Sim, okay?" Autumn bent down to scratch underneath his chin, but he continued meowing in discontent.

Simone walked out from her bedroom, stretching her arms up in the air with a big yawn. "Sounds like someone doesn't wanna listen. That cat'll do what he wants; you know that."

Autumn sighed and shook her head. "Okay, you can come, I suppose. Just don't blame me if your paws are freezing."

Autumn waved at her cousin as she opened the front door. "Be back in a few minutes."

Tavish trotted down the front steps in front of Autumn as she pulled the hood of her cape up over her head. The air felt crisp and chilly this morning, but she loved knowing that meant the season had changed. No matter how warm or cool, the air always gave Autumn comfort, but it was actually the forest where she felt most like herself. There she found the sanctuary she'd had all the years growing up there. Besides the house she'd inherited from Gran, the forest beside it was her home.

She trod gently in her flannel-lined duck boots as she moved through the snow. With each step toward the trees, she breathed deeply and let it out slowly. As she got closer to the tree line and entered onto the dirt path, the air gradually became denser around her, something unusual for these woods. Tavish stopped in the middle of the path to sit and look from side to side. His ears perked up as he listened to the sounds through the trees.

"I sense it, too, Tav. What is it?" Autumn stopped beside him to listen.

The wind swept up around them and howled as it swung through the trees. The voices stirred on the air and spoke strongly.

"Be vigilant. See through the trees."

A chill ran down Autumn's spine as she heard the piercing sound of a bird overhead. She raised her head to see a gliding falcon circling and landing on the topmost point of an aspen tree. He sat there, bending his gaze down toward Autumn and Tavish. The cat meowed at it intently, as if finding an old friend. Tavish circled at Autumn's feet and then sat in front of her as the falcon lifted its wings and flew away.

Autumn lifted her eyebrows in surprise at the two animals. "Friend of yours?" Autumn let out a little laugh as she walked around Tavish. "Honestly, cat, you always surprise me."

Tavish trotted to keep up with her along the path until they got to the clearing in the trees. Autumn turned in a circle, darting her eyes through the trees for anything unusual.

"We'll stick together today, okay?" Autumn looked at Tavish hesitantly as he rubbed up against her leg.

Autumn looked down at the ground and drew a circle with her foot through the snow. She whistled out a breath as she took each step and came back to the beginning. Lifting her arms at her sides, she whispered under her breath.

"Ancestors and spirits of the land, sea, and sky, give me clarity and awareness to see what is currently unseen. Ground my energy so I may calmly walk the path of the elements and restore balance to these lands once more."

The tall trees shook in the wind, and Autumn sensed an unfamiliar energy. She squinted through the trees but saw nothing except the swaying branches and plopping of heaped snow from the boughs.

She stepped up to the circle she'd drawn and put out her foot to extend a straight line outward from the circle. Autumn moved through the makeshift door and toward the tree line. Standing in front of a large, towering pine tree intermixed among the aspens, Autumn placed her hands on the branches of the tree.

Snow fell from the branches onto her boots and sent a reverberation up Autumn's legs. Her earth energy had gained strength lately, and she now felt more of a connection with the trees than before. As her hands grasped the branches and felt the spiky pine needles in her fingers, she sensed a manipulated energy surrounding it. It felt tainted, and her stomach tightened as she moved her eyes around her to find the source.

Tavish meowed loudly and ran toward her just as Autumn heard a cracking sound from above. She looked up to see a mound of falling snow snapping the branches over top of her. Covering her face she ducked as a few branches collapsed. The snow seemed to mound on top of the tree in an instant and continue weighing it down heavily. The entire tree swayed, and with a wisp darting through the air beside her, she heard something strike at the tree's core.

The sound of bark splitting near her made Autumn push herself across the snowy ground as fast as she could on her hands and knees. The pine that just a moment ago towered in the forest now fell at an alarming pace toward the ground with Autumn underneath it. She braced for the impact coming and let out a scream as the heavy tree landed directly on her leg, pinning it firmly to the ground.

Autumn panted heavily with pain as Tavish burrowed under several tree branches to reach her. He brushed his tiny body briskly against her hip, and his warmth eased a small bit of the pain.

Autumn tilted her head back to see if anything nearby could pry the tree away, but all other logs and boulders sat a substantial distance from her reach. She would have to use whatever energy she had to get out of this, but her mind raced and lacked focus. She let her eyes wander up and down the tree, when something caught her eye at the base where the tree had cracked.

A thick translucent arrow stood straight up from the tree's trunk. Its head sat deep in the bark and appeared slick with a shimmering black layer of ice. At the sight of it, a lump formed in Autumn's throat. The same black shimmer tainted the river where Tom Leslie had died and the icy water where Dillon Ross had fallen. This was no accident.

Tavish stepped carefully onto a tree branch next to Autumn and eyed the surrounding forest. Footsteps scurried through the snow somewhere behind her and faded away as a heap of snow fell once more from overhead, covering the icy arrow at the base of the fallen tree. Whoever had been watching through the forest just melted the one piece of evidence showing this was no accident, and then vanished.

Autumn exhaled deeply and reached out a hand to Tavish. She felt her eyes close firmly and her head drop back to the snow below.

Eve's Prosperity Pumpkin Curry Soup

1 tbsp olive oil

1/2 medium yellow onion, diced

3 medium carrots, diced

2 celery stalks, diced

1 small butternut squash (about 1 cup), diced

2 garlic cloves, minced

1/4 tsp ginger, grated

1/8 tsp nutmeg

2 Tbsp curry powder

1 tsp cumin

1 tsp turmeric

3 cups vegetable broth, divided

1 medium apple, peeled, cored and diced

2 14.5-oz cans pumpkin puree

1 14.5-oz can coconut milk

1/2 tsp salt

1/8 tsp pepper

pepitas for garnish

Heat the oil in a dutch oven over medium heat. Add the vegetables and cook until soft, about 5 minutes.

Add the garlic, ginger, and spices and continue cooking for another 2 minutes.

Pour in the vegetable broth and scrape the browned pieces from bottom of the pot. Add the apple, pumpkin puree, and coconut milk. Season with salt and pepper and stir the pot while saying,

With each stir of my spoon and fill of a bowl, bring abundance and prosperity to our days as a whole.

Simmer 10 minutes, or until the vegetables are tender enough to split with the wooden spoon. Let cool for ten minutes. Puree to desired consistency, add desired garnishes, and serve.

CHAPTER 31

Eve stood on the porch as Simone opened the door to greet her in an oversized rock band sweatshirt, black leggings, and black sherpa slippers.

"Hey, Autumn said you'd be here for breakfast this morning. I just put some hot water on for tea, and there's coffee as well."

"Thanks! I brought some warm gingerbread muffins along, too." Eve held up a brown bag from the Forest Brew just as Tavish ran furiously up the porch steps behind her.

The cat meowed furiously and scratched at Simone's leg before jumping back down the steps.

"What's gotten into you, Tavish?" Simone watched the cat curiously as he headed for the woods again. Simone glanced at Eve for a moment and then back at Tavish. They both stood silently while the cat meowed and ran back and forth on the path.

Simone felt her heart drop, receiving an intuitive vision of Autumn lying lifeless. "Autumn!" She ran out the door and burst past Eve down the steps. "Come on! Autumn's in danger!"

Eve dropped the muffin bag on the porch and tried to keep up with Simone as best she could. Tavish ran ahead of them and got to the clearing first.

Simone slowed her breathing and scanned the forest to find where Tavish had gone. She found him rubbing his head against Autumn on the ground under the massive pine bough.

"Oh God, Autumn!" Simone rushed to her side and brushed the hair from Autumn's face. Simone bent her ear to Autumn's nose and heard her breathing. "Eve, over here!"

Eve rushed through the clearing, panting heavily. "I'm here! What can I do?"

"She's still breathing, but it looks like she's pinned down." Simone searched around her, just as Autumn had, for something to pry the heavy tree away. "There's no way we'll be able to move this tree by ourselves. We need to wake her so she can use her magic."

Eve looked up at Simone with worried eyes. "Do you think she has enough strength for that?"

Simone shook her head. "I don't know, but that's our best option. I know there's a bit of mountain mint in this clearing, but who knows if it's still alive."

"Yes! Mountain mint!" Eve straightened up with an ounce of hope. "It should survive the first frost. If we dig under the snow, we should find some to help wake her up."

Simone stood and walked the ground at the edge of the trees. She brushed some of the snow away with her slippers as she shivered. Tavish trotted over and sniffed the ground near her until he scratched at a spot.

Bending down to where Tavish had stopped, Simone dug the snow out with her hands to reveal small green leaves covering the forest floor. "Got it." She plucked several leaves off the stem and crushed them between her fingers.

Eve took the leaves from Simone and hovered them underneath Autumn's nose. "Autumn, can you hear my voice? Simone and I are here, and we need you to wake up. Just follow my voice and open your eyes." Eve rubbed the mint leaves around Autumn's nose to release its oils onto her skin. "Earth energy, revive her. Earth energy, revive her."

Simone put her hand on Autumn's wrist and felt her pulse quickening. "She's stirring. Keep going!"

"Earth energy, revive her." Eve moved the mint leaves under Autumn's nose again as she stirred awake.

Carefully opening her eyes, Autumn saw Eve crouched over her and Simone on her other side. "What happened?"

"Don't move yet. Save your strength for a minute." Simone pressed Autumn back down as she attempted to rise. "A pine tree fell on your leg, and you're pinned down badly. We won't be able to move you on our own, so you're going to need to use your magic."

"I'm calling for help right now, so we'll have a few minutes for you to gather your strength and do what you can to move the tree." Eve glanced down at Autumn's leg under the tree bough. She could see a substantial gash penetrating a couple layers of skin, and bloodstained snow underneath it. There was no doubt some bones had also broken. "Simone, you work with Autumn to move the tree. I need to find that pine sap Penny showed me so I can heal her leg." Eve raised her chin toward Autumn's leg bent awkwardly under the tree.

Simone swallowed hard and nodded. She looked straight into Autumn's eyes as Eve walked away with her phone to search for the sap and call for help. "Autumn, look at me. I need you to call the winds and use your magic to lift either yourself or this tree. Got it? You need to do this."

Autumn glanced down at the massive tree on top of her. Tavish rubbed his head all the way along the side of Autumn's body, and she instantly warmed. Nodding her head, she closed her eyes and channeled the thought of bringing whoever did this to justice.

She remembered the icy arrow standing straight up from the cracked tree trunk. Autumn recalled the black shimmers under the icy lake after Dillon fell in. She brought up visions of the vine-like tentacles in the river, and she could no longer allow the black magic to harm the people of this town, including herself.

As Autumn took a deep breath, her gran's necklace glowed emerald green at her neck. The winds howled furiously around them, and Simone clung her arms close to her chest to stay warm while she worked her magic.

"I am the strength of a thousand hurricanes. I will not be tied down, but fly free." Autumn's heart pounded faster while her legs shifted from beneath the tree branches, but she couldn't quite break free. Simone rushed to her side and put her hands on Autumn's core to send more energy to her center.

The pine needles rustled furiously in the howling wind, and within moments, Autumn's body worked free from the fallen pine. Still lying flat on her back, she rose several feet in the air as wind blew through her hair. Simone looked up at her, and Eve turned from scraping sap off a tree to watch the sight with her jaw dropped open.

"I will fly free. I will fly free," Autumn continued without realizing she had already lifted herself clear of the tree.

"Autumn, you did it. You can stop." Simone reached up to touch her foot gently to make her aware.

The winds slowed as Autumn lowered to the snowy ground. She opened her eyes as Tavish and Eve ran over to her.

"I've got the sap! I found some aspen leaves under the snow as well, so I can work your mother's healing spell just like she taught me. Are you ready?" Eve gave Autumn a hopeful smile and then got to work once Autumn accepted.

Eve had already spread the sap onto the leaves as previously instructed. She now placed them over Autumn's wounds and took a slow, deep breath to calm her energy.

"Medicine of the earth, undo the wounds that run deep. Make them strong once more." Eve firmly pressed her hand over the wound as Autumn cringed in pain. "Laaaammmm . . . laaaammmm," she chanted while continuing to press the leaf into Autumn's skin.

It shimmered with tiny specks of brilliant white light, and Autumn sighed with relief. "I can feel the magic. The pain is subsiding."

Sirens blared in the distance, and Simone's eyes shot up toward the edge of the trees. "I'll go flag them down. Just keep going."

Eve nodded and refocused on the wounds as Simone ran down the forest path. Her chants continued until Autumn relaxed on the ground with normal breathing. Eve sat back on her heels, and Tavish purred loudly beside her.

"She's gonna be okay, Tavish. Don't worry." She smiled and scratched his head, which he graciously accepted.

"Eve, thank you. I knew you needed to be here this morning. Your gifts have gotten stronger, and I'm grateful you were around to use them." A tear streamed down Autumn's face as she turned her head to see emergency responders carrying a handheld stretcher toward her while bounding through the snow. "I'm gonna pass out again now."

Autumn let her eyes close while the falcon that had previously sat atop the tallest tree swung through the air with the strength and grace of a thousand gales.

CHAPTER 32

A knock sounded on Autumn's hospital room door, and she gave her cousin a confused look.

"The doctor just came in. Who . . .?" Autumn paused as soon as the smell of cherry cordial and roasted chestnuts hit her nose. She smiled and tilted her head at her cousin.

Simone shrugged. "I thought you could use a little cheering up."

James poked his head into the room and locked eyes with Autumn. "Hey there." He did what he could to mask his concern and gave her a warm smile. "I heard someone's lucky to be alive."

Autumn sighed. "I am, thanks to Eve and Simone. Tavish, too."

James sat on the edge of her hospital bed and smiled at Simone. "Thanks for calling me. I'm just sorry it took me this long to get over here."

"That was pretty quick, actually. I'm impressed." Simone got up from her seat and grabbed her vegan leather bag. "I'm gonna go down and get some coffee. Want anything?" She pointed back and forth at both of them.

"I'm good, thanks." James shook his head and returned his focus to Autumn.

"No, they should be in pretty soon with my lunch, so I'll wait." Autumn grabbed for James's hand and lost track of Simone as she walked out the door.

"This better not count as the lunch date you owe me. I expect a warm meal and some engaging conversation, but not in this setting."

Autumn chuckled at him but winced at the slight pain in her leg. She leaned over to rub it, and James shifted off the bed.

"I'm sorry, I didn't mean to hurt you. Are you all right?" He sat down in the chair Simone had gotten up from and watched as Autumn revealed a braced leg under the bed sheets.

"I'm healing pretty well, actually. There's some residual pain and discomfort to be expected, but Eve did an amazing job of healing me on the spot. The doctor says she's never seen bone coming back together so quickly, and the wounds have already started disappearing."

"I was so scared when Simone called me." He leaned toward the bed and grabbed Autumn's hand. "I don't know how I didn't see this in a dream. It just didn't come to me." James's voice trailed off with regret. "I'm so sorry."

Autumn sat up straighter in the bed. "You have nothing to be sorry for. None of this was your fault. You know that." She put her hand under his chin, and he raised his warm eyes to meet hers. "I saw your face in my mind when I was lying out in the woods, and I knew I wanted to come back to you. So I'm still here because of you, too."

He kissed her hand and ran his fingers through the long strands of her auburn hair. "I guess my energy felt that you needed me."

Another knock came at the door, and both of them turned to see Chief Walsh and Ben standing there.

"Chief." Autumn gave him a serious look, and he understood there was much to discuss.

He removed his hat and stepped inside the room, along with Ben. "Autumn, James, I hate to be meeting under these circumstances again. How are you feeling?"

Ben closed the door, and Autumn settled back into the hospital bed as she pushed a button to raise the back. "Better than expected. Lucky for me, Eve Newbury was at the house with Simone when the tree struck me. She started the healing process almost instantaneously in the woods."

"Well, I'm glad to hear that. It makes me feel better knowing what you girls are capable of." The chief put his hands on the footboard and sighed. "Why don't you tell us what you know?"

"Well, I knew something wasn't right in the woods. The air felt heavier than usual somehow, but I couldn't figure out why. I was there doing my usual walk to get grounded. When I walked into the tree line, one of the tall trees loaded down with snow cracked and fell right on top of me. It barely missed my whole body. And while I was trying to break my leg free . . ."

Ben stepped up beside his father and looked at Autumn curiously. "You noticed something."

Autumn nodded. "That's right. An arrow that appeared to be made entirely of ice was lodged in the tree trunk exactly where it had cracked off. And the arrow shimmered with the same black magic I had seen before."

"The shimmers from the river and the lake," James interjected under his breath.

"Exactly. It wasn't an accident. Whoever went after Tom Leslie, Dillon Ross, and probably the mayor also went after me."

"Mayor Halpin reported seeing shimmers in the ice as his car went off the road." The chief turned toward his son with concern. "Another founding family member and leader in the community." He sighed and appeared to be exhausted. "I imagine if we went out there to scour the grounds, there'd be no trace of this ice arrow, would there?"

"No, it's likely completely gone. The snow covered it before I passed out, and by now, the sun probably warmed up the clearing enough for it to have melted. Sorry, Chief."

The chief waved his hand in the air to dismiss the apology. "Don't you worry, something will eventually lead us to the person doing this. I'll bank on it. I just don't want anyone in harm's way when it does."

"Chief, what about the other development? Did you want to share that?" Ben waited for his father's go ahead before continuing. "We talked to Emily Campbell, and she confessed to the bribe money. The lumber mill is gonna have a whole slew of investigations into their runoff practices, and they'll probably be slapped with a load of fines. But besides that . . ." Ben looked up at the chief.

"She's got an alibi for the night of Tom Leslie's murder." Chief Walsh slung his fingers over the top of his belt and shifted in his stance. "Not a great one, but it still stands. Turns out, she was with her boyfriend all night, and he confirmed."

James let out an exasperated breath. "All these dead ends and only more people getting harmed to show for it."

"We've got a few more threads we can follow before we're completely down a dead end. But Autumn, I want you to rest up, and promise me this time you'll be cautious of absolutely everything. I don't wanna have to keep one of my deputies with you, but I will if I have to." The chief gave her a stern gaze. "James, help us out, would you?"

"Yes, Chief. I'll keep an eye on her." James put his hand over his heart and stood up as they headed toward the door.

"All right, then. Tell Jo I'll give her an update as soon as I can." The chief placed his hat back on his head and walked out the door with Ben waving behind him.

Simone sauntered in with rosy cheeks from the sight of Ben. "Well? Any news?"

James sighed and sat on the bed. "Not much other than we're getting nowhere."

"Not necessarily. They said Emily Campbell is likely off the table, so maybe we need to refocus our efforts on the last person on our list—Bryce Lachlan." Autumn had a spark in her eye as she spoke. She lifted herself forward and wrapped her hair around itself into a loose bun at her back. "I need to do some digging."

"Autumn, you just had a serious accident that could have killed you. It's okay to go easy for a while." James put his hand on her arm, hoping to slow her down a bit.

"James . . . this is gonna happen again if we don't figure this out. Not to mention, your dream hasn't happened yet. Something is coming, and we need to be prepared so we're not blindsided again."

Simone walked to the window and peered out to see the chief and Ben walking to their police SUV. "I'm totally with you, James. I don't want my cousin in harm's way any more than you do, but . . . she's the four-points witch now. And her destiny is tied to the elements. If anyone can get us through this, it's Autumn."

James rubbed his hand over his forehead. "I don't like this . . . But I have water energy inside me, too, and it's swaying me to follow your lead."

Autumn put her hand on James's cheek and smiled. "Air moves swiftly over compliant waters." She recalled seeing the owl atop the Celtic knot on his family tree. As she touched his face, she knew the day of that owl revealing itself wasn't very far off.

CHAPTER 33

Penny tiptoed across the floor of the girls' living room, and Jo followed behind her. They carried large jute bags to the kitchen counter and plopped them down. Tavish came out of Autumn's bedroom and greeted them with a big stretch of his front legs and a yawn.

Jo smiled and walked over to retrieve the cat. "Good morning, little one. Have you been watching over our girls?" She stroked his fur from head to tail and placed him back down on the ground to help her sister unpack the bags.

They pulled out several bundles of sage and bay leaves, long rosemary stalks, a massive jar of multicolored salts, a round wooden box filled with black tourmaline and clear quartz crystals, and a pastry box from the Forest Brew filled with Eve's warmest collection of baked goods.

Autumn stumbled out with her leg wrapped in a brace. Penny hurried over to her and grabbed her arm.

"Oh, sweetie, I didn't hear you get up. Let me help you over to the stool. I don't want you walking too much on that leg." Penny guided her daughter to one of the kitchen stools.

"Mom, it's okay. That healing spell you taught Eve worked really well, and my leg is practically back to normal. I'm just wearing this brace for more support today so I can rest up and regain some energy." Autumn peeked into the Forest Brew box and eyed all the delectable buns and coffee cakes with anticipation.

Jo put the teakettle on, started the coffeepot, and grabbed a plate for Autumn. "Yes, Penny, you really chose a brilliant apprentice in Eve. She took to that spell like a fish to water, and I'm so thankful that she remembered it in the most pressing of circumstances."

Autumn laughed under her breath. "Me, too. I don't even wanna think about the possibilities if she hadn't saved my leg right away. The pain was almost unbearable. But you know, Tavish took a bit of that away, too. Somehow, when he rubbed against me, I felt the pain subsiding. Is that strange?"

Jo shook her head. "Not at all. Familiars have their own special gifts, too. And aside from this little guy popping up at just the right place and time to support you, he may have a gift for soothing pain as well. Anything's possible."

Autumn looked down at Tavish shaking his tail and stomping his paws with pride. "Well, aren't you full of surprises?"

Simone opened her bedroom door with a bang, pressing her hand firmly against it to prop herself up. The noise startled them all in the kitchen and made Penny and Jo jump.

"Goodness, Sim! What under the moon are you doing?" Jo walked to the edge of the kitchen counter and leaned over to see the bedroom door.

"Why are you here so early? I don't plan to open the shop until noon today for the last lantern pickups. Sleep, I need sleep," Simone grumbled as she rubbed her eyes.

Autumn shook her head. "You always need sleep. But we have the next best thing brewing in here."

"Coffee!" Simone rushed to the kitchen and breathed deeply to smell the rich caramel blend her mother had made. She sighed and took a mug from her. "Thank you."

"I know my girls." Jo pulled out a few pastries onto a large platter and placed it in the center of the kitchen counter.

Penny grabbed a bowl of fruit salad and some organic yogurt from the fridge to complete the breakfast display.

"What's all this about? Why did you bring sage bundles and crystals?" Simone snagged one of the cinnamon brioche rolls, peeled off a piece, and dunked it into her coffee.

"We're doing a boundary spell this morning. Penny and I discussed it, and we don't want to take any chances. So, we're going to set up a safe haven at each of our homes and shops. Oh, and the Forest Brew! Eve is part of your coven now, and the Newburys have been like family to us all these years. Catherine gave me the go ahead earlier when I picked up these scrumptious baked goods, so we're all set!"

"Okay . . . maybe you could have filled us in on this plan before barging in on a Sunday morning. My plan was to get an extra couple hours of sleep." Simone widened her eyes, trying to make the need for sleep go away.

"There was no time. After what happened with Autumn, we needed to get over here as soon as possible. At least once we do this, we'll know our homes and shops are safe and sound. If we keep to those areas and the Forest Brew for now, we can get past all this." Jo fiddled with her rings and stared off into space. "Although, the one thing I am still very much worried about . . ."

Autumn and Simone exchanged glances before turning to Jo with concern. "What is it, Aunt Jo?" Autumn warmed her hands around her tea mug as she stared at Jo intently.

"The solstice festival." Jo swatted at the air with her hand. "It should be just fine. It's just that . . ." She sighed and poured more honey into her tea. "There will be so many people gathered there, and we can't put a boundary around the entire town. I'm worried it'll be an opportunity for serious damage."

"Okay, so we put boundaries where we can, and then we each carry a talisman to the festival. I already have Gran's locket, and Simone retrieved a dried starfish from the ancestral wardrobe."

Jo's eyes brightened at Autumn's words. "The starfish. It called to you, Simone?"

Simone put her brioche down and brushed off her hands. "It has been for over a week now. I didn't want to say anything because I didn't really know where it came from. But then, Autumn and I opened the wardrobe and found the starfish box glowing like her necklace does. It seemed to wait there for me to retrieve it. Do you know what it does?"

Jo moved beside Penny and wrapped her arm around her for support. "It called to me once before, and thankfully I listened. Starfish are a Celtic symbol for spreading messages throughout the seas. The creatures heighten intuition and the ability to sense danger quickly in order to move with intent. The one who bears the starfish also carries the ability for renewal and regeneration, just like the water element itself."

"So it came to you out of necessity?" Simone squinted at her mother, searching for an answer when it automatically came to her. "Someone almost drowned."

Jo nodded as Penny squeezed her tighter. "My friend Abigail."

Autumn gasped and rested her hand on the side of her face. "Dillon Ross's wife."

"That's right. We were just teenagers, and we loved to swim in the lake. A rope swing hung off a tree, and you could swing out pretty far off one of the small docks. Abigail hit her head on the edge of the dock after she swung out into the lake, but no one noticed. Except I had the starfish with me, and I felt a pull from the lake as it called to me. I swam out faster than I had ever swam before and dragged her unconscious body up from the bottom. It was the lightest and strongest I've ever been in the water. And yet it was also the most terrifying."

"You've never told me that story before." Simone felt a new understanding of her mother. Of how she moved so fluidly with each situation while carrying with her a deeply nurturing spirit for all around her. That nurturing spirit allowed her to move between shadow and light without hesitation, if it meant someone's highest good.

"Oh my dear, it's so many years past, and my intention is to be fully here in the present. But I can still faintly hear the call of the seas. Even though I no longer carry the starfish, it has always lived in my heart. I would guess once you connect with it, the talisman will imprint on your spirit as well."

"I had no idea Abigail Ross went through something similar to her husband. She must have been so frightened when he was under the ice." Autumn listened intently, tucking her legs underneath her on the kitchen stool and pulling her long sleeves over her hands.

"She came into the bath shop a few days back, and I spoke with her about it. I sensed from our discussion that you being there calmed her nerves. Abigail knew it was my ancestral magic that saved her that day. She also knew that the magic in my blood passed down to you as well. When you were out on the ice, Abigail set some of her fear aside because she believed in you. In our family. And I know that holds true of everyone in this town, especially the magical families. They believe in the magic of the four points." Jo turned to look at her daughter now. "And if the talisman called to you now, Simone, then I believe the waters are ready for renewal."

Autumn and Simone cleared off the plates from breakfast as Jo and Penny prepared the herbs for the spell at the kitchen island.

"Autumn, as soon as we prepare the ingredients and call the energies, you can unlock the wardrobe for the Book of Spells." Jo eyed Autumn to get her agreement.

Penny went to Gran's tall tea cabinet and bent down to pull out a large black stone mortar and pestle from the bottom. She brought it over to the kitchen island where Jo stood running her fingers along the long rosemary branches to remove the needles. Jo sprinkled them into the mortar bowl as she spoke in a stern voice.

"Rosemary to bind the spell." Jo grabbed the bunch of bay leaves next. She threw them into the bowl and crushed them thoroughly with the pestle. "Bay leaf for the wards."

Penny followed by pulling the tall mason jar full of colorful salts toward her. She unscrewed the lid and used a wooden scoop sitting within the jar to bring out a substantial amount of salts. With a swoop of her arm, Penny drizzled the salts down into the bowl. "Salts of the earth and the sea to absorb negative energies."

Autumn and Simone walked around to the other side of the kitchen island. Autumn opened the round container full of crystals and let Simone choose her preference. Simone pulled out a handful of cube-shaped black tourmaline crystals and sprinkled them in a clockwise circle around the mortar bowl on the island.

"Black tourmaline to shield and remove the unwanted." Jo passed her right hand over the crystals after Simone placed them.

Then, Autumn took a handful of the cube-shaped clear quartz from the container and did the same as Simone.

"Clear quartz to absorb and neutralize the energy." Penny ran her hand over the clear crystals this time and then pulled a couple more items from one of the jute bags. She set a menu down from the Forest Brew, a cinnamon stick tied with what appeared to be Mrs. Newbury's favorite evergreen twine, a small jar of moon water from Jo's garden, a packet of bath salts from Jo's shop, a tin of Gran's homemade teas from the girls' home, a paper invitation from Parchment and Pine, several small sachet bags, and a black pillar candle.

"Items from the safe havens we intend to create." Jo signaled to her sister to begin, and Penny lit the candle in the center of the island.

Each of them took their places at the sides of the island and raised their arms. Jo took a deep breath, and they all followed her.

"Energies of the four points and ancestors, hear our call. We come with the intention to protect these areas from harm and ill will. Our homes and workplaces, our gardens, and our property, and that of our friends, the Newbury family. Bring forth our Book of Spells so that we may maintain our protection and that of these lands."

With Jo's spoken words, Autumn's necklace glowed. She opened it at her chest to reveal the tiny wardrobe key once again. Smiling as she raised it for the others to see, she walked over and retrieved the Book of Spells from the wardrobe, exactly where it always appeared in the wooden box at the base of the cabinet.

"Very good." Jo lowered her arms to her sides, and Penny and Simone followed. "Place the book in front of you on the island, Autumn, and let it fall open as it may."

Autumn did as her aunt instructed and placed the book on the counter. The pages flew around furiously before finally stopping at a page toward the center titled "Boundary Spell to Repel Negative Energies."

Jo and Penny leaned over to check if the book had found the correct page. Penny nodded at her sister. "It's the one we expected."

"Wonderful. Whenever you're ready, dear, proceed." Jo lifted her hand to signal Autumn to read from the book.

Autumn cleared her throat and moved the book closer to her. The instructions read to hover one's hands over the materials intended for the spell sachets. So, Autumn reached her arms out over the island full of spell ingredients. Immediately, she sensed a pulsing energy among them, almost like a beating heart.

"Energies of the earth, air, sky, and water, fill these items with fortitude and will. Let none pass if not with warmth to keep them still. Be vigilant, be strong, be abiding until the first day when my palm touches the earth to return this strength. As above, so below, with my words, make these intentions so."

Simone watched over Autumn's hands as an aura of deep red surrounded the entire kitchen island. "It worked. I see the protective energy settling over the ingredients. But now what?"

"Now, we fill the sachets." Penny grabbed the stack of small bamboo sachet bags and handed them out to everyone. "We'll start with Jo at the north and pass them to our left. Choose one ingredient to insert into the bag until they're all filled."

Jo began with the mixture of herbs and salts in the mortar bowl. She used the wooden scoop from the salt jar to spoon a bit into a sachet and handed it to Penny. They each passed the sachets and put in the herbs and crystals. Simone stacked the sachets in the center of the island when they were complete.

"There." Jo nodded as she looked at the stack. "Autumn, please close the circle for us."

Autumn raised her arms once more and gazed over the sachets on the island. "Elements and ancestors, we thank you for this protection. May our days be many and our land, sea, and sky be in harmony once again. And so it is."

Penny reached out and squeezed Autumn's hand. "You're becoming quite good at leading the circle."

Autumn smiled and closed the Book of Spells to return it to the wardrobe. "Thanks I had some excellent teachers."

"All right, girls. I need you to deliver two of these sachets to the Newburys today. Catherine will know what to do with them." Jo lit a match and tossed it into the mortar bowl with any remaining spell-casting materials as she spoke. The flames turned anything left into ash, and she brushed it gently into a tiny vile to tuck into her skirt pocket. "For the garden."

"Jo and I will take two more of the sachets to the house and the bath shop. That leaves one for here and one for the Pine." Penny divided up the sachets accordingly.

"Sim, if you can hand out the rest of the lantern orders, then I'll take these over to the Forest Brew." Autumn grabbed a couple sachets and walked over to her backpack hanging by the front door. She slid them carefully inside and then brushed her hands together.

"Sounds good. We have about five or six orders left for pickup today, and most of them will be in when we open. So, if you wait for some of them to clear out, then that'll work." Simone squinted at one of the last pastries on the platter and noticed it had a bit of the shimmering red energy around it. She shrugged it off and grabbed it, taking a big bite out of the side.

"Wait a minute." Autumn wrinkled her forehead and looked at their mothers. "Don't you two still need a talisman for when we're outside the boundaries?" Autumn sat back down on her stool and followed Simone in eating the last of the pastries.

Jo waved her hand through the air dismissively. "Yes, but don't you worry. Penny and I will sort that out ourselves. You know I have my moon ring handed down from our mother's mother. That will be mine, and Penny has her charm bracelet. The same one that carried the tree root charm she gave you, Autumn."

Autumn lifted her eyebrows in remembrance. "Right! The charm forged itself to the back of my locket, where the roots took hold and now show an embossed pattern."

Penny hugged her daughter. "It will always keep you rooted and strong, as a MacKinnon woman should be."

Autumn's thoughts went back to yesterday as she had lain pinned to the ground under the fallen tree. She refused to let someone take her strength like that again. As she replayed the scene in her mind, she searched for something to latch on to that could help them gain the upper hand. Her eyes lit up, and she turned toward Simone.

"I think I know what our next step should be." Autumn gave her cousin a smirk as Simone looked at her curiously.

"Okay, let's hear it." Simone crossed her arms at her chest and propped her leg up against the kitchen island.

Autumn lifted the jar of moon water Aunt Jo still had sitting on the counter and sloshed it around a bit in her hand. "The ice archer."

CHAPTER 34

Autumn handed the last pickup order across the counter to a customer and looked at her cousin.

"Well, that's it! Everyone picked up their lanterns. I'm gonna head over to the Forest Brew and take those sachets to Eve. Want any lunch?" Autumn went to the back room to retrieve her chunky scarf, hat, and gloves.

"Yeah, definitely. I'm starving. How about a four-cheese sandwich and some pumpkin curry?" Simone swiveled around on her stool by the computer to wait for Autumn to reappear.

Autumn walked out of the back room with Tavish on her heels. "I'll get you the curry if they have it, but it might be tomato soup today. Are you okay with that, too?"

"Sure, I'll take either as long as it's warm." Simone bent down and grabbed Tavish. "I'll snuggle with this one to keep warm while you're gone."

"I was beginning to think it was just me who's been cold all day. I've felt very off ever since what happened in the woods. It's making me think of Dillon Ross saying the same thing after he fell into the lake. Almost as if that black magic lingers around us or something." Autumn scratched Tavish's chin and gave Simone a serious look. She held up the bag of protection sachets. "These better do the trick!"

"They will. Our magic is powerful, and we're getting closer to figuring this all out. I feel it." Simone walked across the shop floor to the front door with Autumn and held the sachet bag while her cousin grabbed her coat and bag.

"Thanks. I'll be back with lunch in a minute."

"Got it." Simone pointed her finger at her cousin. "Stick to the safe havens and nowhere else. I don't wanna have to rescue you again."

Autumn rolled her eyes and smiled. "Yes, Mom. See you soon."

As she pulled the shop door open, the air felt frigid on the other side. The temperature had dropped dramatically overnight, and it was going to be a cold festival at the river tomorrow evening.

Autumn headed down Main Street to the Forest Brew. As she walked, she sensed the warm bubble of the protective sachets shimmering in the bag for the Newburys. It made her feel more confident knowing they weren't helpless in all of this. She was a powerful witch and wielded more energy than most could imagine. It was time to put that energy to good use and finally rid the town of the black magic hiding within it.

Autumn pulled open the door of the Forest Brew to find it busy inside. Every table was packed for the lunch rush, and she was happy to see business thriving. She stood behind the last person in line to order and noticed it was Anabeth Greenwood. Autumn tapped her on the shoulder.

"Anabeth, hi. How are you?"

Anabeth turned to see Autumn behind her. "Oh, Autumn! I should ask you the same thing. I heard you almost died! How are you out of the hospital already?"

"Oh no, I'm fine. It really wasn't that bad. Mostly my leg, but that's all healed up quickly. I took the brace off this morning, and all's well."

Anabeth lowered her voice and moved up in the line as she leaned back to whisper, "From what I've heard, these have been no accidents. Something's going on in Hollow's Glenn, and I intend to find out. We've gotta keep our town safe, you know?"

Autumn nodded and stood still for a moment as she received an idea. "Actually, Anabeth. Now that you mention it, there may be a way for you to help me figure out what happened. You must be pretty good at finding things out as a journalist."

Anabeth turned around immediately and stared directly at Autumn with a smirk. "I'm amazing at uncovering things. What do you need?"

"Girls! You're next." Mrs. Newbury called from the counter.

Anabeth turned toward her. "Oh, that's me!" She scurried up and put in her order before looking over her shoulder at Autumn. "I'll meet you over at the pastry counter after you order."

Autumn nodded and smiled at her. She stepped up to put her order in next. "Hi, Mrs. Newbury." She handed the bag of sachets over the counter to Catherine. "From my aunt, Jo. She said you'll know what to do with them."

"Right! Yes, thank you so much, dear. I've been so worried! And Eve told me all about what happened. Thank goodness she and Simone were there and you're okay! If I weren't behind this counter, I'd come give you a big hug right now."

Autumn laughed. "I'm fine, Mrs. Newbury. Thank you for thinking of me, but Eve was literally a lifesaver."

"Yes, well . . ." Catherine Newbury glanced over her shoulder at her daughter. "I've taught her well, and now your mother is carrying on where I left off. I'm so grateful to her for that."

"Oh, she loves it. Having a protégé makes her feel like she's continuing to do what she does best and pass on her knowledge." Autumn smiled as she picked up a menu on the counter. "Anyway, I need to order lunch! Simone hoped for some pumpkin curry. Do you have any today?"

"I have a pot in the back that I'll warm up just for her. What else would you like?" Mrs. Newbury rang up the order on the register as Autumn rattled it off.

"Two four-cheese sandwiches, and a side salad with apples and pecans. Oh, and two pomegranate iced teas. Thanks."

"Good choices. I'll have that right up if you wanna wait at the counter." Mrs. Newbury lifted her arm to signal Autumn to move around the corner toward the bar stool seating, and Autumn followed.

Anabeth waved Autumn over and sat inquisitively on a bar stool. "So . . . tell me what you need. I'm all ears."

Autumn sat beside her and kept her voice quiet. "I need to find out who in town may be good with a bow and arrow. Like maybe they're a master archer or something. We need to look into any archery clubs or places nearby with a roster of customers. I'm thinking that's a good place to start."

"Well, right off the top of my head, I know there's a mountain archery club in Ivansedge. They run a camp for kids every summer. I know because we featured it in the paper a few times."

"Oh, I didn't realize there was one so close. Is there any way you could get a list of their customers? That may just be the key to us solving this." Autumn knew Anabeth would inevitably want the inside information for a story. But after she had helped rescue Dillon from the lake, Autumn knew she could trust her to be discreet for now. All she had to do was get Anabeth to feel like part of the team in solving the crime.

"Absolutely. You can count on me, and I'll keep it all very . . ."—Anabeth motioned her hand by pushing it down in front of her—"low key. Just between us."

"I appreciate it, Anabeth."

"Here are your lunches." Eve stood smiling in front of them behind the counter. She lifted two large brown bags up to the countertop and slid them over to the girls. "Autumn, it's so good to see you up and out. I tossed and turned all night after what happened." Eve stopped with her mouth open and eyed Anabeth beside Autumn. "Oh, I . . ."

"It's fine, Eve. Anabeth heard I had an accident, but I told her it wasn't bad. Everything's fine now."

"Oh, thank goodness." Eve sighed with relief. "I was worried for a minute there. But yes"—Eve put her hands out to show off Autumn sitting there—"you look just as good as ever! It's incredible." Eve shook her head, almost in disbelief of her own handiwork with the healing spell she'd performed on Autumn.

Autumn chuckled and grabbed the bag of food. "Anyway, thanks for this. I'll talk to you later. Anabeth, let me know what you find out."

Anabeth nodded and winked as Autumn walked toward the door.

"Are you helping Autumn with something?" Eve had a curious look on her face.

Anabeth pulled her wool beret down on her head, grabbed her lunch bag, and hesitated before answering Eve. "Just a favor between friends." Anabeth waved to Eve and glided toward the door as if someone in town finally saw her for who she truly was.

CHAPTER 35

Simone handed a few lanterns to Autumn out of the trunk of her SUV at the curb of the downtown hill. She searched the crowd gathering in the square as she closed the trunk.

"Why don't you take a couple of these and go find Ben? I'll meet up with our moms. I'm sure they'll be here any minute." Autumn nudged her cousin with her shoulder.

"Are you sure? You don't need help with anything else?" Simone tucked her face into her black knit infinity scarf and grabbed a couple lanterns from Autumn.

"Totally sure. That handsome police officer will be looking for you, and you shouldn't keep him waiting."

Simone turned to Autumn and thought for a moment. "Do you think he's handsome? I mean, I guess he is, in a quiet walled-off kind of way. I do like that about him."

"I know you do. Now go find him before we're much older."

"All right, but pay attention to your necklace. If it gives you any hints of trouble, then find me and head back to the car." Simone raised an eyebrow at her cousin.

Autumn tilted her head and pursed her lips. "Same goes for you."

They parted ways, and Autumn headed down the hill toward the water fountain square with a few paper lanterns in hand. The fountain and the river walk beside it was lit up with the tall path lights glowing in the evening sky. The crisp dusk air seemed to carry a hint of magenta among the shadowy clouds, and Autumn sensed the uncertainty of the winds.

As she watched Simone meet up with Ben at the memorial bench in honor of their gran, Autumn felt someone tap her on the shoulder. She turned to find Anabeth standing behind her with a big smile on her face.

"Anabeth, hey. Are you ready for the festival?"

Anabeth shook her head dismissively and slung her arm through one of Autumn's, nearly dropping the lanterns in her hands. She started leading her toward the river walk to talk away from the crowd.

"Oh, I'm not concerned about all this. Just something I'll cover for the paper, but I wanted to talk to you about the actual story. The one we're digging into behind the scenes."

Autumn stopped and directed all her attention to Anabeth. "You found something. What is it?"

"Turns out, the guy who manages the mountain archery club had a big crush on me in high school. When I went there, he chatted me up. Apparently, he never really got over that crush of his, so I got the entire membership roster out of him." She pulled open the slouchy tote bag slung over her shoulder and brought out a rolled-up paper stack. Handing it to Autumn, Anabeth pointed to a few highlighted lines on the second page. "See anyone of interest?"

"Bryce Lachlan," Autumn whispered under her breath as she read from the page. "Member for fifteen years."

Anabeth shook her head while staring down at the pages. "That's plenty of time to master your archery skills, if you ask me." She put her hand on Autumn's shoulder. "But what's the connection here? I know it has something to do with your accident."

Autumn raised her eyes to meet Anabeth's. "It was no accident. The tree that fell on me . . . I found an ice arrow implanted in the trunk where it cracked. Someone definitely tried to make it appear like an accident, and they knew what they were doing."

"An ice arrow? How would that even work?" Anabeth stood with a confused look on her face.

"It's complicated. But now that I know where the trail leads, it's time to get confirmation." Autumn pushed the paper lanterns into Anabeth's hands and took a step away from her.

Anabeth grabbed Autumn's arm firmly. "Autumn, you need to be careful. Someone's already tried to kill you once."

Autumn put her hands on Anabeth for a moment to calm her. She took a deep breath and thought for a moment. Something told her she needed to go, even though Autumn felt an underlying darkness to the evening.

"Anabeth, I'll only be gone for fifteen minutes. If it's more than that, find Chief Walsh or his son, Ben, and come get me. You know where I'll be."

Autumn grabbed Anabeth's forearms with her hands and pulled them close to her. She stared into her eyes and sent a message through her mind. "You can do this. Watch the clock, get help if necessary, and stay focused."

Without knowing how, Anabeth inherently understood the telepathic message and nodded to Autumn. "I'll watch the clock and keep an eye out for you."

Autumn smiled. "Thank you." She dropped her arms and headed down the river walk, eyeing the icy water beside her as she walked a half mile to the dimly lit marina. She looked behind her on the river trail and noted the desolate distance between her and the crowded town square. If she was going to uncover where the black magic came from, it was now or never.

Autumn only saw a small light at the back of the marina. She walked around the dockside porch and found the shop door unlocked. Quietly, she pulled the door and went inside, careful not to slam the door behind her. The store was quiet and dark, and Autumn felt tension in the air immediately upon entering.

As she took a few steps toward the checkout counter, the familiar hot sensation on her chest crept back up. She put her hand on the locket from her gran and knew it pulsed with light beneath her coat, warning her of potential danger. She moved behind the counter and squinted through the darkness to search the shelves under the register for any clues.

Boxes of fishing and boating supplies lined the shelves. Life vests sat heaped in a pile, along with bunches of rope. Then, something caught her eye underneath it all. On the bottom shelf in the corner, a dark navy-blue hood draped onto the floor from below the life vests. Autumn knelt and pulled on the hood to reveal a heavy ice fishing jacket, just like the one she'd seen in the distance the day Dillon Ross almost drowned.

Autumn gasped, and several life vests tumbled onto the floor. She quickly shoved them back onto the bottom shelf, along with the jacket, when she heard someone muttering in the back room. As she stood up abruptly and took a step away from the counter, someone appeared in the doorway of the back room, lit dimly from behind.

The figure stood still for a moment, staring at Autumn, and then moved closer. "Well, if it isn't the paper shop witch. The one we're all supposed to be dutifully following these days."

Autumn heard the disdain in the man's voice, but it didn't sound like Bryce Lachlan. The voice was more youthful and less gravely. When he stepped out from the doorway and her eyes adjusted, she realized it was the same man who had escorted his mother into her shop several days prior to order invitations for his homecoming. Cory Lachlan, Bryce's only son, stood before her now, and his hand hung low at his side with what appeared in the dim light to be a handgun.

Autumn swallowed hard. "Cory. I thought you came home to take over the family business and follow in your father's footsteps. What's going on?"

Cory laughed under his breath and took a step closer to Autumn. "You tell me. You stick your nose in everyone's business around here. Is that why you're here at the marina instead of over at the festival with everyone else? I should have guessed you couldn't let anything go."

"I came to check on your father. The founders have been suspiciously in danger over the past couple weeks, and the signs pointed here next." Autumn didn't want to reveal her thoughts about Bryce Lachlan being behind it all since she still wasn't sure what was going on.

"You wanted to check on my father, did you? He's in the back of the shop. Why don't you head back there and ask him how he's doing yourself?" Cory nodded his head toward the back room and moved aside so she could pass.

Autumn slowly glided past him and smelled an almost choking scent of sulfur. She wondered how she hadn't picked up on it previously when he was in the shop, but now the scent permeated his entire aura. As she moved through the hallway to the back room, the voices whispered around her.

"The poison pools where the bloodline ceases."

Autumn slowed her steps as she contemplated what the voices said. She looked over her shoulder at Cory, who now raised the gun he held and positioned it toward Autumn's back.

"You're their only son, aren't you?" She paused before moving into the back room with him and saw a smile drift across his face.

"That's right. The one and only heir to our water bloodline. And according to my mother, it's my responsibility to take over the duties of our family and stay in the mountain region. Something I've always resented."

Autumn heard a muffled cry coming from behind her in the back room. As someone raised the lights, she found Bryce Lachlan with bound hands and feet sitting on a chair in the center of the room. Autumn rushed in beside him and put her hands on his arms, searching for what she could do.

"What's she doing here?" a woman's voice interjected.

Standing beside the wall, holding a stack of papers, Emily Campbell glared at Autumn catering to Mr. Lachlan. The name came to Autumn immediately upon seeing her face.

"Emily Campbell. Heir to the lumber mill." The words fell out of Autumn's mouth as she recognized the woman from her library research.

"Very good. It seems you have been doing your research around town, just as I heard." Emily lifted herself from the wall and took a few steps closer. Cory joined her with his gun in hand.

"She stumbled into the marina, looking for answers. Just as well, though, because now we can get rid of them both and be on our way." Cory wrapped one arm around Emily and kissed her lips.

Autumn watched them both intently while in her mind, she called to Simone. She visualized her message swooping through the evening sky like a swift owl finding her cousin amidst the sea of festival goers. While hoping Simone received her message, Autumn turned her attention to the couple in front of her.

"So it wasn't your father after all. You both collaborated on everything, including being each other's alibis." Autumn stood beside Mr. Lachlan and put her hand on his shoulder to comfort him as she spoke.

"Yes, well, being a fairly prominent figure in the community has its perks." Emily's lips cast a thin smile over her face. "No one wants to question your integrity and bring down an economic powerhouse in the region. So having a simple alibi for each other worked nicely, actually."

"And you needed Tom Leslie out of the way so you could stop paying him off and keep him quiet about the runoff permanently. But why did you want to do this to your father and everyone else, Cory?" Autumn worked through the pieces as she spoke out loud.

"My parents and this whole town have made us live up to this ridiculous responsibility for long enough. Why should we be beholden to this town and the shackles it wraps around us for our whole lives? You should understand that. You've inherited the responsibilities, too. It disgusts me they wrap their tentacles around us and keep us from moving beyond anything but this place. Well, now they can all see what it's like to feel the tightening tentacles of a magic that doesn't look out for you. One that only keeps you bound and constrained through life and death." Cory waved the gun around at his father as he spoke. Mr. Lachlan breathed heavier as he sat gagged and bound, staring at his son.

"So you wanted to get rid of all the founders and destroy the magic here. Destroy the very nature of the mountain region through oppositional magic, the dark tentacles."

"That's right. It's only fitting to destroy the magic through its own kind. And as water is in both Emily's blood and mine, what better way to send it through the town? Of course, Tom Leslie always got in the way. First, with the payoffs to keep him quiet, and then he took the wildflowers we needed to perform the spell. Those winter jasmine vines spread the magic beautifully, but the spell had to run its course a few times to truly do enough damage."

"That's why we found traces of it in the river water." Autumn looked down and met eyes with Mr. Lachlan as she thought about the water samples.

"Oh, it's much more than traces now. Those vines permeated the water so much, it's too far gone to save. Too bad they weren't yet strong enough to get rid of that Ross below the ice, though."

"It was you I saw that day across the ice pond. In the ice fishing jacket." Autumn stared at Cory with fierceness in her eyes. "You tried to kill him."

Cory shrugged. "He's another founding member, and in a water bloodline as well. We had to get rid of the water elements that could resist the black magic, or at least largely diminish their power."

"And me and the mayor? We're not predominant water elements."

"No, but the mayor dictates much of what goes on in this town, and he got in the way. We couldn't have fire energy like that blocking our efforts. And you, well, I didn't want to have to hurt you, seeing as you've inherited this just as I have. Our families have spewed these dictatorial edicts about what's required of us since childhood. But once I saw you so determined to uncover what was going on, I knew we couldn't let you go."

Autumn's heart pounded in her chest, and she tried to calm her nerves with slow breaths. "But what do you get out of all of this? Even if you get rid of the magic here, what then? You just leave?"

Emily smiled slyly and started pacing around the room. "We take everything. Cory's father already signed over the rights to the marina to Cory." She slapped the stack of papers against her other palm as she spoke. "Tom Leslie's request to put in a conservation easement should be dropped soon now that he's no longer around. And now that there's no actual witness to the pollution from the mill, we can sell that to the highest bidder. All that's left is to get rid of you two and sell the properties to the developer with the highest bid to fund our new life together."

"That's right. Get what's owed to us and get out of this town." Cory waved the gun up and down. "So come on, both of you. Stand up, Father." Cory stepped over to Mr. Lachlan and pulled him off the chair by his elbow. "You're about to have your own accident in the icy water."

Cory directed Autumn to head to the back door and walk outside as the rest of them followed. As she pulled the door open and took a step out back, an orange ball of fur darted behind the building in her peripheral vision. Autumn instantly felt the tabby cat's energy close by and had a wash of strength come over her. If Tavish was here, then she knew someone else would follow.

Autumn stopped in the snow after she walked off the back porch of the marina.

"Keep going. We're gonna take a little walk down to the dock." Cory pushed his father forward, and he stumbled through the snow.

Autumn stepped slowly, searching through the snow with each step for something she could use as a weapon or to harness her powers, but nothing surfaced. She called Simone in her mind once again. With any luck, Anabeth would bring the chief here soon, and Tavish would have a few tricks of his own.

The dock stretched out into the icy waters in front of Autumn now, and she hesitated before going any further. She looked over at Mr. Lachlan still tied up and took a deep breath. With an exhale, the wind picked up around them and started howling ferociously. Autumn grabbed on to Mr. Lachlan's arm and felt him exchange some of the energy he had left into her own. Her hand shimmered with the magic flowing through it as the wind pushed against them so firmly it almost knocked Cory and Emily over behind them.

"Don't even think about overpowering us with your wind. I'll turn this snow into raging waters and sweep you away with it. Now, get on the dock." Cory struggled to hold up the gun in the powerful winds, but he stood through it and kept moving them forward on the dock.

Autumn's anger built at the idea that Cory would get his way and destroy the town and everyone in it. She wouldn't let that happen. She couldn't. Autumn turned around to confront him on the dock but saw Emily hovering over Mr. Lach-lan sitting on the edge. His feet hung over the dock and grazed the icy waters. Before Autumn had time to react, Cory shoved her entire body over the side, and Autumn crashed through a crack in the ice, plunging into the shimmering black waters below.

CHAPTER 36

Autumn flailed desperately as she sank deeper into the icy lake. The frigid water pierced through her clothes like tiny knives going into her skin. She knew she had to regain composure and make it back to the surface. Kicking her feet in her heavy snow boots, she pushed her way to the top, only to find the spidery black tentacles creeping over the surface and holding her down. Her eyes widened with panic as she pushed away from them.

She looked at her hands in the water and watched them moving back and forth with the water now. The elements resided within her, and all she had to do was harness them. Autumn eyed the black tentacles circling overhead. Anger bubbled within her again, and she watched as her hands shimmered until they were burning with the fire inside.

The waters around Autumn quickly warmed, and she felt the relief of the heat immediately. She shimmied out of her coat and boots and focused her energy on the other elements. She set her intention of transforming the water in front of her. In her mind, she chanted.

"Water, become air. Let each breath resume." Autumn repeated it over in her mind three times until the water molecules before her parted. They shifted up to the surface of the water, creating a tunnel of air from her to the sky above. She gasped and took in as much air as she could while treading water beneath her.

Autumn concentrated on her hands, still seething with fire. She cast them up toward the surface and sent black tentacles cracking down to the bottom of the lake before they disappeared. The flames rose through the ice above and melted it instantly. She breathed deeply, taking in as much air from the tunnel as she could. With another burst of energy, she shot more flames to the surface, joining them to the other flame already there.

The fire spread quickly in a large circle on the ice. Shards cracked off and plummeted around her through the water. Soon, she saw a massive flame wrapping around her at the surface, directing her through, the same as James's dream had predicted. Seeing it play out in front of her, Autumn knew she would make it out.

She called to the air in her mind and asked for the strength to carry herself into the sky. Kicking her legs harder in the water until they became lighter with each kick, she rose forcefully out of the melted surface surrounded by flames. Autumn hung above the lake, dripping wet and covered with shimmering golden light. The emerald glow of Gran's necklace pulsed strongly now around her neck, and she scanned the edge of the waters in front of her.

Sitting on a mound of snow on the shore, a small orange tabby cat meowed and pawed at the air. Autumn's necklace glowed stronger and warmed her body as she stared at the cat in amazement. Tavish always ended up by her side when she needed her magic the most. The cat meowed again and turned his head to focus her attention on the figures beyond him.

Autumn watched the movement near the parking lot beyond the marina. She glimpsed Cory through the dark. He eyed her with fear at the sight of her hovering above the waters he'd thrown her into. Then, he darted into the dark as quickly as he could.

Autumn took a deep breath, calmed the raging energy in her body, and brought herself onto the shore. Just as her bare feet touched the cold snow below her, she heard yelling from behind the marina.

"Drop the weapon! Put your hands up!"

Autumn's eyes darted to the parking lot once again as she wrapped her arms around her chest and dropped to the ground, shaking. A flood of police officers barreled around the corner of the marina, and several pinned Cory and Emily to the ground.

Autumn panted as she rocked back and forth in the cold snow, trying to regroup. Chief Walsh rushed down to her, with Ben, Simone, and Anabeth alongside him.

Autumn looked up at the chief, and he bent down beside her. "I'm okay, but . . ." Autumn turned and scoured the landscape with her eyes. "Bryce Lachlan. Where is he?"

Autumn and Simone both set their eyes on the lake and stared out into the flames still engulfing the surface, melting every bit of ice in their path. They looked at each other and spoke together. "The water."

Simone took off toward the water, unzipping her jacket and throwing it down on the ground as she went.

"Simone, no!" Ben called to her, but Simone didn't look back. Her eyes stayed on the water, and her ears followed the singing beneath it.

Each time her foot hit the ground, she heard the water's call. Watching her run toward it, Autumn noticed the glowing outline of a star in the back pocket of her cousin's jeans. She had the ancestral starfish with her.

Chief Walsh held off his son and watched, hoping Simone knew what she was doing heading into the lake.

Plunging into the center of the flames, Simone dove furiously down to the depths of the lake. The siren call sounded louder in her ears the closer she got to the bottom. As she pushed her arms and legs through the current, her feet flowed swiftly through the water as if they had become fins. Her body torpedoed to the lake floor with the speed of a mermaid, and she found Bryce Lachlan pushing slightly against the bottom with bound hands and feet. Simone saw his aura diminishing with each second. She grabbed under his arms and pulled him up through the water with her. Letting the fin-like movements of her arms and legs do the work, she worked her way up toward the surface amidst the remaining vines.

Autumn focused on the water from above and stood up to get closer.

"Autumn, wait." The chief put out a hand to stop her from moving, but she waved him away.

"Chief, hold off the rescuers. She's got him."

The chief turned over his shoulder and gave a halting motion to the rescue workers rushing down to help. "Hold."

Autumn stood at the water's edge, steadying herself as best she could. "Water, become air. Make a tunnel for them to rise. Fire, light the way. Earth, rise to meet them."

With a deep breath, Autumn closed her eyes and focused her heart and mind as one. She envisioned the water spreading apart, just as it had for her, and the flames creating a line for Simone to follow.

As she opened her eyes, Autumn saw the waters push aside before her. A ramp of earth lay out before her, stretching the shoreline out further into the water. Simone slowly emerged, crawling out of the water with Mr. Lachlan under her arm.

Ben ran past all of them toward Simone and grabbed them both instantly, dragging them further up the shore.

The chief gave the signal for the medics to go ahead, and a flood of people rushed around Autumn to the water's edge. They placed Mr. Lachlan on his back, removing the gag from his mouth and checking his vitals and faint breathing.

"What were you thinking, Simone? You could have drowned or froze to death in that water." Ben wrapped his arms around her and closed his eyes. He opened them and pressed his lips firmly to Simone's, holding the side of her face in his hand. "You're infuriating. You know that?"

Simone smiled and grabbed at her back pocket. "I know. It's part of my charm." She pulled out the dried starfish, holding it up so Autumn could see it as well. "But have I ever mentioned that I swam competitively in high school? I dominated the four-hundred-meter breaststroke, the freestyle, and the butterfly. No one touched my times."

Autumn walked over to her cousin and flopped down on the snowy shore. They both nudged each other, still shaking from the stress and the cold. Several emergency workers wrapped them in blankets and gave Autumn warm compresses for her bare feet.

Anabeth ran to their sides with a worried expression on her face. "I waited fifteen minutes like you said, and then I got the chief. If I'd waited any longer, I . . ." Anabeth shook her head, and tears welled up in her eyes.

"Anabeth, it's okay. You did great. If it weren't for you, Cory and Emily would have gotten away, and who knows what else would have happened. Thank you for getting the chief here."

"But you just . . . you saved everyone. You moved that water and made those flames. How was that possible?" Anabeth swallowed hard and looked between Autumn and Simone, searching for an answer.

Autumn turned directly toward Anabeth and searched her eyes for whether she was ready and able to hear the truth. "Anabeth, how long have you lived in this town?"

Anabeth shook her head in confusion. "All my life, except for a few years at college. Why?"

"You've been in the exact right place to help when we needed you more than once now, and I see that as a sign."

"A sign of what?" Anabeth sat apprehensively beside them, but more curious than ever to hear what was about to be said.

Just as Autumn opened her mouth to speak, the sound of an owl swept through the air to the side of them. Through the darkness, a white owl swooped through the darkening sky and landed on her shoulder. It peered out into the crisp air and then back at the girls. Autumn sat quietly for a moment, connecting to the bird and admiring its beauty.

With a quick push, the owl took off through the diminishing flames over the lake, dipping its claws gently into the surface of the melted lake and then picking up speed to soar higher into the air.

"The outstretched owl over the elements," Autumn whispered under her breath.

Simone squinted at her cousin, intuitively reading into her thoughts. "You are the owl, Autumn. It flew to me with a vision of where you were." She nodded at Autumn. "Your energy is one and the same. You are the owl presiding over the land, fire, sea, and sky. It's your rightful place." Simone's eyes looked up past the marina to see James being stopped by two officers. She raised her chin for Autumn to look. "As an owl intended to join a raven moon, perhaps."

Chief Walsh waved the officers off James and allowed him to pass. James ran down through the snow to the water's edge. Simone and Anabeth helped Autumn stand up to meet him.

James scanned the scene and noticed the flames putting themselves out over the lake's surface. He recognized the shimmering lights on Simone's skin and Autumn's, and his eye caught a strange glow on the inside of Autumn's wrist. He gently lifted her arm to find the outline of an outstretched owl carrying a Celtic quaternary knot in its claws. As soon as they both saw the marking on her skin, it vanished.

He sighed with relief and pulled her close to his chest. "You're the owl that's been watching over my dreams all these years. And the circle of fire in the water? From this latest dream?"

Autumn lifted her head and looked up at him, nodding. "I did that."

He brushed the air away from her face and put his forehead to hers. "I was so scared when I saw the smoke from the downtown square and I couldn't find you."

"I'm okay, and it's all over now." Autumn turned to the other girls and Ben behind her.

James looked at them all and squinted at Simone. "Let me guess." He dipped his chin down and gave Simone the eye. "The mermaid."

Simone gave him a sly smile and raised her eyebrows at him.

Anabeth threw her hands up at her sides and shook her head. "Will somebody please help me understand what's going on here?"

"Right . . . Anabeth. There are some things about this town and the mountain region that are important enough to be left . . . undiscovered." Autumn stepped forward and grabbed hold of Anabeth's hands. She focused on warming them gently and holding a sincere tone in her voice to comfort Anabeth. "If you're ready to know the truth, then you must keep it protected. As you've seen today, the price goes up when the wrong people take advantage of what they know and can do."

Anabeth stared into Autumn's eyes, ready and willing to take a chance if it meant more knowledge. "I understand."

Simone stepped forward beside Autumn. She scanned the green glow of Anabeth's aura and felt the genuineness of her energy. "This isn't like anything you've ever uncovered for your stories before, and you can never expose it. Are you willing to swear to that?"

Looking around the scene before her, Anabeth let out a deep breath that fogged up the air. "Yes, I am."

Autumn and Simone exchanged glances and nodded. "Head back to the house with us tonight. Our gran always said a good pot of tea and a long conversation always put things right."

Autumn put her arm around her cousin and turned to glimpse soft, glowing lights in the background sky. Hundreds of paper lanterns floated up one by one into the air over the far side of the lake. They stretched over the tall pine trees and spotted the sky with an illuminating glow that Autumn knew as the enduring light of Hollow's Glenn.

CHAPTER 37

Anabeth set her teacup down on the kitchen island and looked up at Autumn, Simone, and James across from her. The story they had just told her of centuries' old magic in the mountain region was hard to believe, yet somehow she trusted it was all true.

"How did I not see any hints of this magic before? It stared me right in the face, and as a journalist, I should have picked up on it."

"Anabeth, it's not meant for people to see. We intentionally keep things under wraps to protect the energy here and all the people. The slightest imbalance affects everything. And to be honest, that day at the lake when you helped us save Dillon Ross . . . I had to help you change your memory of it a bit. I'm really sorry about that, but if you'd like, I can try to help you recover the memory of what really happened." Autumn wrinkled her forehead, cringing at the fact that she'd had to alter reality for Anabeth previously.

Anabeth turned the teacup in her hands, considering what Autumn said. "You can do that? Change people's memories around?"

"Well, only if the person is open enough to it. If you want to remember, then yes, we can recover your memory. But please understand, we only use our magic for healing, protection, and caring for one another. The magic Cory and Emily did here was toxic, and if it would have spread, we all would have been in danger."

"Listen, you've all been through a lot tonight." James started cleaning up the kitchen island as he spoke. "Anabeth, why don't you take some time to process all this? We're not going anywhere, and I for one want to get some sleep. Autumn, you need to restore your energy, and so do you, Simone." James put the dishes in the sink and turned to rub Autumn's arm beside him.

"He's right. I can't keep my eyes open anymore. I'm sorry." Autumn rubbed her hand over her face and started heading toward the bedroom. "Anabeth, I know this is a lot. Just call us whenever you want to talk more. We'll be here."

Anabeth nodded and smiled. "Okay, but once I sleep on this, I'm probably going to have a million more questions. Just promise me you'll answer them."

Simone laughed. "We will as long as you promise to share important information when we need it most. Trust goes both ways, you know?"

James and Simone both stared at Anabeth to get her confirmation, and she nodded in agreement. "I may be a snoop, but I'm also steadfastly loyal to the people and causes important to me. And besides, you'll be able to tell if my aura is off, anyway, right? So there's nothing to hide."

"Quick learner. I like that about you. Okay, I'll walk you out, Anabeth. And put some lavender under your pillow tonight for better sleep." Simone grabbed a small lavender sachet out of their gran's tea cabinet and handed it to her.

"Right, thanks." Anabeth lifted the sachet in appreciation. "I'll try it out."

Simone led her to the door as James gave Autumn a helping hand into bed.

"Careful going home. There'll be lots of traffic after the lantern festival." Simone paused for a moment as Anabeth put on her coat to head out. "And thanks for tonight. You did good, calling for help and getting the police to the marina. I can tell you've got spirit."

A slight smile crossed Anabeth's lips as she pulled open the door. "Yeah, you, too. Night." Anabeth walked out into the night toward her car as Simone turned to check on Autumn.

James tucked Autumn gently under a fluffy down comforter, and she reached a hand toward him.

"Could you stay for a little while until I fall asleep? The warm chestnut puts me at ease."

James looked at her with confusion, and Simone let out a little chuckle from the hallway. She leaned into Autumn's bedroom and whispered, "She picks up on scents in the air. You're chestnut and cherry cordial."

James looked over at Autumn already with her eyes closed. He couldn't help but smile at the thought of her recognizing him as a warm, comforting scent. After all, he felt the same about her, except she was the air he'd always wanted to breathe. And now he knew for sure, after seeing the owl with the Celtic quaternary emblazoned on her wrist, that she had always been the one slipping into his dreams.

He slid onto the edge of the bed and rested one leg along it. Autumn shimmied over onto his chest as he wrapped his arm around her and pressed his chin into her hair. One raven and one owl, finally where they were supposed to be.

The sunlight crept in from the edge of the curtains, and James squinted as he opened his eyes to recall where he was. In the same place where she'd fallen asleep the night before, Autumn lay quietly on his chest.

He wiggled his way out of the bed and pressed a pillow firmly underneath her. Making his way to the cottage kitchen, James found a large pot to start up a batch of oatmeal and put on some hot water. He grabbed a few apples out of the fridge and placed them on a cutting board at the counter, when someone peeked through the front door.

"Hello," Josephine whispered as she eased her way inside. She caught James's eye from the kitchen and perked up. "James! Oh, thank goodness someone has been here with the girls. How are they? Tell us everything."

Penny fumbled inside behind her sister, carrying several fabric tote bags full of food, flowers, and other provisions. "Are the girls still asleep? We shouldn't wake them."

Tavish wandered out of the bedroom hallway and straight up to Aunt Jo. She smiled and instantly bent down to pick up the cat. "Looks like you two are taking care of the house this morning and letting the girls sleep."

"Yeah, they're both still asleep. I was pretty worried about them last night, but I think they've had some good rest now. I just wanted to make some breakfast so they wouldn't have to do anything. Autumn didn't say much, but I could tell what happened last night drained her energy."

Jo and Penny looked at one another with concern, and Jo headed straight for a bag with a few healing crystals inside. She pulled out a white selenite wand, a large black hematite palm stone, and a raw red jasper. Placing them in the center of the kitchen island, she grabbed a sage stick from Penny and began smudging the space to clear the energy.

"Chief Walsh called to tell us what happened last night. He told us the girls could have died, but they were strong enough to save themselves and Bryce Lachlan. The chief was extremely grateful that everything turned out the way it did." Penny pulled out a large batch of golden speckled flowers brought from their magical winter garden as she spoke. She found a glass pitcher inside one of the kitchen cabinets, filled it with a little water, and arranged the flowers inside as they sparkled with light.

Autumn stumbled out of the bedroom alongside Simone just as Jo moved past them with the sage stick.

"Oh, wow. Mom, how many times in my life do I have to be woken up with smudging? I could smell that in my sleep." Simone sighed and rolled her eyes. "Honestly, what are you all doing here so early?"

"Oh, I'm sorry, dear." Jo hugged her daughter and Autumn before continuing to waft the smoky smudge stick around the house. "You know we couldn't stay away after hearing something happened to both of you last night. We came over first thing to make sure you were okay. Of course, I sensed you had someone watching over you throughout the night." Jo patted James on the arm and smiled at him. "So that calmed my nerves, along with Penny and Chief Walsh agreeing that you would be fine for the night."

Penny glanced over her shoulder as she poured several cups of tea. "Tell us what happened. We heard some from the chief, but fill us in on the details."

Autumn sighed and sat down on a kitchen stool as Tavish hopped up on her lap. Simone headed straight for the coffeepot and then checked to see what was bubbling on the stove.

"Anabeth put the pieces together. She figured out Bryce Lachlan had been a member of the archery club in the mountain region. So I headed over to the marina to see what I could find, and it turned out Cory and Emily were in on everything together. Cory was the archer we were looking for, not his father. And the two of them planned to sell everything passed down through their families and destroy the town before skipping out."

Jo shook her head as she processed it all. "Water energy can be so volatile. It must have consumed both of them with rage to do such things."

"It was resentment." Autumn took a cup of breakfast tea from her mother and poured a few drops of honey into it. "They resented being beholden to the magic handed down through their families. They described it as having bonds holding them to this place and the responsibilities here, and they wanted to wipe it away forever."

"I mean, it's no wonder they felt that way." Simone sipped her coffee and looked at everyone over her mug. "Mrs. Lachlan was pretty insistent that Cory take over the family business and stay here in Hollow's Glenn. That family made it abundantly clear there was no other way but to uphold the family name and responsibility."

Penny nodded with understanding. "The Lachlans always leaned more toward forceful tidal waves rather than bubbling brooks. Growing up, Cornelia's specialty was bending things toward her will."

Jo sighed and fiddled with her rings. "I'm just so thankful this is behind us now and that you girls are safe and sound. But this brings up a troubling part of our responsibilities as the original family." Jo pulled the quaternary knot out from her skirt pocket and placed it next to the crystals on the counter.

"That's right." Penny stared at the knot amulet as she continued her sister's thoughts. "Jo and I have discussed the repercussions of this for a time now. We knew one of the founding families could be at fault, and it turned out that was the case. Therefore, we need to make a determination around the continued use of their magic."

Autumn squinted at her mother. "You mentioned before that I would be the one to implement the consequences. But it was Cory who used black magic, not his parents. They're the founding members, and they were as innocent in all of this as any of us."

Jo grabbed Autumn's hand from across the island. "Yes, but it's within their bloodline now. And once black magic seeps in, there's greater opportunity for it to return. That's why binding their magic can be the only way forward."

"Binding? As in, never to be used again?" Simone perked up her ears to listen as she scooped up a cup of oatmeal into a bowl and sprinkled some cinnamon apples into it before sitting down.

"Yes. Binding is a serious act that should never be done lightly, but in this case, Penny and I feel it is necessary." Jo poured some tea into her cup and stood silently for a moment. "However, Autumn is correct. She is the four-points witch now, and she must seal any decision we make with the founding families. Which also means Autumn has to set the terms of the binding and perform the spell."

Autumn swallowed hard and moved her eyes amongst them. "How can I take someone's magic from them? That seems so cruel and final."

James came over to her and wrapped his arm around her. "Maybe it doesn't have to be so cut and dry. Autumn, you perceive things differently than we do, so use that to your advantage to make the right decision."

"James's thoughts are valid as well, my little ladybug." Penny's face warmed toward her daughter. "Earth, air, fire, and water bend to you. Use your heart and mind to find the right decision, and the founders will back you, I'm sure of it."

"You haven't called me ladybug since I was a child." Autumn looked at her mother curiously.

Jo nodded and took a breath. "Did I ever tell you about the beautiful nature of the ladybug? It stays close to the ground naturally. When it's ready to fly, its front wings protect its delicate back wings, allowing it to glide with strength. It also swims through the water with ease, taking in what it needs, and then drawing toward any heat and the light that it brings. So, my sweet Autumn, when you were a child, I glimpsed these traits within you as only a mother could. And some went dormant for quite some time, but I knew in my heart they would emerge again. Now you are my ladybug once more, and I know the elements will guide you."

Autumn looked down at the amulet before her on the counter. Under the skin on her wrist, the same emblem burned within her. No matter how much it weighed on Autumn to be the one making this decision, she knew her mother was right. The elements had chosen her, and even with pangs of empathy in her heart, she had to act.

CHAPTER 38

Simone stood over the icy river behind Jo and Penny's house. She held the dried starfish firmly in her hand as the water sang to her.

"I think I know what I need to do." She watched the ice and listened to the water asking for a reprieve from the remaining black magic tentacles swirling within it. "I'll use the water's own power to push the tentacles out, but I may need a little backup if I don't have enough energy."

Autumn stood up from a boulder and walked to the water's edge. "Got it. I'll be ready with some extra power."

"And so will we, dear." Jo looked over at Penny, who nodded in agreement. "We'll put our full intentions behind you."

Simone took a deep breath, nodded, and closed her eyes. "Okay, let's do this." She stretched her fingers wide and turned her palms upside down at her sides. "Waters of this region, hear our call. No more shall you struggle under black magic's hold.

Break free from the vines that hold you. Let your rapids rage and push out the dark to be balanced once again."

Simone pulled her hands up toward her chest with a forceful motion. A rumbling noise sounded from underneath the ice in front of them until it cracked from the edge all the way to the center of the river. Simone repeated the motion of her hands with more force this time, and Jo and Penny joined her in performing the motion.

Autumn whispered under her breath, "By my coven sister's side, I offer the water within me. Be forceful, be deliberate, and be free."

A rush of water blasted through the remaining ice at the surface and flung heaps of long, shimmering black vines up through the air onto the sides of the river, only to melt away instantly. Simone bent down to the water's edge and let the dried starfish touch the cold surface. A golden shimmer spread over the entire river, and Simone heard the final gracious song of the water before the singing stopped.

"It's done. The water sent its thanks." Simone stood up, letting out a warm breath into the cold air.

"Ancestors and elements, we reestablish the energy balance to honor you and all that the mountain region provides." Jo blew out a long breath to release the energy.

Autumn bent down and placed her palm to the ground. "As the earth gave us its strength, I return it once more. Through our words, our energy flows. And so it is."

The other three women nodded and repeated after Autumn. "And so it is."

Jo hugged her daughter and moved over to give Penny a squeeze as well. "I'm so relieved! We can sleep well tonight knowing all is well again."

A faint smile ran across Autumn's face as she sat back down on the boulder by the river's edge.

"Or . . . will we? What's wrong?" Simone stood over Autumn with a questioning look.

"Nothing. It's just that now . . ." Autumn shrugged and eyed the ground below her feet.

"It's the binding spell, isn't it? You don't like the idea of taking someone's magic away." Simone knew her cousin better than anyone, and she empathically felt what Autumn was going through.

"One person's faults shouldn't decide the outcome of an entire family. Just as one season of drought won't devastate the lands for centuries. I have to figure out the best way to handle this." Autumn leaned over and put her forearms on her knees. She groaned at some lingering pain from her leg being pinned only a few days prior.

Penny rushed to her daughter's side. "Easy. The wounds may have healed, but the aches under the surface take much longer to subside."

"Autumn, think of it this way." Simone sat beside her on the boulder. "We're reestablishing the balance in all things here. Cory never wanted to have this magical responsibility, anyway. It came to him through the bloodline, but from his perspective, it cursed him. Now is your chance to set things right. Instead of considering it a binding of his powers, look at it as a means of mercy shown to someone who never wanted it at all. It's a realignment of what always should have been. You're not the one serving up a punishment. The police and the courts do that part. Your job is to adjust what was off all along."

Autumn squinted her eyes as she thought for a moment. "A realignment?"

Simone nodded. "For when something gets out of whack and needs to be put back on track. That's all it needs to be."

Autumn leaned over and nudged her cousin with a smile. "Thanks."

Simone raised the corner of her mouth. "You know I've got you. Anyway, it's better you than me explaining all this to the founders. Good luck with that."

"Hey! What happened to being helpful?" Autumn laughed as Simone shrugged.

"Girls, let's wrap this up and get back to the house. Jo requested the founders be there in less than an hour, and we need to be ready." Penny gathered up a few of their things and guided them toward the trail to the house.

Autumn followed their mothers into the trees and turned back to her cousin. "Coming?"

Simone lifted her head to the dusk sky and nodded. "Yeah, just a second."

The waning gibbous moon shone its face down from above onto the surface of the chilled water. Simone watched as the water bubbled over the rocks once again and made the harmonious gurgling sound she remembered. It made the tension in her body melt away, and for the first time in a long while, she felt her own energy unleash again.

Autumn stood beside the roaring fire in the living room as Jo and Penny greeted the founding families at the door. She turned a glass mug of hot cider in her hands as she contemplated what came next. Looking into the fire, she took a breath and asked the ancestors for guidance.

"Ancestors, make my words and actions wise. Give me the strength to wield my power with compassion and understanding for what is now and what is to come. As I say it, so shall it be." Autumn's breath floated into the fire and sent the flames rising higher with each whispered word. The fire sent a hint of cedarwood through the air, and she knew instantly her gran was there with her.

"I love you, Gran." Autumn smiled to herself just as someone touched her shoulder. She turned from the fire to see Bryce Lachlan standing in front of her. "Mr. Lachlan, how are you?"

Bryce nodded his head and looked down at the floor. "All right, considering everything that's happened. I wanted to tell you personally how very sorry I am to put you in harm's way, and how grateful I am to you and your cousin for being there to save me."

Autumn tilted her head at him. "Oh, Mr. Lachlan, I'm just glad you're okay. I can't even imagine what you're going through right now, but at least you're alive."

"Listen, Autumn, I know this meeting is going to be about consequences, and you must do what's best for the region. But if you can, please go easy on my wife. Cornelia's heart already broke, and I don't know if she could bear much more being taken from her."

Autumn shook her head and looked over his shoulder at Cornelia Lachlan sitting on the edge of the couch. Autumn pursed her lips together and moved her eyes to meet his. "I understand."

He patted her forearm and went to sit next to his wife. The remaining families made their way inside, gathering in the living room. Penny and Simone served hot cider to everyone and laid out a couple trays of toast and baked brie overflowing with cranberries and walnuts. When everyone got situated, Jo gave Autumn a nod to proceed.

Putting down her cider on the coffee table, Autumn cleared her throat and looked around the room. "Good evening, everyone. Before we start, would each founding family please present your amulet?"

One by one, a representative from each family pulled out their Celtic quaternary knot from under wraps and held it up for all to see. "MacKinnon, Halpin, Newbury, Ross, Lachlan, and Carmichael." Autumn drew her finger across the room, pointing to each amulet in approval. "Thank you, everyone." She signaled for them all to be tucked away again.

"Now, I'm sure you heard the police now have the people in custody responsible for recent events. Thankfully, no one else got hurt, and we cleared the waters of the remaining toxins just this evening." Autumn gave them all a reassuring smile as she glanced around the room.

"Oh, thank goodness!" Dr. Carmichael put her hand to her chest and sighed with relief. "I was seeing more and more virus cases at the hospital, and I knew they were from the contaminated waters. Hopefully now it'll put a stop to all the sickness."

"Yes, and the authorities are working on cleaning the pollutants caused by the lumber mill. Even with the black magic out of the water, some traces of harmful chemicals remained. But the energy will rebalance itself now, and we need to move to another pressing matter." Autumn paused and searched the room for Simone. She locked eyes with her cousin and received a validating nod to keep going.

Autumn took a few paces in front of the fireplace and grasped her gran's necklace around her neck for guidance. "Unfortunately, those who performed the black magic were from a founding family. The water bloodline. And as those of you who have experienced the black magic know, as I do now, it lingers and leaves you vulnerable to its darkness."

Bryce Lachlan stood up from his place on the sofa. "Autumn, could I speak for a moment?"

Autumn paused to read his intentions. She picked up on overwhelming shame and hurt within him, but she knew he still had a strong sense of duty. "Go ahead, Mr. Lachlan." Autumn raised her arm to signal him to come forward.

"Thank you. My friends, our families have known each other for centuries now. We have proudly carried the elemental duties of this region alongside you. But I'm afraid our bloodline let you down, and for that, I am truly sorry. We understand the nature of our covenant and know that consequences must be given. My wife and I still honor our responsibilities and care deeply about this community, but we wish no more harm to come to it. So I will stand by our new four-points witch with the decision that she comes to tonight." Mr. Lachlan exhaled deeply and sat back down beside his wife. Cornelia clutched his hand in hers and sat with a grave face.

"Mr. Lachlan, we appreciate your words." Autumn watched all the stunned faces around the room. Each of the families whispered to each other, and Autumn gave them a moment to process his speech.

"We've never experienced someone infecting the energy of our town from within our circle before. And while unprecedented, we still have a longstanding relationship with the Lachlan family." The mayor put his hand on Bryce Lachlan's shoulder to console him. "It would be an injustice to remove the family completely from their rightful place here."

Dr. Carmichael leaned forward in her chair. "But we can't risk any dark magic seeping back into the bloodlines. We just mentioned how vulnerable we are now. The tainted water bloodline must be bound."

"I agree with Rose," Graham Newbury chimed in. Eve's mouth dropped open beside her father as he spoke, and she made an audible gasp. "As much as it pains me to say this, we cannot allow any magic to remain past Bryce and Cornelia in the family line. It's too dangerous. Even the two of them will still be vulnerable. We have to do what's right for the collective."

Jo stepped to the center of the room from the archway to the hall. "All right, everyone. This is a highly sensitive situation, and it's important we understand the consequences for everyone before we move forward. Bryce and Cornelia Lachlan were victims in this situation, just as many of you were as well. They have been faithful founding members, and continue to be. And we should appreciate that fact in our decision-making. However, if we choose to bind their bloodline, only a four-points witch can reinstate it. I need to remind you all that binding takes away all magical ability and will leave the person or family line powerless. Autumn will make the final decision here tonight, but we as founders must give her our insights."

"Actually . . ." Autumn stood tall in front of the bright fire behind her. "I have a way forward." She looked over at Simone.

"My cousin reminded me that our whole purpose here is to establish balance. To realign the energies when things become out of whack. And that doesn't mean that we must become the punishers of what we see as wrongdoing, only that we must keep the energies of the land, sea, and sky intact."

She paced the room, weaving in and out of the founding members as her necklace glowed with a gentle blue light none of them had yet seen. "Therefore, it is our responsibility to find the most aligned path for all parties. Even those who used black magic are still within our charge to help in realignment. And while we must protect the strength of the elements, we must also set things on the course that should always have been."

"So what is that course, then?" Dillon Ross spoke up.

"To me, it's as clear as day now. A course of allowance, just as the water allows for changes in flow. We must also be willing to let the bloodlines determine within themselves where the magic lies. Every new generation must have the choice. To accept the covenant that we have all chosen to abide by, and serve the elements throughout their days, or to choose a more traditional life. But for those who have already chosen to live along a path of darkness, we shall bind their magic. They have made their choice. And for the others in the bloodlines, we will protect ourselves. But no one bloodline should carry the burden of this. The elements are one, and so are we. If we are to maintain harmony, then we must first do it within ourselves and know that we are nothing without the whole of our parts."

Penny stepped toward her daughter as Autumn stopped pacing. "There's a reason Autumn became our four-points witch. The compassion she holds in her heart is clear, but her grounded wisdom is far beyond what we've seen these many years. It's time for us to stand beside her and create the way ahead."

"I agree!" Mrs. Newbury sat up from her seat and emphatically joined in. "I want my daughter and the sons and daughters who come after her to have a choice. This is an opportunity rather than an obstacle. If we don't give our children the chance to self-select, then we'll just find ourselves with this same problem further down the road. The problem here wasn't one or two people with bad intentions and access to black magic. The real problem derived from the lack of freedom in our structure. And what is magic if not the manifestation of true, free-flowing intention?"

"Well, I believe you've all made quite a convincing argument." Dillon Ross put his cider mug down and stood up. "I agree to proceed."

Mr. Newbury nodded his head and thought for a moment before standing. "As do I."

Mayor Halpin walked around to the front side of the sofa and nodded. "You had me with the whole of our parts. I don't believe in standing alone."

"Dr. Carmichael?" Autumn turned and waited for a response from her.

She stood up with a sigh. "My biggest concern is the health and safety of this town. If more choice means less pain and suffering, then that's what we should do. I agree."

Mr. and Mrs. Lachlan looked at one another. Cornelia's eyes welled up with tears as she tried to speak.

"I . . . I never fully recognized what it meant to be one part of the whole until now. But to see you all take up our burden as your own, I don't know what to say except thank you. Our son never wanted this responsibility. Now, not only will he be relinquished of it, but others will know what it's like to accept the magic with an open heart. That's all I ever wanted for him, but now I realize the magic can only live within you if it's accepted willingly, not forced."

Bryce and Cornelia Lachlan stood up as everyone took the hands of the person standing next to them.

Autumn took her place at the head of the circle and closed her eyes. The fire sparked behind her, and the wind howled beyond the front windows.

"Elements of earth, air, sky, and water, we call to you now. As the founding families of these lands, we ask to realign the energetic path that has faltered. With each of our bloodlines, may every new generation have a choice. To open to our magical path and be one with the elements, or to deny that right and lead a traditional life. As we connect our energies together, protect these bloodlines from harm. Seal the vulnerabilities with strength and fortitude. Let no darkness seep through our lines, only energy of truth and light. And for those who have chosen the dark, bind their magic by the power of the four points. Bound once by the earth. Bound twice by the sky. Bound three times by fire. And bound four times by water. So that no more harm may come and only the elements of the light shall persist. As I say it, so shall it be."

As Autumn spoke the last few words, the window panels flew open with a gust of blustery wind. Each member held tighter to the hand of the person beside them's hand and locked eyes with those across from them. The flames danced furiously in the fireplace before slowing to a gentle sway along with the wind.

Jo dropped hands and hurried to the windows to shut them. "I think the elements have spoken."

"Yes, and it seems they've left us a message." Mayor Halpin directed everyone's attention to the coffee table in the center of the room.

Sitting in the warm fire's glow on the wooden coffee table, a white owl perched silently for all of them to see. Autumn stared in awe before it looked directly at her and flapped its wings before resting gracefully upon her shoulder.

CHAPTER 39

S imone turned the music up in the back room of the shop and danced her way to the front counter. Autumn laughed while Tavish stared with a curious look.

"Looks like someone got their flow back." Autumn carried a basket of winter berry branches over to a wall display and lined the shelves with them as she spoke.

"I feel like the floodgates opened on my energy again. Now that the water is clear, I'm free and clear, too. And all I want to do is dance and do whatever makes me happy." Simone grabbed her cousin's hand and spun her around just as the chime rang at the front.

Lainy wandered in, pulling the tall collar of her camel wool coat down from around her neck. She stomped the snow off her heeled boots and came further into the shop.

"Well, well, well. Look who it is." Simone crossed her arms at her chest and gave Lainy a look.

"Yeah, I'm sorry. I've been swamped with work at city hall, and there was no way I was getting out of there in time to make the gathering last night. But . . . I've heard a lot about you two over there."

"Oh, really?" Autumn swiveled her head around from adjusting the wall display to look at Lainy.

"Mmm hmm. The mayor mentioned how you've both been getting into trouble and out of it. Something about fire engulfing the icy lake again?" Lainy squinted her eyes at Autumn.

Autumn smirked and walked back to the counter. "Can you believe it? Fire over the ice twice in just a couple weeks. It's a wonder how that all started."

"Right . . . a wonder. Seems to me someone's getting quite good at wielding her strengths." Lainy removed her fur-lined leather gloves and sat on a stool at the counter. She looked between Autumn and Simone. "I should have been there to help. Why didn't you call me?"

"Everything happened so fast. There was no time to call anyone. My telepathic messages somehow made it to Simone, and it was lucky Anabeth attended the festival. She's the one who sent the police to the marina. Otherwise, who knows if we could have stopped it all." Autumn fiddled with a spool of twine and tied it carefully around a few new journals as she spoke.

"Well, I'm glad you're both all right. I got nervous when I heard there was another mishap."

"You, nervous?" Simone scoffed. "You eat stress for breakfast. Who are you kidding?"

"Well, I was concerned but confident in both of your capabilities. I know what you both can do. I've seen black magic, though, and it's not something to take lightly."

"You're right. It's not. But it's clear now thanks to Simone. And since you missed the gathering last night, we might as well tell you. We performed a spell, so from now on those in our bloodlines must choose to take this magical path. It won't automatically pass down to them, but the lines won't force it either."

"A choice?" Lainy leaned over the counter to watch what Autumn was doing with the twine.

"That's right." Simone gave her cousin a nudge and sat down at the computer. "Autumn came up with a pretty genius way of binding only the person responsible for the black magic, protecting our bloodlines, and giving any new heirs a choice in all this. It was brilliant, if I say so myself."

"I got the idea from you, you know? When you mentioned things needed to be realigned, it got me thinking. I don't want to be a four-points witch who doles out punishments. I want to be the one who creates positive change and moves us forward as a collective, you know?"

"There's that fire coming out. I love it." Lainy pointed her finger at Autumn and smiled.

"Yeah, well, as much fire as I've harnessed lately, I could always use help in cultivating more, seeing as how it's a pretty important piece of the four elements. And I can't always focus on that one." Autumn lifted her eyebrows and stared at Lainy.

"Okay . . . you know I'm more than happy to help teach you how to work with it." Lainy looked at Autumn, confused.

"Lainy." Simone peeked out from behind the computer. "She's asking you to be a permanent part of our coven. Not just someone who comes and goes occasionally to help, but someone who holds the actual fire element place."

"A permanent part of your coven? As in, the fourth piece of the quaternary?" Lainy sat and considered the offer.

"Yes, the fourth piece. What else would it be?" Simone sighed.

Autumn laughed at both of them. "Just say yes already. You know you belong here, and we need you. Fire can be temperamental, but you have a way with it I've never seen before. Plus, you're family, and you've grown on us. So be our fourth and complete the circle."

Lainy pushed her lips to the side and glanced over at the blazing fire in the hearth room. "On one condition—we trust each other implicitly and aren't afraid to get out of our comfort zones to follow another's lead."

Simone raised one eyebrow. "Interesting. You caught me on a good day when I'm ready to go with the flow again, so I'm good with that."

"Me, too. And I think Eve already pushed herself to do just that. So it looks like we've got ourselves four points to make a solid coven!" Autumn held a finger up and started walking to the back of the shop. "Let me get some celebratory tea for us."

Autumn headed back to put the teakettle on, when the door chimed again. This time James wandered through the front door, waving a letter in his hand to say hello.

"Hey, Autumn just went to the back. Come on in," Simone called to him.

"Thanks. I wanted to stop by and see how everyone was doing. Oh, and I have something important for you both."

Simone grabbed the stack of letters from him and nodded just as Autumn came out holding a tray of tea mugs.

"James! I didn't expect to see you today. Are you on a break?" Autumn handed out the warm mugs of rooibos tea to the girls and eyed James curiously.

"It's kind of a late start today. We need to wait for some weather to clear before we can head to the job site. Anyway, I thought I'd check up on you, and my mother asked me to deliver this note as soon as possible."

"Oh, okay. Well, we're doing good, thanks. But since you're here, I actually wanted to ask you for a favor." Autumn turned from James to Simone with a smile.

"Why are you looking at me?" Simone wrinkled her forehead at her cousin. "What are you up to?"

"Nothing. It's just that now that we're both living in Gran's cottage, and it's ours, I thought we could fix it up. I hoped James could help us make some improvements. I mean, I want to keep the character of the house and all the charming parts, like the archways and creaky floors. It's just that I also want to make it our own, you know?"

"Aw, cuz. That's really sweet of you. I like it." Simone nodded in agreement.

"Well, I am pretty handy, and I've got quite the tool collection. So if you throw in a few lunches or dinners, then I could definitely spare some time." James smiled warmly at Autumn.

"Oh, just a few lunches or dinners, huh?" She smiled back at him, thinking she'd be happy looking at that smile for the rest of her life.

Simone rolled her eyes and exchanged a glance with Lainy as she stared at the letter James dropped on the counter. "Lainy, you need to come by more often, too. We need to plan a regular gathering." Simone squinted her eyes and leaned down to read the writing on the letter before her. She looked up and nudged Autumn. "Autumn, Mrs. Allan's letter has a hazy gray aura around it. I think we better open it right now."

Autumn grabbed the letter from the counter and looked up at James. "Strange. I feel a denseness to it as well. James, do you know what it's about?"

James shook his head. "No, she didn't say anything but to give this to you right away, and then she left for her sister's house again. I could tell something bothered her, though."

Autumn ran her finger inside the flap of the envelope and opened it hastily. Pulling the note out, she read it aloud.

"Girls, I have a predicament, and I knew I could count on you once again. I went to see my sister for our regular get-togethers. When I got there, she was nowhere to be found. I'm so worried, as I've checked for several days now with no trace of her." Autumn grabbed her tea mug from the counter and made her way to the hearth room as she read the letter. The three of them followed behind her.

"I thought you could help before I go to the authorities, seeing as how you've been so good with other recent events. Since I haven't been able to get a hold of you lately, I had James deliver this letter. I'll be back in town in a couple days to meet and discuss in person. Signed, Sorcha Allan."

Autumn flopped down in a wingback chair next to the fireplace, and Tavish hopped up onto her lap. "I didn't realize your mother had been gone, James. I know you said she visited her sister sometimes, though."

"She visits her sister, Ayla, all the time, and she went a few days ago to clear her mind after the recent dreams." James trailed into the hearth room and paced the floor. "I saw her when she got home, but this time she didn't tell me about the visit. She just gave me the letter and said she had to go back for a while. I could tell something was wrong, but she wouldn't say anything more."

Simone propped herself up beside the mantle and leaned over to view the note. "What's that ink stamp at the top of the page?"

Lainy peeked over Autumn's other shoulder. "Looks like two overlapping circles similar to the eclipse we had the other night," she interjected before walking over to the opposite wingback chair. "It could be the lunar eclipse with the earth's shadow over the moon. Maybe it references the water energy in the Allan family. James, do you know?" She looked up at him as he shook his head with uncertainty.

Simone walked over to the hearth room archway and pulled the heavy curtains down from either side of the doorway.

James moved behind Autumn and squinted at the letter. "My aunt stays in tune with the moon's energy. But I'm not sure how this symbol relates to her. I guess whatever this is, we'll figure it out together this time." James gave Autumn the eye.

"That's right. Power in numbers, and we've got that in spades now." Lainy laughed under her breath. "Never thought I'd say that, but it's true."

Autumn nodded and looked around the room at all of them. "Well, it looks like we have our work cut out for us." She raised her tea mug up high and then took a sip. As she stared at the letter in her hands, Autumn knew this time, with a full coven, they were prepared for anything.

Will the coven discover the reason behind the strange disappearance of Sorcha's sister? Find out if they'll get to her before it's too late in the next installment of A Hollow's Glenn Coven Mystery Series, *An Eclipse of Evidence*.

Next In Series

Get the next book in the Hollow's Glenn Coven Mystery Series!

An Eclipse of Evidence, book 3 in the series, is available at the link below.

The lunar eclipse brings the strange disappearance of Sorcha's sister and the discovery of a dead body on her property to complicate matters. Find out if Autumn's coven can uncover the mysterious happenings in Hollow's Glenn and recover Sorcha's sister before it's too late. Don't miss another great story with your favorite characters from Hollow's Glenn!

Grab your copy now!

https://kristenkingwrites.com/hollowsglennseries

A Note From The Author

Thank you so much for reading my cozy paranormal mystery, *A River of Resentment*. I hope the characters spoke to you and that you fell in love with the inviting mountain town of Hollow's Glenn. If you'd like to share the enjoyment with fellow readers, then leaving an online book review would support those interested in cozy reads as well. That way, we can create a movement of magical readers in love with the worlds and possibilities in each story.

Now, as this book is part of the Hollow's Glenn Coven Mystery series, there will be more opportunities to get immersed in the world of the MacKinnon girls and the founding families. Plus, with each book, I'll share some practical magic such as Gran's tea recipes, Autumn's seasonal journaling prompts, and Eve's pastry recipes.

You can also hop onto my newsletter list to get the prequel with Penny's story of how she left for the mountain region and why she stayed so long. You may even find out how Autumn's gifts started.

To read the free prequel novella, *A Land of Consequence*, and hear about the latest releases and other goodies, scan here:

ACKNOWLEDGMENTS

This book came rushing through like an eager waterfall ready to burst over the edge . . . Just like my little Scorpio, who teaches me every single day to embrace life fully, imagine all possibilities, and enjoy the ride. With you in mind, I felt my creative soul open up each time I sat down to write. Your inspiration led me to think less and let the muse take over more. Thank you for being one of my greatest teachers, Maddie Cat.

About The Author

Kristen is an Amazon best-selling author, coach, and creative. After years of doing project management and design, she now lets her air and water energies lead through creative fiction writing. She finds that a good dose of magic sets the coziest tone for any day. When not channeling her writing muse, Kristen spends time snuggling in her mountain home next to a cozy fire and her calico cat. She loves to lose herself in taking photos, baking for her family, and pulling tarot cards or charging crystals by the light of the moon.

For more from the author and to find her books and offerings, go to:

https://www.kristenkingwrites.com